Contribution

– CAROL CLAYTON –

An environmentally friendly book printed and bound in England by
www.printondemand-worldwide.com

This book is made entirely of chain-of-custody materials

FastPrint Publishing

www.fast-print.net/store.php

CONTRIBUTION
Copyright © Carol Clayton 2014

All rights reserved

No part of this book may be reproduced in any form by photocopying or any electronic or mechanical means, including information storage or retrieval systems, without permission in writing from both the copyright owner and the publisher of the book.

All characters are fictional.
Any similarity to any actual person is purely coincidental.

The right of Carol Clayton to be identified as the author of this work has been asserted by her in accordance with the Copyright, Designs and Patents Act 1988 and any subsequent amendments thereto.

A catalogue record for this book is available from the British Library

ISBN 978-178456-040-9

First published 2014 by
FASTPRINT PUBLISHING
Peterborough, England.

Acknowledgments

To my wonderful dad, I thought you were gone for ever. It took me a long time to realise you were watching over me and always within my heart. For my mum who presented many challenges but taught me unconditional love, and for my loyal and talented brother, I love you all. If I have any choice in the matter I would always choose you as my family!

To my aunts, uncles and cousins, I always feel I never give you enough credit and tell you how much I love you but I hope you know!

To my ex-husband, thank you for your love and all you gave me. To my wonderful husband, David, thank you so much for your love, endless support and for encouraging my creativity. My love has no bounds. To my stepchildren and their families, thank you so much for the joy you have brought into my life! I love you all.

To my very best friend in the whole wide world, Marie, my life would just not have been the same without you in it all these years! And to all my other dear friends, old and new, thank you so much for the wonderful gift of friendship.

To all the people who have come my way, some for longer times than others, and those who have yet to come into my life, thank you for the lessons you have taught me or have yet to teach me, helping me along on my journey of spiritual growth.

To www.dbmaesworldimages.com for the photograph on the front cover which inspired much of this story.

To the spiritual and self-help writers who have pointed me in the right direction and through the words in their books have motivated and encouraged me to be the best I can! Thank you!

To the team at Fast-print including my copy editors, thank you for all your support and patience with the publishing of both my novels!

And last but not least to all my readers, thank you! Whether you bought the books for escapism, to know you are not alone with life's challenges, to help find other books or just to have a jolly good read, I hope you got something out of them to take on your journey in life. Even if I have helped just one person to overcome an obstacle then I feel the books have been a success. Once again thank you!

With much love and gratitude to you all,
Carol

Prologue

By the time Poppy was twenty-four, she was already a well-known celebrity and spokesperson for numerous environmental projects and had appeared on the front cover of many popular magazines. She was often quoted in newspaper articles and interviewed on talk shows. She also had her own cable programme promoting conservation, in particular marine life, and was top of the ratings.

She was well respected by her colleagues and admired by people from all walks of life. Her exotic looks caught people's attention but it was her devotion and dedication to our planet that held their interest. She was intelligent, charming and very passionate about protecting the environment.

The media found her intriguing because if there was any scandal they couldn't find it. She rarely dated and when someone once asked her why she didn't have many boyfriends she simply told them she was waiting for the right man and anyway she was far too busy for love!

Tonight, as she walked up the red-carpeted stairs to the stage, she wore a beautiful long white and silver backless gown that accentuated her natural tan and long dark hair. She was here to receive an award recognising her work on her latest documentary. Her parents, Toby and Annabelle, were in the audience, watching proudly.

Poppy stood at the podium, adjusted the microphone and started by saying, 'I'm not going to thank everyone individually, you all know who you are and you know how much I love you and am grateful to you!'

Indeed they did, she always wrote a note of thanks to those who helped her and included a thoughtful gift that she knew would mean something to them.

'But tonight I really want to thank the one person who inspired me the most and helped make me the woman I am today and that person is my grandmother Jasmine. She was a wonderful lady, kind and caring, but more than anything she taught me to believe in myself and to make my dreams come true. She always said whatever you do, do it with integrity, compassion and above all do it with love! So this is for you Gran,' Poppy said, raising the trophy in the air. There was loud applause from the audience.

After the ceremony, people gathered around to offer their compliments. Poppy was standing with her parents when a handsome man came up to congratulate her.

'Excuse me Miss Anderson,' he said, 'I hope you don't mind me saying, but I am a big admirer of your work and I enjoy watching all your documentaries!'

'Thank you!' she said, slightly blushing. She was used to hearing high praises but not from someone as attractive as he was. 'But please call me Poppy!' she smiled engagingly. The young stranger was tall, broad shouldered, with compelling blue eyes and curly brown hair that framed his handsome face.

Poppy instantly felt her heart jump and instinctively knew this was the connection her gran used to tell her about when she first met Ben, her true soul mate who would later become her husband - when that energy swirled around your body - and you know, you just know that this is the person you have been waiting for!

They stood gazing into each other's eyes. For some reason the lights flickered slightly. Everyone looked up to the ceiling and a small white feather floated down in front of the handsome man.

'An angel feather!' he said, as it gently settled into his hand and he passed it to Poppy. 'That's for luck' he said, with a twinkle in his eye, 'not that you'll need it, I'm sure!'

Poppy thanked him and, as she reached for it, their hands brushed leaving an exciting tingling sensation between them.

Poppy knew with all her heart that her gran had something to do with it. She looked up to the ceiling, and silently thanked her, as the cycle of love was about to begin…

CONTRIBUTION

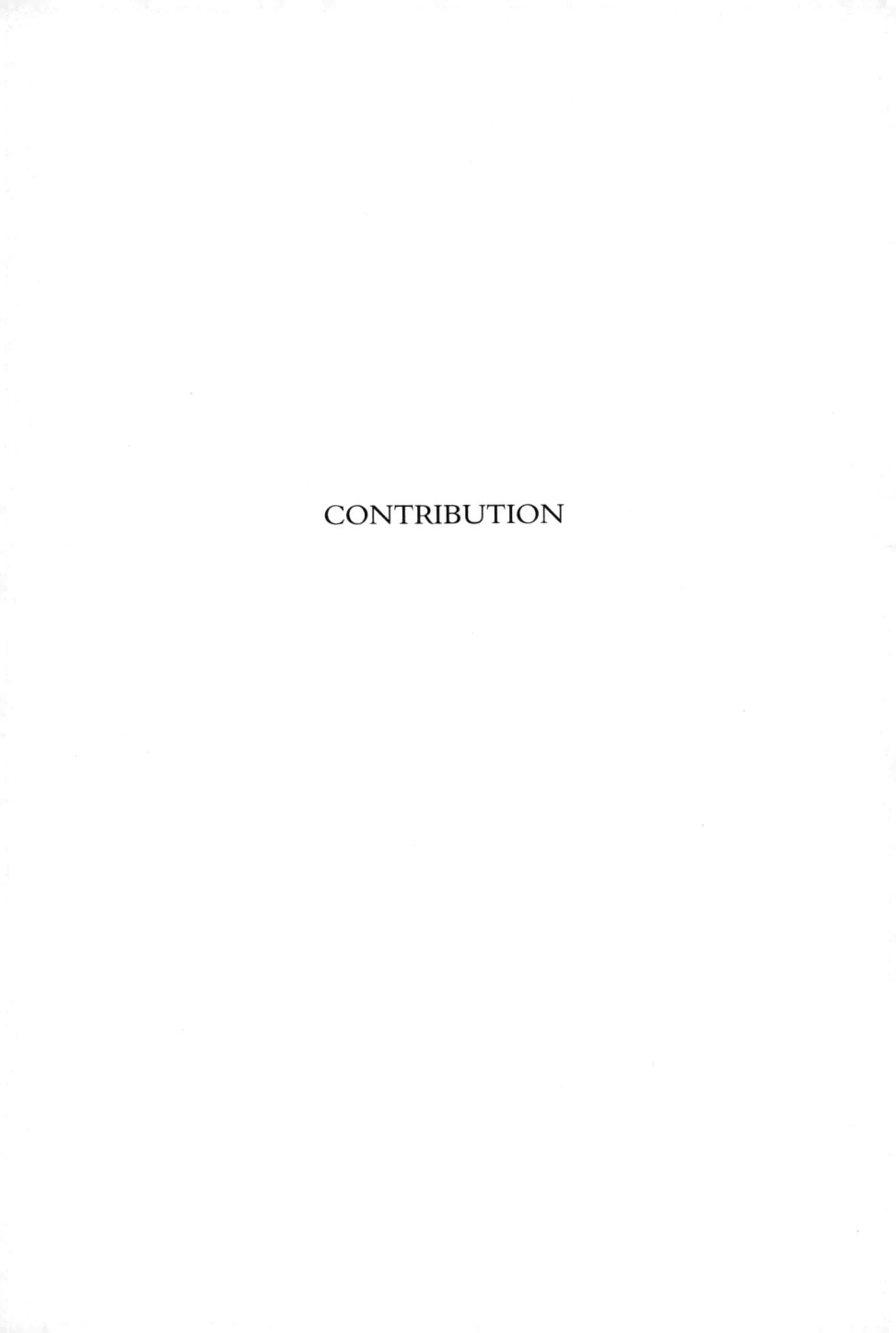

Chapter 1
Growing up!

Among the noise and multitude of people Annabelle couldn't help but notice the immediate attraction between the young man and her daughter. Only the other day she had been saying to Toby that she sometimes worried that Poppy didn't have a steady boyfriend in her life and felt she still hadn't got over the heartbreak of Sam, her childhood best friend and sweetheart. Toby agreed and was also worried that Poppy worked too hard, took on too many projects and had gained international stardom at too young an age. But then Toby always concluded that Poppy was level-headed and had the energy of youth on her side!

Annabelle shot Toby a sideways glance before stepping in and asking the stranger his name. He replied, 'Gregory'. She then asked if he would like to join them for dinner.

'I would love to, thank you!' He didn't hesitate in accepting the invitation and the chance to spend some time with Poppy. 'But first I'll just have to let my crew know I'll be disappearing. There's an awards party afterwards but I must admit I would rather have a nice quiet dinner with such an engaging group of people!' he smiled charmingly before excusing himself to find his production crew.

Annabelle, smiling, turned to her daughter and declared, 'What a lovely polite young man!' as she watched him disappear into the crowd.

'Gorgeous!' Poppy agreed, her eyes twinkling.

Annabelle turned to her husband. 'I hope you didn't mind me inviting him?'

He smiled back. 'Not at all. Besides, how could I refuse such a request from my lovely wife!' He thought she looked beautiful in her elegant burgundy evening gown with her long dark hair secured at the nape of her neck and draped in a loose roll over her shoulders. They were so busy with their careers he couldn't believe how quickly the years were passing. Toby squeezed Annabelle's hand and she smiled tenderly into his eyes.

Gregory seemed to have been gone only a few minutes before returning with a broad smile on his face.

'Was that okay with your crew?' Poppy enquired politely.

'Sure. No problem at all.'

Toby then took the lead. 'Come on then let's go and get something to eat, I'm starving!' He smiled at his beautiful wife and daughter as they left the noise of the auditorium and headed towards the restaurant where he had made reservations.

When they arrived Toby spoke quietly to the maître d' and asked him if they could accommodate an extra person? He was told that would be fine if they could wait a few minutes. So they ordered cocktails in the bar which gave them a chance to relax with some light conversation.

'That's better,' Toby sighed, as he undid the bow tie on his white shirt and tucked it into the pocket of his black dinner jacket. 'Now I can actually hear people talking!'

They all laughed, knowing what he meant.

'So tell us all about you!' Toby enquired, wanting to find out about Gregory but not wanting to appear to be the over-protective father.

Gregory wasn't sure where to begin. However, he told them he was head cinematographer on a movie, which had been nominated in the category for best new science fiction film, although this time they did not win an award.

'So do you enjoy your job?' Poppy enquired, keen to find out all about him, noticing that he had followed her father's lead and taken his tie off, leaving his white shirt open at the neck and looking particularly alluring. She sensed, quite rightly, he probably didn't feel too comfortable in his black tuxedo.

'Oh yes,' he enthused passionately. 'I enjoy the creativity, working on location, travelling the world and I have a great crew too!'

Poppy appreciated the life he led. It was very similar to hers in many ways, except she was in front of the camera, the star of the show and did a lot of the writing and directing herself, whereas he liked to be unobtrusive and work behind the camera.

Then, as an afterthought, he added, 'But it's not really what I want to do!'

'Oh really?' Poppy enquired, curious to find out more about him.

'No…' he paused, thoughtfully, 'as exciting as it is being on location with a multi-million dollar budget movie, what I really want to do is make a film that will one day make a difference to the world!'

Poppy smiled at him, fully understanding. 'If that's what you really want, then that's what will happen… you've just got to take small steps and work towards it each day and believe in yourself!' Poppy shrewdly told him, giving him the benefit of her grandmother's wisdom.

He smiled in return. 'You're absolutely right… I do and I will!'

At that point, the maître d' returned and led them to a quiet table.

They continued their conversation and learned more about each other.

Like her, Gregory was an only child. He was born and raised in the picturesque maritime state of Rhode Island, also known as the Ocean State, whereas Poppy came from a small seaside village in the tropical paradise of Costa Rica. She spoke both Spanish and English fluently and could also get by with French,

German and Italian which had been particularly beneficial in her career.

The evening quickly wore on and they were having a wonderful time, becoming comfortable in each other's company as the wine flowed and they ate their delicious meals. All the while Toby and Annabelle were warmed by the visible connection between the young couple.

They finished their after-dinner coffees and far too soon the evening came to an end. Poppy was disappointed to hear that Gregory was on a flight out of LA early in the morning but they exchanged e-mail addresses and cellphone numbers, promising to keep in touch.

Gregory politely thanked Toby, Annabelle and Poppy for a wonderful evening, and shook their hands. He told them that it had been a great pleasure meeting them all.

Poppy replied, 'It has been a great pleasure for us too!' and as she said this, their eyes lingered and their hands locked momentarily.

They each got into their respective taxis and Gregory waved back at them all, before they were whisked off to their hotels.

'What a delightful young man!' Annabelle once again declared to her daughter and husband.

Poppy nodded and smiled in agreement, thinking of the vibrant man who had suddenly walked into her life.

The next morning Gregory still felt the excitement of meeting the one woman he admired most, not only because of her obvious good looks but because of her inner-beauty, passion and enthusiasm for life! He felt light-hearted as he quietly whistled a soft tune and confidently strolled towards the check-in counter at the airport, unaware of the admiring looks from women of all ages as they stole glances at the handsome young man, with brown curly hair, casually dressed in cream slacks and light green short sleeved shirt, with his suit carry-case nonchalantly slung over his shoulder.

Toby, Annabelle and Poppy were catching a flight back to Logan airport, Boston later that morning. Her parents still owned an apartment near the city centre from their university days. They earned their medical degrees at Harvard School of Medicine and liked to go back to Boston at least once a year to catch up with close friends and spend time wandering around the exquisite cosmopolitan city. They especially enjoyed the history of the city and the delights of the restaurants there. Poppy always liked to make the most of any family time they had together as these days, with their respective schedules, the opportunities were rare.

Toby and Annabelle read the latest medical journals on their flight back to Boston. They both thought flying was a good opportunity to catch up on journals and other books they hadn't had time for in their hectic lives.

Contribution

Poppy sat next to the window and let her thoughts drift to Gregory and then back to Sam. She'd been so busy lately she was surprised she hadn't thought of her childhood friend in a while.

Poppy closed her eyes and remembered when she first met Sam. They were nine and it was his first day at school, shortly after moving from England to Costa Rica. His father was a civil engineer and had been commissioned from London by the Costa Rican government to oversee the construction of a huge suspension bridge over an enormous river canyon. Frank loved Costa Rica so much that before the bridge construction had even started he knew he wanted to live there for ever. So he bought a large new property, built to American standards, and enrolled his only son into one of the most prestigious private schools in Costa Rica.

Poppy recalled how the teacher made Sam sit next to her, as she knew Poppy would look after the new boy. They had instantly got on well and soon realised they both had a love of nature.

The weeks and months flew by and they would often go on long walks along the beach and into the jungle, studying birds and animals, writing about them and illustrating their work. Both children were extremely intelligent and curious about the world in which they lived, studying it with a sense of wonder!

Poppy and Sam were inseparable except for several weeks a year when Poppy's parents' friends from California sailed into Costa Rica in the boat they had remodelled into a floating marine research lab. It was those special weeks spent each year with Carmel, Ely and their team that had fuelled Poppy's passion for ocean research. Her parents' friends had been impressed with the young girl's acumen and enthusiasm to learn as much as she could and they in turn did whatever they could to encourage her appetite for knowledge.

Over the years, both Sam and Poppy were constantly top of their class at the prominent school. They were often in competition with each other, seeing who could get the best grades but were always pleased for the other. Their teachers were amazed with their progress and encouraged them to take advanced courses. When they were in their early teens they were both on track to graduate a year early.

Poppy thought back to that life-changing sunny afternoon at the age of sixteen when she felt both totally loved and then completely abandoned all at once! Even now she had never experienced two such conflicting emotions at the same time.

That day Poppy and Sam had been for a long walk in the jungle and had been excited to see a sloth and watch his slow movements high in the tree tops. Afterwards they ran back down the hill, both hot and sweaty, to the cool pool of water at the foot of their favourite waterfall. They were excitedly shouting over to each other about their find and without thinking they had both stripped naked, ready to plunge into the refreshing water, something they had often done when they were younger. Suddenly aware of the other's body and how much they had matured they stopped in their tracks.

Poppy's eyes were tight shut and her heart was pounding, remembering Sam's every word and his youthful muscular body like it was yesterday.

'My god Poppy, you are truly beautiful,' he said, looking at her slim, bronzed body.

'You are too. You look like a handsome Greek god!' she said, astonished at his toned body. At sixteen he was almost a fully grown man. His blond hair glistened in the sunshine. His strong jaw line and twinkling blue eyes made him look confident and noble.

'For as long as I live Poppy I don't think I'll ever see anyone as perfect as you. I truly love you. Never forget that, no matter what happens in our lives!' he said, almost choking with emotion.

'I truly love you too!' she said, taking a step forward but inadvertently breaking the magic spell.

He took a huge breath and with every ounce of willpower he could muster, turned abruptly and said, 'Come on I'll race you!'

'What?' She was totally confused.

Turning his back to her, he repeated and shouted over his shoulder, 'Come on, last one in the water's a cissy!'

Poppy was totally bemused, and before she realised what was happening, he dived into the invigorating pool of water. He came to the surface and shouted, 'Come on in, it's fantastic!' He was relieved to feel the cold water cool his over-heated body and help quash the excitement that had abruptly arisen within him.

Mesmerised and still confused she followed him into the water, gasping as the coldness washed over her body. She didn't know what she had done to cause the sudden change in him.

He was laughing and splashing water at her. She in turn splashed back at him, trying to disguise her inner turmoil. They played in the water until they had thoroughly cooled down. They then returned to the rocks where their clothes lay, this time quickly drying off and putting their clothes back on, feeling shy and uncomfortable, not daring to look at each other.

'Are you ready?' Sam asked.

She nodded, still dazed at what had just happened in the last ten minutes.

'Come on then let's head back home,' he said. 'Everyone will be wondering where we are!' He put his arm amiably around her shoulders and they strolled back home over the long grass, overgrown weeds and uneven paved areas.

Her arm automatically tucked behind his back and it seemed the most comfortable feeling in the world. Sam broke the silence, 'You know I meant what I said. I will always love you and be there for you!'

Contribution

Her heart skipped a beat again. She looked up at him, but as their lips were about to meet, he quickly turned away. She was again feeling confused and now she was exasperated. 'What's the matter?' Poppy asked.

'We can't do this!'

'Why is it so wrong? We both love each other with all our hearts! We are truly best friends. Nobody could ever love you like I love you!'

'Yes, but we can't get any more involved than we already are!'

'Why not?' she almost wailed in frustration.

While fighting back his youthful desire and at the same time with a sense of maturity well beyond his years he looked into her eyes and said, 'Because we're too young Poppy and what we have is incredibly powerful and special. I really don't want to do anything to spoil it and I know if we let things get out of hand we will!'

'I don't see how?'

'Poppy, we've got the rest of our lives ahead of us. There is so much we both want to see and do - so much to create and experience. There are lots of adventures for us to have and we need to find our place and make our own mark in the world!' He paused and before she could say any more he added, 'Besides, my parents want to send me back to my aunt and uncle's in England so that I can finish off my education there!' He hadn't meant to blurt it out just yet and had wanted to wait until he felt the time was right.

Poppy was stunned and thought about it for a few minutes. 'But I could wait for you to return after getting your degree and we could do all these adventures together!' she tried to reason. 'Just because we're involved doesn't mean we can't do what we want!'

'Poppy, we've got to be sensible here. We both want to have great careers, see the world and do all sorts of things.'

'But we can do it together!'

He shook his head sadly. It wasn't going well. He knew what he had to do for both their sakes.

'Poppy, we need to give ourselves some space here. Yes, we'll always be best friends but there's a whole world out there full of people that we need to meet!'

She was shocked at what he was saying. It just didn't make sense to her. By now they had reached her house.

'If you ever need me or just want to talk, you know I'll always be there for you but we really can't let things go any further!' He looked at her beautiful bemused face. 'Poppy I want you to enjoy life. You deserve the best of it! We both do!' With that he gave her a brief kiss on the top of her head and quickly walked away, without looking back.

She was too stunned to say anything and just stared at his retreating back.

Poppy remembered being a shell-shocked teenager having gone back inside her home, pouring a glass of water and telling her gran she was going to her bedroom for an afternoon siesta.

'Are you all right dear?' Jasmine asked in a worried voice, she wasn't used to seeing her granddaughter look so forlorn.

'I'm fine thanks Gran, just a bit tired.' She really didn't feel like talking and needed to mull everything over.

'Well let me know if you need anything. Dinner will be at the usual time!'

'Okay, thanks Gran,' Poppy replied, trying to put on a brave face and smile.

Jasmine busied herself at the kitchen sink. She was concerned, but knew Poppy would tell her what was bothering her when she was ready to.

One warm evening, several months later, Jasmine and Poppy were sitting on the swing sofa on the back deck. Jasmine had once again been worried that her granddaughter didn't seem her usual bright and breezy self. When Jasmine asked her what was wrong Poppy burst into tears. It took a long while for the flood of tears to stop. Jasmine held her, gently stroking her hair like she used to do when she was a little girl and had fallen down and hurt herself. 'Tell me what's bothering you sweetheart.'

'It's Sam,' Poppy gulped in between sobs.

'I kind of guessed it was, since he hasn't been around here for a long time,' Jasmine said sympathetically. Ever since he had moved here the two children had been almost inseparable and he had spent much of his time at their house. 'So what happened?'

'He was worried that we were getting too involved and said we needed to have our own space and that he would be going back to England soon! I think that was just an excuse because he's been seeing lots of different girls!' Poppy didn't say that he was starting to get quite the reputation as a "Romeo". Girls were automatically drawn to his good looks, easygoing manner and ability to put his mind to anything he chose from sports, music, academics and artwork.

'Well, I guess he has a point... You know sweetheart it's all a part of growing up, even though it's very painful at times!' Jasmine had also been worried that they had been getting too close and in a way was kind of relieved that they were having some time apart but she hated to see her granddaughter so unhappy.

'But Gran, I miss him so much! He was my very best friend. Life is so lonely without him. He's broken my heart!'

'Honey, I'm sure he's still your best friend and this is probably just a passing phase. You two will always have that very special bond between you but maybe it's time you were spending more time with other people in your class!'

Poppy could see her grandmother's point of view but she had never felt so hurt or deserted in all her life.

Contribution

The weeks and months passed by and Poppy's heart still ached. It didn't help that she saw Sam at school all the time. However, she tried to block him out of her mind and dedicated every minute to her studies, graduating top of the whole year group, with exemplary results. Sam came second.

Finally the last day of school arrived and after graduation a party was held in the main hall of their small school with all the pupils who were a year older than they were. Sam caught Poppy's eye and she quickly turned away as he moved purposefully towards her.

'Hey Poppy, how are you?' he asked, above the noise of laughter coming from the happy students and loud music playing in the hall.

'Good thanks!' she said, trying to put on a brave face. 'How about you?'

'I'm fine thanks.' He paused. 'Poppy, I just wanted to say I am so very sorry for hurting you.' He paused again, and before she had chance to say anything he added, 'And to say goodbye!' Poppy took a deep breath as he continued, 'Tomorrow I'm flying out to England!'

'Oh!' she said, trying to quell the disappointment inside her.

'You knew I was going!

'Yes, but I guess I hadn't expected so soon!'

- 15 -

'Well mom and dad think it best I get settled with my aunt and uncle before starting university and I must admit I'm keen to get going.'

'What are you going to do?'

'I've been accepted at Oxford. I'm going to follow in dad's footsteps and do a civil engineering degree and in my free time I'll help my uncle in his construction company.'

'Oh, I hadn't realised you wanted to be an engineer!' Poppy responded, suddenly feeling that she didn't know him as well as she thought she did.

'Well, to be honest, I don't know what I really want to do, except surf and draw, of course!' He smiled, 'But dad wants me to do this and he says as long as I get a good degree I can go on and do other things after that! Anyway, we'll see!'

'Well,' Poppy sighed, 'I wish you luck!'

'Thank you and what about you?' he asked, good-naturedly.

'I still want to study marine biology like we both used to say we wanted to do,' she said, hoping she would remind him of their hopes and dreams when they were younger. 'I've been accepted at Stanford University in California.'

'Congratulations! But I'm not surprised you're going to do something like that. You've always loved nature and the ocean!' he said warmly, but not wanting to get caught up in the memories of their earlier life together.

Poppy smiled and nodded in acknowledgement.

Sam then added, 'Poppy, I wish you all the luck in the world and please, please be happy! You have so much talent. I know you can do wonderful things with it,' he almost pleaded.

Poppy smiled, as she tried to fight back tears and dislodge the lump in her throat. They both simply nodded and hugged each other tightly. She wanted to hang onto him for ever but he briefly kissed her on the cheek and gently untangled himself before going back to the crowd.

Poppy watched him say goodbye to his friends and then walk out of the hall. She knew things were going to be very different and there was a huge emptiness inside her. Yet she was glad they were finally leaving school so she didn't have to see the girls flirting around him so much now that he was no longer with her all the time.

After saying her own goodbyes to friends, it was with a heavy heart she returned home.

When Jasmine heard Poppy open the door, she greeted her. 'Hi, sweetheart, are you okay?' she asked, already knowing the answer.

'Yeah, I guess,' Poppy replied unenthusiastically, before continuing, 'I talked to Sam at the party and he told me he's going to England tomorrow!'

Jasmine gave a deep sigh and put her arm around Poppy's shoulders. 'But I thought you knew that!' her gran said quietly.

'I did, I just didn't think it would be quite so soon!'

Jasmine understood and nodded. She tried to lift her granddaughter's spirits, 'Well sweetheart it won't be long before you're off to Stanford and making your own way in the world too! Come on let's have some ice cream and make a list of all the things you think you'll need. We can go shopping in San Jose tomorrow. How does that sound?'

Poppy smiled and tried to put on a brave face for her grandmother's sake. They both knew they were going to miss each other and Poppy was worried that her grandmother would be left all on her own.

Chapter 2
The Road to Success!

Several weeks later Jasmine was fussing around Poppy at San Jose airport. 'Now you will e-mail me and keep in touch on *Facebook* won't you? Jasmine asked, pushing a strand of her granddaughter's hair back behind her white T-shirt.

'Of course Gran,' she smiled, 'but will you be all right? I'll worry about you too, you know!'

Jasmine, laughed. 'Ha, I'm a tough old bird you know!'

Poppy smiled. 'I know, but mom and dad were away so much it was always just you and me for the most part!'

'I know and I'll miss you every waking moment and I'll worry about you too but equally know you have your own life to lead! Having taken advanced placement courses and starting university a year younger than most I kind of feel my baby is leaving too soon but I know you have a very bright future ahead and I don't want to put any obstacles in your way!'

Poppy gulped, trying not to let unshed tears spill over. 'Gran, you know how much I love you and I've never really thanked you before for everything you've done for me!'

'I do and there's no need to thank me. After Ben died, you were my greatest joy and kept me going. I needed that! So it should be me thanking you!'

Poppy smiled in return. 'You know, I always wish I'd met him. Sometimes I feel as though I know him from stories you or dad have told me.'

Jasmine smiled back. 'I wish you had too. You would have really liked him, he was a real character. I'm sure you two would have got on really well.' Her thoughts drifted back to the man she idolised and still missed every day.

They clung to each other. 'Come on sweetheart, enough of all this sentimentality, it's time you were checking in!'

They hugged one last time as they reluctantly let go of each other, knowing that life was changing yet again for them both.

At university Poppy still couldn't get Sam out of her mind and would lose herself in her studies, reading as much as she could to try to forget him and move on with her life. She decided she would never get that close to any one person again so she set about making as many friends as she could. She was very popular and being such a young student, her mentor and lecturers always made sure she was all right, which was easy really as she was already self-sufficient and a great student.

Poppy's grades were excellent and she formed many friendships with people who shared the same interests and passion. Her gran used to tell her that when you were on the right road in your life and living your destiny, doors always seemed to open and the right person was in the right place for you at the right time! Poppy was finding this to be the case and loved what she was doing. When she had long vacation time she would return to Costa Rica and excitedly tell her gran all about what she had been doing.

'And any special boy in your life?' Jasmine would always ask, with a mischievous twinkle in her eye.

'No Gran,' Poppy would sigh good-naturedly with a slight smile, 'you know I don't have time for boys!'

'Well don't burn yourself out dear.'

They would continue with the charade both knowing the real reason why she didn't want a boyfriend.

'No Gran, I won't!'

They would catch up on all Poppy had been doing and she would then ask her gran if she had heard how Sam was doing, even though she would get the occasional brief e-mail from him. Sometimes she just liked to talk about him and hear his name but the reply was always the same: Jasmine had heard that Sam was enjoying his time in England and was doing well.

Poppy's vacation would always pass far too quickly. Each time she returned to Costa Rica she felt that her gran looked a little older and frailer. She worried about her but was heartened by the fact that on occasions

Aunt Millie from England would visit. She wasn't really her aunt but being her grandmother's best friend Poppy had known her all her life and affectionately called her Aunt Millie. From the stories her grandmother had told her she knew that Aunt Millie's visits would be light-hearted occasions with lots of laughter as they recalled their memories and past adventures.

Poppy's time at university in California was a challenging yet exciting time in her life which afforded her many opportunities to gain valuable marine experience out on the ocean. She continued to study and now offer findings to her research. She had quickly achieved a reputation as a future star and people would deferentially listen to what she had to say, drawn in by her beauty and enthusiasm for ecology at such a young age.

Poppy opened her eyes and stared out of the plane window, remembering the last time she saw her gran. At the age of nineteen, she had gone back to Costa Rica on vacation. It was at that time her grandmother's health rapidly deteriorated. This time Aunt Millie was there too and other family members.

Even now Poppy still felt an unbearable loss as she thought back to her grandmother's last day. Jasmine looked so serene and peaceful as she offered the last of her worldly wisdom in her final moments.

Poppy remembered how beautiful the church looked, filled with white gardenia, freesias and white candles, but inside she felt a huge dark void. She had been inconsolable as she wept into her father's arms. He had held her close with one arm, wiping his own eyes and blowing his nose, trying to comfort his daughter in their time of sorrow.

Yet now, especially in quiet moments, Poppy sensed that her grandmother wasn't totally gone but felt she was with her, guiding her.

Poppy remembered how after the funeral she had returned to university life in California, this time with a heavy heart, mourning the loss of the woman who had always been in her life and who had always been there for her.

Once again Poppy threw herself into her studies and research with even more vigour, if that were possible. Her parents were worried about her and told her to slow down but Poppy didn't want to. She wanted to block out her pain and pursue her dreams as swiftly as possible.

Despite, her loss, time did pass quickly and after finishing university Poppy graduated with a master's degree, being the top of her class in marine biology. She knew her gran would have been proud of her and wished with every ounce of her being that her gran could have been at her graduation.

Sam also graduated from university with a first class honours degree. It had been a breeze for him and he had enjoyed university life. He had become an expert boat rower. Anything to do with water he loved. He had had several girlfriends but now realised he couldn't get Poppy out of his heart and thoughts and so would occasionally e-mail her to see how she was and she would respond with a quick note.

Sam felt bad that he hadn't been there for her after her gran died. He had begun to think that Poppy had been right that they could have both pursued their dreams and still been together. But then he would think he didn't want to take that risk and he didn't want to mess her about, so his answer was to go out and date another girl!

By now Poppy had learned to scuba dive and after leaving university her internship was on a small scientific research boat, similar to the one she used to spend her summers on when Carmel, Ely and their team sailed into their bay in Costa Rica.

Poppy had stayed in California and loved working with the elite team of marine researchers and after a year their findings were becoming world famous. The crew were interviewed by a well-known TV documentary team while docked for a short while near LA.

The producer was so impressed with Poppy's charm, looks and ability that she offered her a job at the TV station helping to research information for marine projects. Very soon Poppy was co-starring with the main anchor. Her parents were very proud of her and often e-mailed a quick note to tell her so.

Poppy's popularity soared and very quickly the ratings rocketed. From there she was offered her own conservation show. Poppy often thought back to her gran's words of support when she had told her she knew she wanted to work with conservation and ecology but also wanted to be in the limelight. Poppy remembered how her gran had told her that she could do anything she wanted, if she thought it, felt it, believed it and worked hard towards her goal. Poppy once again wished her gran could have been there to share in the glory of her success.

Meanwhile, Sam had stayed on in England for a year working in one of the finest engineering firms. But he hated the confines of being in an office all day and almost felt claustrophobic. He yearned to go to back to Costa Rica. So he tendered his resignation and booked a flight home.

Having said farewell to everyone in England he was happy to be flying back to the lush green jungles and beautiful sandy beaches of Costa Rica.

However, after several weeks of surfing and spending time in solitude, playing his guitar, on the soft sandy beach, he began to feel restless again. He had re-connected with some of his Costa Rican friends but a lot had left to go and work in cities and it just wasn't the same without Poppy.

Sam knew Poppy was very busy in the glamorous world she was carving for herself and he followed her progress with the interest of a life-long friend. He spent hours on the beach, thinking and meditating, until one day his inner voice urged him to visit India and try to connect with his spiritual roots.

Sam's parents were not happy about this but nonetheless he felt compelled to do it. He corresponded with a spiritual leader a college friend had recommended and they made arrangements for his arrival.

Sam loved his journey through India, spending time in ashrams, meditating, helping people where he could and really connecting with his spiritual self. He had also become firm friends with a young Indian man of similar age named Akbar. They were great companions and said they would always stay connected and be best friends no matter where they were in the world or what they were doing.

After Sam left India he continued to travel the world, visiting spiritual sites, in particular spending time in the south-western region of the US, where many ancient American Indian ruins held mystical powers. Spiritual teachings were passed down through generations from one Shaman to another. Sam absorbed all the spiritual teachings he could, feeling connected and at one with the universe. However, no matter what he did he never stopped thinking about Poppy.

As the years wore on Sam was true to his word and kept in touch with Poppy. He often sent an e-mail saying he'd seen her latest show, or magazine article, and that he was immensely proud of her. He would also tell her what he had been doing.

Poppy had dated a couple of other men in her life but they hadn't lasted long - they could never measure up to Sam in her eyes. Besides she was totally focused on her career and did sometimes wonder if Sam had actually been right – that they could only pursue their lifelong dreams on their own.

Her thoughts then wandered back to meeting Gregory and she excitedly imagined them spending time together...

Poppy dozed off for a short while and was woken by the pilot announcing that the cabin crew should now prepare for landing.

'Are you okay?' Toby asked his lovely daughter, whom he adored with all his heart.

'I'm fine thanks Dad. How about you?'

'I'm fine too,' he smiled in reply. 'Looking forward to some quality time with you and your mom!'

'Me too!' she agreed.

They only had small carry-ons so it didn't take them long to disembark and make their way through Logan airport.

Chapter 3
Brief Encounters!

When they arrived back at the apartment in Boston, Poppy quickly unpacked her small suitcase and removed her laptop. She always had lots of e-mails to check and liked to keep on top of her work even when she was supposed to be taking a break. But this time she was eager to see if there was an e-mail from a certain special gentleman she had recently met.

Poppy was delighted to see a highlighted e-mail nestled in between all the others and eagerly opened it. Gregory told her how happy he had been to meet both her and her parents, thanked them all for sharing a wonderful evening and he hoped he hadn't come across as a "star-struck fan", which of course he was, he told her good humouredly!

Poppy in return sent Gregory an e-mail telling him how delighted they were to have met him and spend time getting to know him.

Over the next few weeks Poppy and Gregory e-mailed each other on a regular basis, asking questions and finding out more about the other.

She already knew that, like her, he loved his work and nature. She also found out that, like her, he enjoyed reading, listening to music, hiking in the forests and walking along the beach, whenever he could. He lived on his own, close to his parents, in Rhode Island. He was especially attached to his faithful and loving golden Labrador "Misty". He had named her that because on the day he brought her home it had been particularly foggy.

Misty had been part of his life for several years now but, as he travelled so much, she lived with his parents when he was away and he would look after her on his return home.

Gregory also liked to cook, loved sailing and told Poppy he hoped that one day she would come and visit him in Rhode Island and he would make her a delicious three-course meal and take her out on his boat!

In her reply, Poppy told him she would love to visit Rhode Island, as it was a place she had never been to and would be more than happy to sample his cooking and go sailing with him! However, she wasn't sure when she could get over there but told him she would be in Boston with her parents until the end of the week. Toby and Annabelle wanted to combine some free time following on from several medical seminars. Rhode Island was only a short flight to Boston, and she wondered if he might want to join them before she returned to Costa Rica? He replied he would love to and booked the first flight out of Rhode Island for a few days visit.

Toby dressed casually in jeans and red sweater that accentuated his swept-back dark hair, which now had specks of grey showing through. He expertly drove the rental car to Logan airport to collect Gregory. Annabelle sat next to her husband, dressed in light grey slacks and black sweater with her hair swept up into a loose bun, making her look sophisticated but relaxed. Poppy's parents were looking forward to getting to know Gregory.

Poppy sat behind her parents and let her thoughts drift to Gregory. She was very excited about seeing him again, especially so soon after their first meeting. She wore tight blue jeans with a thick white sweater and white scarf bejewelled with deep blue and purple gems, which highlighted her dark skin and hair. Having been used to the tropical temperatures of Costa Rica for much of her life, she always felt the cold when she was in Boston, even though today was a bright sunny day.

Gregory also dressed in jeans but was wearing a blue sweatshirt, which emphasised his blue eyes. He hurried through arrivals and almost came to a standstill as his eyes settled on Poppy. He'd seen her many times on television and even after meeting her he was still dazzled by her beauty. Gregory forced himself to walk at a reasonable pace towards the small party waiting for him, instead of running at full speed to take Poppy into his arms, which was what he really wanted to do. They all briefly hugged and said how good it was to see each other.

'Not sure if you're hungry Gregory, but we thought you might like to go out for breakfast,' Poppy's father said.

'That would be great,' Gregory enthused. He didn't care what they did. He just wanted to spend as much time as he possibly could in the company of Poppy.

'So where are you staying?' Annabelle asked in a casual voice. She noticed him blush, looking embarrassed.

'Ah... well... I managed to get my flight booked and then got so busy I forgot to book a room but once we've finished breakfast I'll make some calls. There are usually plenty of rooms at this time of year,' he said. He hadn't wanted to admit that his thoughts had been so full of Poppy that he'd totally overlooked booking anywhere!

'Well don't worry, you can stay at our place... although I'm afraid you'll have to sleep on the sofa as the apartment is only small!' Annabelle quickly added.

'Oh I couldn't possibly put you to any trouble...'

'No trouble at all, in fact it would be a pleasure,' Toby said, agreeing with his wife.

'Well if you're sure?' Gregory replied sheepishly.

'Of course, I wouldn't have suggested it otherwise!' Annabelle smiled at him, also thinking it was a good opportunity to get to know him better.

They ate a light and pleasant breakfast and caught up on what they'd been doing since their last meeting.

Contribution

When they returned to the apartment, Annabelle reiterated apologetically, 'Sorry it's just the sofa.'

'I really don't mind. I'm just glad to be here and I certainly don't want to impose on you!' he replied sincerely with a warm smile. He would have slept on the roof if he thought it would have meant being closer to Poppy, he thought to himself.

Gregory quickly unpacked a couple of small gifts he had brought for Poppy's parents and then turned to Poppy. 'Would you like to take a walk around the city?'

'I'd love to,' she smiled. Even though she knew the city well, nothing would have given her more pleasure than to be in his company.

They strolled comfortably down the interesting streets in the sunny New England spring air, feeling as though they already knew each other well after sharing so much of their thoughts and dreams through e-mails and long phone conversations.

Poppy and Gregory walked hand in hand along the Freedom Trail and talked about the history of this fine-looking city. They then went into Faneuil Hall and Quincy Market before stopping for a drink and light bite to eat. They talked and laughed and felt totally at one with each other.

'You know Poppy, I almost feel as though this is a dream,' he said, shyly and pausing. 'I've seen you so much in the media and yet I find myself sitting here across from you, holding your hand and spending time with you!'

Poppy laughed light-heartedly and blushed at his heartfelt compliment.

'You are one of the most beautiful women I've ever seen! he said, admiring her. He was only too aware of the appreciative glances she got and people nudging each other saying, 'Isn't that the girl who does the wildlife shows?'

'Thank you,' she said, still blushing.

He also liked her modesty and the fact that she didn't take her stardom for granted but used it as a tool to educate people about the natural living planet.

For her part, she was totally smitten with him - not just his boyish sexy charm but his soft voice and his strength and gentleness at the same time, giving an attractive magnetism.

'I hope you don't mind spending some of the weekend with my parents,' Poppy said, almost apologetically. 'It's just that with our hectic schedules I couldn't see when we could fit it in sooner if we hadn't have done this!'

He smiled endearingly. 'Poppy, if it meant sharing you with a hundred people this weekend I would have done it just to be near you!'

She laughed again and was delighted he felt the same way.

The afternoon shadows grew longer and there was a definite chill in the air so they returned to her parents' apartment. After exchanging pleasantries with her parents they quickly changed to get ready for cocktails and evening meal at the old *Union Oyster House* which, according to Toby, had the best lobster and oysters anywhere.

'Wow, you look stunning!' Gregory said, once again admiring Poppy. She was wearing a short black cocktail dress and black high heeled sandals with her long dark hair swept down over one side of her shoulders.

'Thank you!' she replied, noticing how smart Gregory looked in his charcoal grey slacks and silvery blue open-necked shirt. 'You don't look so bad yourself!'

Toby and Annabelle were pleased to note the heightened colour in their daughter's cheeks and mischievous twinkle in her dark eyes, something they hadn't seen in a long time.

Although Poppy had been to the old *Union Oyster House* many times before, she had never felt as excited about the place as she did tonight. Once seated, Gregory and Poppy continued with their easy banter and devoured the hors d'oeuvres of oysters, laughing and watching the other as they each swallowed the savoury appetisers whole.

After they finished eating the oysters they continued telling each other about their latest projects and gazed into each other's eyes. The waiter brought them a huge plate of lobster each. They tucked into the fine meal and both declared it was one of the best they had eaten in a long time. When they finished dinner they held hands across the table, totally at ease with each other.

After they drank their coffees and liqueurs they thanked the waiter for his excellent service and Gregory promptly paid, leaving a generous tip. They walked slowly through the brightly lit streets, bustling with evening shoppers and street entertainers. They enjoyed the hustle and bustle of city night life and made their way back to the apartment, arm in arm.

Before they entered the main doorway Gregory turned slowly and pulled Poppy firmly to him, bringing her face close to his. 'Poppy, I've got to tell you, this has been one of the most enjoyable evenings of my life!'

'Mine too!' she agreed. Before she could say anything else his lips tenderly found hers. They embraced and the kisses became more passionate. They could feel an exciting energy swirling between them and both reluctantly tore themselves away from each other with a heady sigh and walked to the elevator, arms still around each other.

They entered the apartment, still arm in arm.

'Did you two youngsters enjoy yourselves?' Annabelle asked, already knowing the answer. She could see excitement and new love shining brightly in their eyes.

'Oh yes Mom we had a fabulous time thanks,' Poppy said, laying down her purse and removing her shawl. She then poured them all a nightcap and Gregory told Toby and Annabelle about their evening.

It was getting late so Annabelle turned the sofa into a bed for Gregory.

It suddenly felt awkward as Toby and Annabelle hovered in the open-plan living room. So Poppy just went up to Gregory and briefly kissed him on the cheek, and they both thanked each other for a wonderful time.

All the subtle exchanges were not lost on Annabelle and Toby. They really liked Gregory and were glad someone had finally whisked their beautiful daughter off her feet. They had been worried that Poppy still hadn't got over Sam, although they knew they were still friends and would probably be there for each other for the rest of their lives.

Everyone said goodnight and Poppy left to go to her room and get ready for bed. As she got into bed her thoughts were full of Gregory. It felt strange to her knowing he was lying in the room next to her and so close.

Gregory's thoughts were also of her and the energy between them was almost tangible.

The night wore on and Poppy tossed and turned - she just couldn't get to sleep.

Gregory was also restless in the next room.

Poppy wanted to sneak through to him but didn't dare.

Gregory lay on the sofa, his thoughts drifting to Poppy. He wanted to lie next to her and feel her heartbeat but would never offend her parents' hospitality. So they both remained in their own room in the dark, imagining and dreaming of what it would be like to be together.

The next morning Poppy and Gregory both awoke early and quickly dressed for the day, wanting to make the most of their time together. They skipped breakfast at the apartment, telling Annabelle they would grab something later on when they were out.

Once again they both wore jeans but this time also wore hooded sweatshirts over T-shirts, after feeling the chill in the air last night. Gregory wore a dark green sweatshirt and Poppy a light grey one. She was glad they didn't look too identical!

After they started walking through the city, they found a lively place for breakfast. When they finally finished the huge plate of bacon, eggs, hash browns, toast and coffee, they continued walking.

They visited the *USS Constitution* which was docked at the Charlestown Navy Yard. Gregory really enjoyed the tour of the old warship before going on to have a light lunch of clam chowder and fresh bread. During their lunch, Gregory leaned over, taking her hand. 'You know, I feel I know so much about you but the one thing you haven't told me about is your love life! I'm kind of thinking you may have had your heart broken. Is that right?'

Poppy looked a little uncomfortable and shuffled slightly in her seat.

'Sorry, I shouldn't have asked,' he said apologetically.

'No, it's not that, and of course you should ask! It's just where to begin?' She thought about Sam, remembering the day when he turned her world upside down. Poppy wanted to start her relationship with Gregory on the right footing so decided to give Gregory an abridged version.

'You see he wasn't my boyfriend as such but my very best friend! Sam had been in my life every day until he decided he wanted different things in life. I guess I had a crush on him during all that time!'

Poppy and Gregory fell into a companionable silence as she let her thoughts drift back to a different time and place, and he patiently waited for more information.

Time was getting on and Gregory broke the silence with a gentle touch of her hand. He could see remnants of pain in Poppy's eyes as the memories came flooding back. 'If you don't want to tell me I understand, but I was just wondering if you still see him?' Gregory asked in a tentative quiet voice.

'Now and again, it just depends on what we're doing. He's still on this huge quest to find himself so it depends on where he is and what he's doing! But when he's back home in Costa Rica he fills his time creating exquisite artwork and fine pieces of furniture from driftwood he finds on the beach. Then when he has enough money he travels around the world in pursuit of inspiration for his art and spiritual fulfilment!'

'He sounds like an interesting character. I'd really enjoy meeting him some day!'

'Well, maybe we can arrange it, especially if you come over to Costa Rica some time!'

'Is that an invitation?' Gregory asked with a flirtatious smile.

'Maybe…! Would you like it to be one?' Poppy replied, equally flirtatious.

'I certainly would!' He smiled mischievously.

'Well in that case we'll have to see what we can do!' She grinned teasingly, before continuing, 'So come on, tell me all about your love life!'

'Nothing much to tell really,' he shrugged. 'I've had a few girlfriends that lasted a while but nothing serious, well not on my part anyway.' He paused. 'And like you I always wanted to focus on my career and travel, which isn't too good for relationships!'

She nodded, understanding.

'Besides, I think I always had a secret crush on you!' he schmoozed and she blushed once more.

During the afternoon they continued their tour of the city and went to the Museum of Fine Arts. They admired the impressionist paintings and especially loved the Monet collection. They discussed each painting then moved onto the Asian and Old Egyptian collection and finally the classical art. They both had a love and appreciation of all types of art and were delighted to realise they had so much in common. He thought Poppy was the most intelligent woman he had ever met.

That evening they joined Poppy's parents for a delicious home-cooked meal prepared by Annabelle and served with fine Italian red wine. The conversation was light, good-humoured and full of laughter.

Having had an early start to the day, and neither getting much sleep the night before, they were both feeling tired. Poppy yawned and finished helping her mother clear away the last of the dishes. 'I think I'm going to have an early night if that's okay with everyone?'

'Of course, dear.' Annabelle replied.

'Thanks for a wonderful meal Mom,' Poppy continued gratefully.

'Yes, thank you,' Gregory chimed in, also grateful to his hosts. 'And once again thank you for putting me up at such short notice!'

'No trouble at all and you are very welcome!' Annabelle smiled graciously. She already really liked the handsome young gentleman who had suddenly come into their lives. 'Let me make up the sofa again.'

'No, no, let me do that!' Gregory insisted, picking up the pile of blankets.

They all said goodnight, and even though they were both tired, Poppy and Gregory thought they would have another restless night thinking of each other.

As it happened, they both fell quickly asleep in their separate sleeping areas, content and thankful at finding a new friendship and the start of what they both hoped would be something more.

The next morning the four of them had a leisurely Sunday breakfast together, lingering for as long as possible, knowing all too soon their time together would be over and Gregory would have to leave for the airport.

Gregory thanked Toby and Annabelle for their hospitality, and in turn they told him it had been a real pleasure.

This time Poppy took him to the airport herself and before he went through departures she told him how much she had enjoyed their weekend.

'I have too, Poppy. I'm really going to miss you. I feel like I've known you for ever and that we have something very special… Although I'm not sure how we're going to manage to make time to see each other with our hectic schedules, but I really want to make this work!'

'I know what you mean, and I feel the same way. I was thinking, I've got a month's shoot in Mexico then I've got a week off at home in Costa Rica. Is there any chance you could join me then?'

He beamed. 'I'll move heaven and earth to be with you. I'll let you know.'

They lovingly embraced, and as they kissed a beautiful sensation soared through their bodies. Neither of them wanted it to end - it was almost as though time stood still. He reluctantly pulled himself away.

'I'll e-mail you every day and call you whenever I can,' he said earnestly, with his arms around her, looking steadily into her eyes.

She nodded, barely able to speak such was the incredible feelings he had stirred within her. 'I'll be counting down the days until we see each other again.'

'Me too!' he said, before briefly kissing her on the forehead and making his way through departures, turning and waving to her before disappearing.

Poppy wanted to shout over to him that she loved him, but felt it was too early to express such a strong emotion and knew it could wait until they were together again. She waited until she could no longer see him in the crowded terminal and then turned and walked back to her car with a sense of excitement at the way her life had suddenly changed.

Later that evening Gregory e-mailed her to say he had arrived back home safely in Rhode Island. He thanked her once again for such a wonderful time and told her he was already missing her. He also asked her to thank her parents once again for their kindness. He thought she had lovely, caring, intelligent parents so it wasn't surprising that their daughter was so dynamic!

The next morning a massive bouquet of deep red roses arrived at her parents' apartment. Poppy opened the envelope with a card enclosed and her mother looked over her shoulder at the beautiful flowers.

Poppy read the note from Gregory out loud saying that he was already missing her and counting down the days until they could be together again.

Annabelle smiled knowing that her daughter had found a very special man. Poppy was delighted to receive the thoughtful gift and was on cloud nine all day.

Poppy e-mailed Gregory, thanking him for the exquisite flowers.

He replied telling her they were going to be on location in the Colorado Rockies for the next few weeks and then in Canada, but he should be able to get a week off to join her in Costa Rica by calling in a few favours. They were both delighted and couldn't wait for the next time they could be together. In the meantime, they worked hard to keep up with their arduous schedules on location.

Whenever Poppy and Gregory had a spare moment their thoughts would wander to the other...

Chapter 4
Meant to Be!

The e-mails continued to fly back and forth at a furious pace until four weeks later Poppy was finally going to meet Gregory at San Jose airport. She would then drive him down to her family coastal home.

When Gregory came through arrivals she ran up to him and he hugged her tightly. 'Hey, how are you?' he asked, pulling her close to him.

'I'm great now that you're here!'

'I know what you mean. How was the filming in Mexico?' he asked, reluctantly letting her go but leaving his arm around her shoulders. They sauntered slowly back to her car.

'Hectic, but good thanks. We studied a pod of dolphins and filmed off the Yucatan Peninsula. It was extremely hot and humid, but thankfully we spent much of our time in the water,' she said, smiling.

'That's good!'

There was a slight silence before Gregory added, 'You look fantastic!' He was admiring her short, white, halter-neck sundress, showing off her bronzed body. Her white flat sandals accentuated her shapely legs and her long dark hair glistened in the bright sunlight.

'Thank you. You too!' Poppy replied, observing his white shorts and pale blue polo shirt, noticing, once again, how the colour matched his soft blue eyes. He looked incredibly relaxed, confident and sexy.

'Thank you!' he smiled. 'I must admit it's great to be back in a warm climate and wear shorts again after having worked in the cold Rockies!'

'Other than being cold, did the filming go well?'

'Yes thanks. We got everything done we wanted to and now we just need to do some final studio work later this month.'

Poppy confidently drove from the airport towards the coast and they chatted about everything they could think of.

After an hour's drive she pulled over to a nice small, family-run restaurant overlooking the ocean. They couldn't take their eyes off each other, and if they weren't holding hands their legs or knees were gently touching each other. The feeling between them was electrifying. They had an enjoyable traditional meal of beans, rice, pork *Carnitas* and *pico de gallo* before continuing with the last part of the journey.

About half-an-hour before arriving home, Poppy approached the closest town to her village. 'I thought I would just stop off here and get some pastries for breakfast and show you a little of the town if that's okay with you?' she asked, turning her head to him as she expertly drove through the busy streets.

'That's fine.'

'Good, it gives us chance to stretch our legs a bit too!'

'Sounds good to me!'

Once Poppy found a parking spot on the busy high street, they got out of her air-conditioned car and strolled hand in hand, passing many small shops. She told him stories about the people she knew working at the various places ranging from liquor to tourist souvenir shops and attractions. Many people sat outside relaxing and eating at the wooden tables of the friendly restaurants. The sun beat down on them and Poppy asked him if he would like an ice cream. 'You read my mind!' he smiled at her.

They sat under the shade eating ice cream, watching the world go by. Once they finished their refreshing treat they walked over to the bakery and bought what she needed for the next few days before getting back in the car and finishing their journey.

Poppy drove along the winding roads of the rugged coast, lined with tropical trees, and they continued chatting. Brightly coloured scarlet macaws and other birds circled above before landing on nearby branches.

'Wow what a beautiful coastline,' Gregory observed.

'Yes, I must admit even though I spent much of my life here I really love it. The scenery makes such a lovely drive!'

He nodded in agreement.

It wasn't long before they arrived at her family home, which originally had been her gran's. Poppy now lived here alone when she wasn't on location. Her parents were currently living and working in Panama.

Poppy drove up the steep hill, lit by lamps on top of the elaborate block walls, surrounded by palm trees and brightly coloured hibiscus, ginger and other tropical plants.

'Wow, is this your home?' he asked, looking at the magnificent house painted white with lots of huge windows and black railed balconies surrounding it. The property overlooked well-cared for gardens and out to the roaring ocean.

Poppy nodded proudly. 'Well, family home. It was originally Gran and Grandpa Ben's, although I never met him. He died just before I was born.'

'Oh I'm sorry,' Gregory said, sympathetically squeezing her hand.

'Yes, it was a shame. I wish I'd met him. Gran always talked about him and he sounded like an amazing man.' Poppy paused, recollecting her gran's stories. 'He was a firefighter in America and had a long and distinguished career. When he retired he travelled the world with Gran, taking photos and becoming quite famous for his fine art photography. He was very talented. They eventually settled here in Costa Rica and he actually built this house himself. That large building over there used to be his art gallery but a long time after he passed away gran converted it into accommodation for our property managers who care for the house, gardens and guard dog as we were all away so much.'

'Wow, it's gorgeous!' he said, mesmerised by the size and splendour of it all.

'It's my oasis... my little piece of heaven to come home to! Come on, I'll show you around,' Poppy enthused. They entered through the front door into the huge open-plan living room full of light with the large kitchen window overlooking the ocean. She showed him the guest bathroom and bedroom downstairs and explained the story behind each of Ben's large photographs strategically placed throughout each room.

'My grandparents had absolutely loads of photos but we only keep on display those that have sentimental meaning to the family.'

'They're stunning and very creative too,' Gregory said, studying each one and fully appreciating the artistic technique behind them. 'They must have gone to some fantastic places!'

'They certainly did! They spent a good twenty years travelling the world and taking in all its beauty and wonders. Gran used to tell me stories of the fun and sometimes dangerous adventures they used to have. Gran also sold her artwork too and they were really making quite a name for themselves!' Poppy told him proudly. 'They were very talented but gran always said you can do anything you choose to if you think it, feel it and believe it!'

'You two sound like you were really close.'

'We were, especially as she more or less brought me up when my parents went to medical school in Boston just after I was born. They only came home on the holidays and then when they started working they worked in local hospitals before coming back to Costa Rica to work.'

'I thought they lived and worked in Panama?'

'They do now but have only been there the last couple of years. They like to go where they feel really needed. As mom mentioned last time we were all together, she's a cardiologist. Dad has always specialised in trauma and emergency room medicine because his natural mother was killed in a car accident when he was a child.'

'Oh really, that's so tragic!'

'Yes, my grandparents are really my adopted grandparents but I always think of them as my own which they are really, especially as gran was the one who brought me up! Gran and Grandpa Ben found dad and his mother at the scene of a horrible car accident. Dad's mother died in Ben's arms just as he pulled her from the wreckage before it was engulfed in flames. Gran carried dad away from the wreckage. He was only a small boy then. Apparently, he constantly clung to her in the police station afterwards. Gran and grandpa took him back to their home and consoled and cared for him. They later went through the lengthy legal process of adopting him!'

'Gosh that's amazing!'

'Gran used to say that I look very much like my birth grandmother as she also had long, dark, straight hair and dark skin.' Poppy paused, taking a sip of the icy cold lemon water she had poured. Gregory too drank from the tall glass of water Poppy had handed him before they started the tour of the house.

'That's a photo of Grandpa Ben over there,' she said, pointing to the photo of him in his fire-fighting gear, 'and that's him with gran,' Poppy said, looking at the photo of Ben with his arms protectively around Jasmine who was looking lovingly into his eyes. 'Those are my two favourite photos of them, although I have loads tucked away in albums.'

'What a handsome couple. They looked good together.'

'Yes, they were,' she agreed. It surprised her that even now she still missed her gran so much.

'Did they have children of their own?' Gregory asked, breaking into Poppy's thoughts.

'No. By the time they met, Grandpa Ben had grown-up children by his first marriage. But gran loved his children and grandchildren as much as if they had been her own and always thought of them as her family too. They were the family she never had. That's them all together,' Poppy said, pointing to the large family photo of the rare time when they could all be together at once.

'What a lovely looking family,' Gregory said, taking the photo off the shelf and admiring it.

'Yes they are,' Poppy agreed.

'Do you still keep in touch?'

'Yes, sometimes, more on *Facebook* than anything, especially as we all have such busy lives these days and live so far away!'

Gregory smiled. 'That's nice.'

Poppy nodded. They continued looking at the pictures. 'You know, one day I would really love to do the same tour gran and grandpa did on their first year of travelling together,' Poppy said casually.

'Where was that?'

'Well, let's see,' Poppy said, recollecting her gran's words. 'They started in England, toured Scotland, went back to Colorado which is where grandpa was originally from. Then onto the Napa Valley, San Francisco and then Hawaii, Fiji, Australia, Thailand, India and came full circle back to the UK. They then returned to Colorado for a short while before going to live in Costa Rica and finally building this house!'

'Wow, that's quite the tour!' Gregory said, before continuing, 'and maybe one day you'll be able to do the same!' he smiled encouragingly.

She smiled back at him. 'Maybe I will! Anyway come on, let me take you to the best part of the house.'

Poppy led him up the spiral staircase which brought them to the huge master bedroom. There was a large king size bed in the middle of the room with luxurious white linens. The whole bedroom was decorated white with comfortable chairs and occasional tables dotted around.

Gregory noticed a small bookcase discreetly tucked away and an array of books neatly displayed. He walked over to them and read the titles on the spines of the covers.

'This is quite the collection of inspirational and thought-provoking books you have here!'

Poppy smiled. 'Actually they were gran's and really just a small selection of what she had but these were her favourites. She was quite an avid reader!'

'So have you read them?' Gregory enquired amiably.

'I've read some but there are still a few I would like to read when I have more time!'

He pulled out a small thin book entitled *As A Man Thinketh* and looked at it thoughtfully. 'I read this one a long time ago!'

'Really, did you like it?'

'Yes, and it's pretty much the way I try to live my life! I really do believe our thoughts make things happen in our lives!'

Poppy smiled in response, pleased they were on the same wavelength. 'That's what gran used to say. I'm sure you would have got on well with her!'

He smiled in response, pleased he was making a good impression on the woman he was so smitten with.

'So what's your favourite out of the ones you've read so far?'

'Uumm, that's a good question. There are so many great books I've gained wisdom from... but I think I would have to say that *The Road Less Travelled* is one of my real favourites.'

'Why's that?'

'Mmmm... I guess because the author was an actual psychiatrist and he guides and suggests ways that help people reach a higher level of self-understanding when facing difficulties and suffering.'

Gregory nodded, picking up another book and as he did so a small white envelope fell to the polished wooden floor. They both stared at it, surprised by its sudden appearance.

'It's addressed to you!' Gregory said, as he stooped to pick it up.

'Yes, it looks like gran's handwriting,' she said, as he passed it to her.

'And you haven't read it?'

'No, I've never seen it before!' she said intrigued, wondering what it could be about. 'But I'll read it later. First I want to finish showing you the rest of the place!' she said as she carefully placed it on top of the books.

Poppy led him through the airy bedroom onto the huge veranda with outdoor wooden seating and tables. It was now getting late and it had turned pitch black outside. The sky was illuminated with bright twinkling stars. Below, lights shone from distant houses and there were even some dazzling fireflies darting about.

'Poppy this is so beautiful and tranquil!' he said, feeling totally at ease.

'I know. I just love to get away from things and come back here!'

They stood very close to each other, looking out, listening to the sound of the ocean and their hearts beating. It was pure magic. Gregory turned to Poppy. Their eyes held each other and he put his hand behind her neck and felt her long soft hair fall over his hand. Their lips found each other in a hungry, passionate embrace. They held each other tightly and he gently picked her up in his arms and carried her back through to her bedroom, all the time studying her exquisite face. He didn't utter a word but the expression in his eyes asked, 'Is this okay?' She barely managed a nod. Gregory gently laid her down on the bed and tenderly undid her sundress revealing her flawless body.

He kissed her fervently, while swiftly removing his own clothing until they were lying naked next to each other, their bodies on fire. 'Are you sure about this Poppy?'

She could barely breathe let alone answer, so once again she just nodded. Her eyes roamed from his handsome face over his perfectly toned body and she felt her own body quivering with anticipation...

The balcony's low lighting dimly lit the room and outlined their bodies as they found their rhythm and made sweet love. Neither of them had ever felt this way before.

Afterwards, feeling hot and clammy in the humid evening, they lay contentedly in each other's arms, amazed at the love and wonderful feeling between them.

Gregory fell quiet and Poppy realised he'd suddenly fallen asleep! She lay awake, thinking about the wonderful sensual man lying next to her and the love she had for him. Never had she felt like this. The excitement of meeting a new man and finding out all about him was different to the love she had had for Sam and she thought that maybe he had been right after all! She was now so grateful for the way things had turned out and thanked the heavens above for bringing Gregory into her life!

Then she remembered the small white envelope that had fallen to the floor. Curious, she quietly slipped out of bed, picked up the envelope off the top of the bookcase where she had previously placed it and tip-toed out onto the balcony. She sat under one of the dim exterior lights and caught her breath as she read the all too familiar writing:

My dearest Poppy, by the time you read this I will have passed over to the other side. I hope things are going well for you and that all your dreams are coming true!

I want you to know that from the moment I first held you in my arms, when you were a newborn, I could see the light in your eyes and knew you were an extra-special baby!

Contribution

As you grew, your curiosity and sweetness were a joy to behold and I knew, without doubt, you would grow into a very special woman and do great things with your life!

You and Sam gave me so much joy as I watched you grow into teenagers. He was always an old soul in a young body. He was wise beyond his years and I feel sure that he has carried over the lessons learned from past lives very well. I know he really hurt you but I am hoping that with the passing of time you two have become the firm friends you always were and I hope you will have moved on and have now found true love in your life! If I have anything to do with it that will certainly be the case!

However, as you know, there will be tough times in your life that is for sure. We cannot escape these! As well as being on this earth to love, create and experience, I believe we are also here for valuable lessons that we have to learn to help us in our spiritual growth! When those tough times are with you, that's when you face your greatest lessons and it is in those times that I want you to know I will be watching over you, along with your Guardian Angel! And remember, my beautiful Poppy, we are never faced with anything we cannot handle, no matter how tough it may seem at the time!

I will be with you always, all my love Gran xx

Poppy felt a lump in her throat as she fought back tears and yet at the same time she felt completely at ease with herself and the universe. She gently folded the letter and looked up to the stars, giving thanks for her life and the part her gran had played in it.

Poppy then tip-toed back to her bed and slipped in beside Gregory, without disturbing him. She lay very still, thinking about Gregory and Sam, and decided she should really tell Sam about her new man. Maybe they could all have dinner together soon? She would call him in the morning. She then fell into a blissful sleep, dreaming about the amazing time she had already had with Gregory.

Poppy opened her eyes to find Gregory lying on one elbow, seductively smiling at her. She returned a slow smile.

'Good morning sleepy head. I hope you don't mind but I put the coffee on and made some breakfast,' he said softly.

'Mind? Not at all! That's great!' She smiled delightedly, loving the feeling of being indulged.

He bent his head down and their lips touched. Feeling very relaxed, she held on tightly to him and returned his kisses, and very soon his naked body was on top of hers.

Later, feeling sedated, she said, 'Let's sample your breakfast out on the bedroom balcony!'

'Good idea! I'll just go and get it,' he said, making himself at home.

Out on the balcony, they sat eating their breakfast of pastries and fresh tropical fruit they had bought yesterday, looking out over the ocean. They talked about what they would like to do that day and she suggested that perhaps they should see if Sam could join them for dinner?

Gregory thought that was a good idea but in all honesty he didn't care what they did as long as they were together!

Later on Poppy made the call to Sam.

'Hey, that's a coincidence, I was just about to phone you and invite you out for dinner since I'd heard you were back!'

Sam planned to tell Poppy how much he loved her and couldn't get her out of his head and that no-one ever measured up to her. He hoped she would give him a second chance. However, the wind was taken out of his sails when Poppy rushed in telling him about the wonderful man she had met and had fallen in love with! He knew then he couldn't tell her and confuse her all over again!

They agreed that the three of them would meet up for dinner at Jose's cantina later that evening.

They had a lovely evening and Poppy was delighted that the two men in her life got on so well and really liked each other. She had been worried that it might have been a little uneasy but she should have known better she told herself. They were both so easygoing and quietly self-assured that there would never have been any awkwardness. They finished their evening together with Sam saying he would keep in touch.

Their week in Costa Rica was bliss. Poppy and Gregory spent their time walking hand in hand along the beach every day, once early in the morning and then again before sunset. She had taken him into the rainforest and pointed out all the beautiful birds and plants she knew so well.

As promised, Poppy had also taught him how to surf and was impressed that after his first few attempts he was up on the board, steadily surfing the waves, but being so athletic she guessed she shouldn't have been surprised. His confidence quickly grew on the surfboard and he started catching larger waves. He was thoroughly enjoying his new found skill. Afterwards they walked along the beach and found one of Poppy's favourite spots to watch the sunset. They gazed out onto the horizon and then into each other's eyes and deep into the other's soul. They once again felt such an awakening deep within, such was their connection.

They had walked down to the village and bumped into people she had known most of her life. She proudly introduced Gregory and they in turn were delighted she had found such a nice young man.

On an evening they would make love. The ocean breeze would gently ruffle the white voiles at the large windows of her patio doors leading to the balcony from her tranquil bedroom, casting shadows over the intimate couple.

All too soon their week was at an end but they made arrangements to see each other in eight weeks' time, when their respective schedules permitted. And this time she would visit his home in Rhode Island.

Chapter 5
Gratitude!

It had been the longest eight weeks of Poppy's life, even though she had kept herself very busy. When Gregory met her at the airport they threw themselves into each other's arms, kissing each other over and over again, declaring how much they had missed the other. The long weeks without each other seemed to simply melt away.

Poppy loved the quirky main street on which Gregory lived and the nearby marina. His New England style loft had white and light blue walls painted throughout and maritime paraphernalia dotted around the spacious rooms. Poppy thought it was masculine in a light and airy way and suited both him and the fishing town he lived in.

'Do you like it?' he asked, arms stretched out and smiling proudly.

'Oh yes. It's so you!'

'Thank you! I must admit I enjoyed putting it together, with a little help from my mom!' Gregory smiled impishly.

'Well, it all looks very good!'

'How about I take you sailing in *Little Annie* - my pride and joy?'

'That sounds wonderful,' she smiled in return at his boyish enthusiasm.

He quickly gathered a few things together before locking the door. They strolled the short distance to the marina. Gregory put his arm around Poppy's shoulders and she melted into his strong chest and the delightful smell of his Armani cologne.

'There she is!' he smiled, pointing to the neat little yacht.

'Wow, she's a beauty!' Poppy agreed.

Gregory held out his hand for her to jump on board and expertly set the yacht in motion. And soon they were riding the waves in the sunshine of early summer! They sailed away from the marina and Poppy could see much of the quaint fishing port he lived in.

'Do you like my little town?'

She looked up at him and smiled. 'It's gorgeous. I can see why you enjoy living here.'

Gregory nodded. 'I truly love it and miss it when I'm working away so much but I guess it gives me more of an appreciation of it, not that I needed it!'

His town began to disappear out of sight and they could no longer see any other boats nearby. Poppy enjoyed the delights of the open ocean and the sun glistening on the waves. She hadn't noticed Gregory studying her intently. 'Are you enjoying this?' he asked, already knowing the answer.

'Oh yes, it's almost like we are the only ones in the universe!'

'I know!' They then fell into a long silence as they studied each other, content and happy in each other's company, each knowing they had found their true soul mate.

All too quickly the sun was starting to set and they returned to his home, joyful and thankful for having the opportunity of spending such a beautiful and serene afternoon together.

This time when they returned to Gregory's home they kissed passionately and he carried her to his large masculine bed where they made love. They declared how much they loved each other and were both amazed they felt like this in such a relatively short time.

Afterwards they got up, showered and he took her out to one of his favourite restaurants just a short walk from where he lived. Gregory proudly introduced her to people he knew when they walked along the street and then the staff he knew so well at the lively Italian restaurant.

On Sunday morning Gregory drove Poppy the short distance to his parents' home. They had obviously seen her on TV and in magazines but couldn't wait to actually meet the woman their son had so quickly fallen in love with.

Poppy was given a very warm welcome and she instantly liked Gregory's parents. She was surprised at how much Gregory looked like his father. They were both tall and easygoing, although Jim's hair was now white. He was looking forward to retirement soon, once he sold his business, he told Poppy.

Jim knew he would miss the dynamics of being a portrait photographer although he wouldn't miss photographing the weddings – he just didn't seem to have the energy for them any more. Besides, he was looking forward to doing a lot of travelling with his wife and not having to get up so early to keep his records up-to-date before opening the studio.

Nancy had spent her working life writing weekly columns for the local newspaper and doing a lot of voluntary charity work. Between them they had kept themselves pretty busy being an integral part of the community and bringing up their only son. Then, as he got older, waiting for his return from assignments.

Nancy was quietly spoken and was always keen to listen to what people had to say. She had such a nice way about her, which was one of the reasons people opened up to her so quickly. These days, her mousey-coloured hair was styled into a bob that neatly shaped her pretty face and accentuated her soft blue eyes. Poppy noticed that Nancy's eyes were the same shade Gregory's were.

After serving coffees, Nancy said, 'Here let me show you a few of my favourite albums of Gregory growing up!'

'Aww Mom, do you have to?' Gregory said good-naturedly, knowing there was no way his mother wouldn't show them.

'Of course, it's a mother's prerogative to show off her only child!' She smiled mischievously.

Poppy had already noticed several of the larger pictures of Gregory dotted around their living room. They were clearly a close-knit family and, not for the first time, Poppy realised how much time she had missed growing up with her parents when they were away so much. But then each time she thought that, she chided herself for she knew her gran had given her so much love and a great start in life. Besides her parents often rang or texted and always tried to make up for lost time when they were all together.

Nancy proudly turned the pages of the albums and Poppy said what a beautiful baby and toddler he had been. Gregory was always smiling. When he got older the photos showed him playing baseball and all the other things he liked to do, including sailing with his father and hiking.

'He was such a good boy,' Nancy continued. 'We had wanted to start a family early in our marriage but he didn't come along for a long time. So we always felt he was our special blessing, especially when we realised we couldn't have any more children despite the doctors telling us it would happen one day!' Nancy said wistfully. Poppy touched Nancy's hand in an understanding manner and Nancy appreciated the gesture.

After Nancy finished showing Poppy the photo albums, she smiled and said, 'I hope you guys are ready for a little lunch I prepared.'

Contribution

They all filed through to the kitchen and looking at the huge spread on the table, Gregory said good-naturedly, 'Aww Mom you shouldn't have gone to all this trouble!'

'Oh don't be silly, I just wanted to make Poppy feel welcome!'

Poppy smiled in response. 'Thank you and I do feel very welcome. But Gregory is right you shouldn't have gone to all this trouble!'

Jim chimed in, looking at Gregory, 'Now come on Son, you know wild horses wouldn't have stopped your Mom from preparing a feast!'

They all laughed and continued chatting. After the delicious lunch Poppy and Gregory insisted on clearing away and afterwards thanked his parents for their wonderful hospitality.

'It was a great pleasure meeting you Poppy. We had heard so much about you!' Nancy said, and Jim agreed.

'Thank you. It was a great pleasure meeting you two too!' Poppy concurred. 'It's no wonder Gregory is the wonderful man he is with parents like you two,' she said, meaning every word sincerely.

Afterwards Gregory expertly drove Poppy to the beach in his dark green Range Rover. On the way she told him how much she liked his parents.

He smiled. 'I'm glad. They are good people and, of course, I love them dearly. And they liked you too! Although it's not surprising! I could see they were immediately smitten with you!'

'Thank you!' Poppy said, squeezing his leg.

The whole weekend was truly joyful. They shared wine, meals and walks, making the most of every minute, aware that once again they had only a limited amount of time together.

Poppy and Gregory wanted to be together so much it was almost unbearable. They once again wondered how they could manage their demanding careers and find time to be together. Poppy's stay in Rhode Island quickly came to an end and each time they said goodbye it seemed to get harder; this time they reluctantly returned to their busy lifestyle.

Chapter 6
The Cycle of Love!

In between e-mails, phone calls and the occasional visit for a couple of days every few months, when they were at least on the same continent, they would do their utmost to snatch some time together.

When Poppy travelled to her next destination in Argentina and Gregory was on location in Europe they continued e-mailing each other, while they filmed in different corners of the world.

Then, much to her surprise, she received an e-mail from Gregory saying he had to stay in Europe for another four weeks but asked if there was any chance she could get away for three or four days and meet him in Venice?

She checked her schedule and could manage a couple of days just before he was due to return. It seemed to be an enormous wait but Poppy excitedly looked forward to meeting him there.

Gregory met her off the plane and they hugged each other tightly. 'Oh god Poppy I can't tell you how much I've missed you,' he said with deep passion.

'Me too!' she said, as she nuzzled into his chest, smelling his Armani aftershave. She felt dizzy with delight and thought her legs would buckle beneath her. They gazed lovingly into each other's eyes and then he put his arm around her shoulder and whisked her back to his hotel where they made passionate love, making up for lost time. Hours later, after showering and getting changed, they strolled out into the bright sunshine.

Gregory had changed into grey slacks and a white short-sleeved shirt open at the neck. Poppy left her long hair loose over a cool white-spotted navy blue summer's dress. She wore matching navy blue sandals and had slung a large leather navy blue handbag over her shoulder.

They both wore sunglasses and looked perfectly relaxed and very much in love. People snuck admiring glances and smiled at the striking couple sauntering confidently through the cobbled streets of Venice into hidden alleyways and onto the Piazza San Marco and the Doge's Palace, brimming with colourful delights and artistic treasures.

They found a shop that specialised in selling the gorgeous ornate red Venetian glass Venice was famous for. Gregory bought an exquisite vase for her.

'Now all I need are some flowers!' she smiled up at him.

'Well we'll have to see what we can do for the lady!' he said, squeezing her hand and leading her outside.

They made their way towards the gondolas and he waved at one of the traditionally dressed Italian men. The gondolier greeted them, seemingly knowing who they were. Gregory smiled and nodded at the man who steadied Poppy as she stepped down into the colourful boat. Once seated, they glided smoothly through the water and Poppy was inspired by all the aged buildings. The gondolier serenaded them and then Gregory reached into his pocket and pulled out a little square box.

'My darling Poppy, you know how much I love you don't you?'

She nodded, her heart pounding excitedly. She looked steadily and questioningly into Gregory's eyes.

'I know it's only been a short time but you truly are the woman of my dreams! Poppy would you do me the honour of marrying me?'

She caught her breath. She hadn't expected this! He opened the box, revealing a stunning square cut diamond ring. She threw her arms around his neck.

'Of course, you know I would be delighted to be your wife!' she said, and they once again passionately kissed each other. The world seemed to be spinning and yet still all at the same time!

The gondolier looked on and smiled. This, he thought, was the best part of his job!

Poppy felt giddy watching Gregory place the ring on her finger. She continually gazed at it and admired the stunning stone.

'Do you like it?' Gregory asked hopefully.

'Like it? I love it! I wouldn't have chosen anything different,' Poppy beamed.

Gregory was relieved to hear this.

All too quickly their time in the gondola came to an end but neither would ever forget the magical time they had just shared.

Although Poppy was used to the paparazzi being around, she was startled to see such a large crowd of photographers waiting for them when they returned to the dock. There were sounds of cameras clicking and flashing and she heard shouts of, 'Look this way, Poppy!'

Out of the crowd one of the reporters shouted, 'Can we see the ring?'

For a moment Poppy wondered how they knew they were there and had just got engaged. But she was so blissfully happy she didn't care and she relaxed into the security of Gregory's arms while both smiled at the cameras.

Gregory, quite rightly, guessed he perhaps shouldn't have mentioned what his plans were to Poppy's friend and agent, Bev. She never missed an opportunity for some good publicity for her favourite client!

Poppy and Gregory agreed that the paparazzi could take a few more photos while they posed together against the backdrop of the harbour and Rialto Bridge.

After the impromptu photo shoot and the photographers had dispersed, Poppy and Gregory walked hand in hand to one of the best restaurants in

Contribution

the area. He had already telephoned ahead to book a table in a secluded corner. Poppy continually gazed at her eye-catching ring.

Once seated at their table, the waiter deftly poured champagne into the crystal flutes and another waiter presented a beautiful bouquet of orchids and lilies that Gregory had previously arranged.

'You have made me the happiest man in the world,' Gregory told Poppy.

'And you've made me the happiest woman! Thank you so much my darling,' she beamed.

They smiled at each other and their eyes sparkled as much as the diamond ring he had placed on her finger.

'So where would you like to get married?' he asked.

'I really haven't had a chance to think about it! Do you have any ideas?'

'Well, really it's the bride's prerogative, and I only have a small family so I really don't have any preferences. I just want us to be together for ever!'

She smiled. 'Me too!'

Gregory then said, 'But I think I would like to get married in a church and I did wonder if you might want to get married in Costa Rica?'

'I would love that,' she agreed.

After some discussion they decided to get married early in the spring of next year at the oldest Catholic Church in San Jose, the capital city of Costa Rica. They realised it needed to be a huge building to accommodate so many friends and colleagues they wanted to invite. Afterwards they would have a grand reception nearby. The next day they would return to her home and invite everyone from the village to witness a blessing. Caterers and musicians would be brought in to provide food and entertainment for their guests. She wanted the latter part to be very much like Gran and Grandpa Ben's wedding. She remembered her gran telling her about their wedding and Poppy always thought how intimate and magical it sounded.

'And how long would you like our honeymoon to be?' Gregory asked.

'Oh, I think about a year should do it!' she replied, half-jokingly.

'Oh I wish! But what would you say to two weeks after our wedding and then a month somewhere else later on in the year? How does that sound?'

'Really? Honestly? That would be wonderful!'

'It would wouldn't it? I think we deserve a good long break after our demanding schedules and what better time than our honeymoon?'

'I agree!' she said, feeling full of joy. 'Where do you have in mind?'

'I don't know, but I would like it to be somewhere neither of us has visited before!'

'Well that doesn't leave us too many places!' she smiled in return. They discussed every country they had been to.

Contribution

In the end Gregory said, 'Well, what about going to a private Fijian island, where we can be away from the limelight after the wedding? We could spend our time scuba diving and relaxing on our own island? And for the month away later in the year what do you think to going to India?'

'Really? That would be fantastic!' Poppy was especially excited because these two countries were places her grandparents had visited on their first world adventure. Poppy remembered how her gran had told her so many amazing stories about India and its people. Gran Jasmine had often referred to it as Incredible India.

'Yes, I think it would be too but you know in the end it doesn't matter where we go as long as we're together!' Gregory paused. 'You know how much I love you don't you?'

Poppy nodded before Gregory continued, 'I just wish we could have done the whole tour that your grandparents did all those years ago but sadly our careers won't give us that kind of time!'

'I know,' Poppy agreed, smiling and leaning back in her chair. 'I still can't believe we're getting married and going to go on our own first adventure as husband and wife!'

Gregory smiled, 'Me neither!'

Poppy continued, 'I think you're going to have to pinch me!'

Gregory continued smiling, 'Well, how about a kiss instead of a pinch?'

'That'll do me just fine!' she said and he leaned over. Just then the waiter returned with their appetisers of oysters.

'Oh, just like we had when you first came over to Boston!' Poppy said, delightedly picking one up.

'Of course!'

'Is there nothing you haven't thought of?'

Gregory smiled, elated she was so happy, and once again picked up her hand and caressed it. 'I know it's been a whirlwind but it all seems so right to me! I can't imagine anyone else in the world I would rather marry!' he exclaimed.

'I feel exactly the same,' she said, smiling and squeezing his hand gently.

After Poppy devoured the last of her delectable oysters, she said, 'I think when we get back to the hotel we need to make a few phone calls before our family and friends see it in the papers!'

'I agree,' he smiled in return, 'if it's not already too late!'

Poppy nodded, still smiling. 'So who do you think told the press - the gondolier?'

Gregory looked a little sheepish. 'I'm not sure,' he said, 'but I wouldn't mind guessing it was Bev! I told her my plan! And we both know how she likes to get as much publicity for you as possible! I was so excited I had to tell someone but perhaps it shouldn't have been her! Sorry!'

'I really don't mind,' Poppy said. 'I'm so happy I could shout it from the roof tops!' And then Poppy had a thought, 'But where we will live?'

'Hmmm, that's a good question with our lifestyles. What do you say to sharing our time between my place in Rhode Island and yours in Costa Rica until we have more of an idea of where we want to be?'

'Sounds good to me!' she agreed, basking in the warmth of his love.

The waiter returned with their main course of lobster but both Poppy and Gregory were too excited to tuck into it and instead just nibbled away and continued talking about their future plans.

After their meal, Poppy and Gregory made their way back to the hotel to make their calls, even though it was getting late. Annabelle, Toby, Gregory's parents and their closest friends were all delighted to hear the wonderful news. After they finished their phone calls they were exhausted but elated and got ready for bed, this time just cuddling each other and quickly drifting off into a blissful sleep.

The next morning they were woken by a light knock on the door and the voice behind it saying, 'Room service!'

Gregory got up and wrapped the white towelling robe around him that the hotel had provided. He opened the door and the waiter wheeled in a full breakfast trolley with a red rose in a vase.

'For you my dear,' Gregory beamed.

Poppy sat up in bed. 'You're spoiling me!' she said jubilantly.

Both Gregory and the waiter smiled, and Gregory discreetly handed the young man a large tip before he quietly slipped away.

'So what would like to do today?' Gregory asked, while they both tucked into their large fried breakfast.

'Stay here and snuggle up to you all day!' she smiled gleefully.

'I like that idea too! But it would also be good to see a little bit more of Venice while we're together, especially as today is our last full day!' he declared.

She felt a jolt at the thought of them being apart again, but tried to put that thought at the back of her mind. She didn't want to put a damper on their day.

'Mmm, what to do? Okay! How about this? What about wandering around the inside of St Mark's Basilica and then finding more artists' areas? I love seeing so many beautiful paintings!'

'Sounds great to me,' he agreed good-naturedly.

Once again they spent a lovely day together, strolling through the unique ancient city, enjoying watching artists at work and ladies selling exquisite lace. However, they were both acutely aware that their time together was fast drawing to an end again.

Contribution

The next morning Gregory took Poppy back to the airport.

'I'm going to miss you so much,' she said, as her eyes filled up with tears.

Gregory nodded. 'Me too, it doesn't get any easier does it?'

She shook her head. 'Sometimes I'm tempted to just stay with you but I've really got to see my work through at least to the end of my contract!'

'I know, I really understand. But one day we'll be able to spend more time together and have more of a normal life!' Gregory said brightly, trying to cheer her up.

She nodded. They kissed passionately before she once again made her way to the check-in desk. She turned and they sadly waved goodbye to each other.

'Until next time my love!' he mouthed to her.

She nodded and smiled.

Poppy sat on the plane twirling her fine-looking engagement ring around her finger. She felt euphoric at the thought of being Mrs Taylor and yet forlorn at being apart from her beloved Gregory once again. But at least now she knew that one day they would be able to share their lives together as a regular couple and she couldn't wait for that day.

After their photos appeared in the press and their engagement was officially announced, the media wanted lots of interviews and to know all about their romance and how they had managed to keep it a secret. Poppy and Gregory were almost treated as royalty.

Chapter 7
Exciting Times!

The months following were even more hectic. Poppy and Gregory would try to snatch a weekend together wherever they could. On one such weekend at Gregory's in Rhode Island they were discussing their wedding plans, schedules and the future.

'I was thinking...' Poppy said, snuggling into his chest. They were sitting out on the deck overlooking the marina.

'Mmmm?' Gregory replied contentedly.

'My current contract comes to an end just a few weeks before the wedding and as we will be going to India later on in the year, I was thinking about not renewing my contract until we come back from there. What do you think?'

He looked down at her, surprised and delighted at the same time. 'If you can do that it would be great! You could have a nice break at home or, better still, come on location with me and then we wouldn't have to be apart so much. How does that sound?'

'Wonderful! Let's do that,' they agreed and sealed it with a kiss.

Once again their weekend came to an end all too quickly but this time they were also making plans for their next visit which would be a week over Christmas and neither of them could hardly wait. Because of their respective schedules they both felt it would be easier to spend it at Gregory's home in Rhode Island. They had also been invited to his parents for Christmas dinner, which Gregory's parents were thrilled about, aware that it would give them more time to get to know their future daughter-in-law.

Gregory drove Poppy to the airport and as usual it was hard saying goodbye, but as they finally let go of each other they reiterated it wouldn't be long before they would be back together again for Christmas.

Poppy was flying back to California this time. She had some more research to do there. Although miles away, it seemed a little more comforting that at least this time she was in the same country as her beloved fiancé.

Throughout their hectic schedules they slipped back into the routine of sending an e-mail or text every chance they got. In the weeks leading up to Christmas Poppy also kept herself busy buying presents for her family, friends and colleagues and sending them around the globe to arrive on time. And soon she was back on a plane leaving LA to return to Gregory.

Gregory excitedly met Poppy at Providence airport in Rhode Island and immediately swept her up in his arms. They were talking and laughing in between hugs and kisses. He carried her bags and parcels out of the airport.

As soon as the cold winter air hit them Gregory pulled up the collar of his sheepskin jacket and Poppy tied her red scarf tight over her black woollen coat. She didn't think she'd ever get used to the cold weather.

On the way out of the airport Gregory found a *Starbucks* and bought them both a hot chocolate to warm them up before the drive back home.

When they finally arrived at his place, they ran up the wooden stairs to the deck leading to his front door which he eagerly opened. Poppy was astounded to see his loft style apartment looking so festive. She entered the kitchen and walked through to the familiar living room.

'Like it?' Gregory asked her, feeling pleased with himself. This was the first time he had really gone to town on decorating his home for Christmas.

'Wow, it's gorgeous! I hadn't expected you to have done all this!' She smiled, admiring the brightly coloured festive decorations lining the walls and shelves of the large rooms.

'I wasn't sure whether to wait or not so I thought I'd do all this and then tomorrow we can go and buy a real tree and decorate it together. How does that sound?'

'That sounds wonderful,' she agreed, taking off her coat and making herself at home.

'I thought you might be tired so I bought a lasagne to heat up after I've drawn a candlelit bath for you!'

'Wow, your spoiling me again... and I love it!' she said, wrapping her arms around his neck. He in turn put his arms around her waist. They stopped talking and started kissing each other passionately before he led her to his bedroom...

The next morning they slept in and then made a leisurely breakfast together before going out to finish the last of their Christmas shopping and buying a real tree. They talked and laughed every step of the way. They finally chose a medium-sized tree and brought it home to decorate.

Gregory produced a box of family ornaments. Poppy happily looked at each one and carefully hung it on the tree while Gregory explained its origins.

Several hours later they sat back and admired the brightly decorated tree before he poured them each a glass of mulled wine to celebrate their work. They then finished wrapping all the presents to put under the twinkling tree.

On Christmas Day Poppy and Gregory excitedly opened each of their presents and exclaimed how much they liked them. For his main present Poppy bought Gregory a Rolex watch which he was delighted with. Gregory had bought Poppy a diamond necklace with matching earrings but her favourite present was an angel holding a heart in a snow globe. The message on the heart read *Expect Miracles Every Day* and she truly adored it. She threw her arms around his neck and thanked him over and over again.

After they showered and dressed, Gregory drove them the short distance to his parents' house. They were greeted with open arms and hugs. They had a lovely day talking, laughing and playing games. Poppy helped Gregory's mom, Nancy, prepare dinner and they all enjoyed the fruits of their labour.

Nancy and Jim were overjoyed with their son's choice of bride and they too discussed options for the wedding. All too soon their time together was coming to an end. They hugged each other tightly and said goodbye with promises of phoning each other soon.

Poppy and Gregory's last few days of the holidays were spent watching movies and going out to restaurants. They discussed the final arrangements for their wedding, knowing that the next time they would be together would be just before their special day and they couldn't wait.

Once again their parting was sad but this time they eagerly anticipated their wedding day in a couple of months' time when they would be spending the rest of their lives together.

This time Gregory would be working in New Zealand and Poppy had to finish her contract out in California. There was so much to do preparing for the wedding, but they knew time would pass quickly and each counted down the weeks to their huge lifestyle change that neither could wait for.

Annabelle also helped plan and prepare for the wedding, long distance in between her many appointments in Panama. She was very grateful for the opportunities internet and e-mail gave her, especially on an evening.

Poppy wanted her dress to be a sophisticated gown made of white lace. She had found a designer in San Jose who would make the perfect dress. Other than that everything else was going to be made in her village. Her family had always tried to put money back into their local economy and this occasion was no exception.

Andrea, Poppy's personal assistant, who had become her close friend and confidante over the years, was to be her matron of honour, and Andrea's two children, Becky and Connor, would be a flower girl and a ring bearer. She was also going to have Bev, her agent, and Gregory's young cousin, Elaine, as bridesmaids.

The matron of honour and bridesmaids were going to wear knee-length purple dresses nipped in at the waist. Becky, the flower girl, would be wearing a tiered-lace, purple dress adorned with pale pink roses and green leaves with a pale pink ribbon tied at the waist. Gregory would be wearing a white suit as would his best-man, ushers and the ring bearer.

The bridesmaids' dresses were going to be made by a family friend and another friend was going to make the huge, four-tiered cake which would be iced in white and exquisitely decorated in matching purple and pale pink roses that Poppy and her attendants would be carrying.

Poppy wanted the wedding to be a magical event with an abundance of flowers and candles in the church and her home grounds in celebration of their love.

Chapter 8
Bliss!

Several days before their wedding, Gregory flew into San Jose with his parents. He'd managed to have a few days back in Rhode Island after his contract in New Zealand had come to an end.

Poppy and Gregory were thrilled at being together again and knowing that this time their life was going in a new direction. They couldn't believe it and wanted to pinch themselves! They were on cloud nine and deliriously happy.

Finally the big day arrived. Many of Poppy's and Gregory's family and friends had flown in from all over the world during the previous day. Some stayed in San Jose but others stayed in her small village which for the first time was brimming with guests. Several famous people enjoyed being in the relative anonymity of the remote village, although there were several paparazzi roaming around both the city and the small community.

Poppy's attendants put the finishing touches to her hair and makeup and made sure her gown, with its long train, was flowing perfectly. At the age of twenty-five,

Poppy looked stunning. Her hair was tied up in a loose knot under a long veil of white lace draped over her beautiful gown.

There was a light knock at the door and Toby entered the dressing area. He caught his breath at the spectacle of his dazzling daughter.

The attendants quickly left to take their places.

Toby could barely speak. Tears filled his eyes and emotion overwhelmed him. 'My darling little girl you've grown into such a beautiful woman. You truly look amazing!'

'Thank you Dad!' she said, smiling at him before her eyes fell to the dressing table and her favourite photograph of her gran smiling back at the photographer. 'The only thing I wish is that gran could have been here with us today!'

'I know sweetheart and she would have been very proud of you - for everything, not just today. She would have been delighted to have been here and overjoyed at seeing you look so stunning and to be marrying such a wonderful young man!'

'I know,' Poppy said, swallowing the lump she could feel forming at the back of her throat.

'But she'll be happily watching you!'

'Yes, I think so too! It's strange, I almost feel my relationship with Gregory has been so similar to hers and grandpa's.' Toby nodded and Poppy continued, 'We both had long distance relationships and I wanted the latter part of the wedding to be a lot like theirs. I'm still convinced she brought Gregory to me!'

'I'm sure of it,' Toby agreed. 'Now come on, they're waiting for us,' Toby said, bending his arm for Poppy to link hers through his.

There was a large crowd of well-wishers outside the church and in the surrounding grounds. The crowd had been patiently waiting and craning their necks to see all the famous people who had been arriving but in particular they wanted to see their very own Poppy Anderson.

The paparazzi had a field day taking photos of Poppy, arriving at the church in a horse drawn carriage and waving to the crowd. White, purple and pink ribbons and flowers adorned the old-fashioned transportation.

Poppy straightened her gown as she got out of the carriage. She was radiant, her love illuminated her. She felt so much joy she thought she was going to burst! She once again linked her arm through her father's and waved to the waiting crowds. There were gasps of approval, shouts of good wishes and loud applause from the crowd watching Poppy and Toby walk up to the huge church doors. Dozens of cameras continually clicked and flashed. Poppy turned around, waved one last time as Miss Anderson, and blew kisses to the crowd before entering the church.

Poppy and her father walked down the aisle to the sounds of the wedding march and guests turned around. Once again there were gasps of approval and

Contribution

smiles at the beautiful spectacle. Poppy smiled back at the congregation. She finally approached the altar and Gregory turned around. He thought his heart would stop with pure joy as he took in the beauty and radiance of his bride. Their eyes and souls locked together. Poppy moved towards him, almost in a trance. She still couldn't believe they were about to become man and wife!

The ceremony was long and touching, and sniffles were occasionally heard from the guests. The ceremony came to an end and the newlyweds embraced each other, sharing a long and tender kiss. The priest, smiling, presented them as Mr and Mrs Taylor. Once again many photographs were taken as the couple left the church.

Afterwards, the reception was an amazing event. Over three hundred guests filed into the old hotel ballroom. After the magnificent feast of regional and international cuisine, Gregory's best man and best friend, John, tapped his wine glass.

The gathering fell quiet in anticipation. John then went on to give a heartfelt and moving toast to the happy couple. When he finished his speech there was loud applause. The groom stood up and before thanking everyone individually, Gregory turned to Poppy and said, 'Although I've admired you for years, I could never have imagined the love and magic you would have brought into my life and I want you to know, my darling, that you have made me the happiest man in the world!' He smiled, taking her hand and kissing it.

Poppy could feel emotion overwhelming her and tried not to let tears of joy sting her eyes but instead smiled at the man of her dreams. The guests once again applauded loudly.

After the reception luncheon, the newlyweds drove back to her home where local villagers were gathered in the tropical gardens bathed in sunshine to give their good wishes. The minister was waiting to offer his formal blessing. Chairs were adorned with white, purple and pink ribbons and flowers.

Sam and his new girlfriend Maria had left the wedding reception early and rushed back to Poppy's house to help put the finishing touches to the final arrangements and make sure everything was in place.

Sam and Maria sat at the front of the congregation and Sam proudly watched his best friend walk down the entrance of the beautiful gardens lined with pots of colourful plants. It wasn't lost on people how much, in many ways, Maria looked like Poppy.

After the blessing, a simple and traditional wedding meal was served on locally made platters garnished with banana leaves and flowers.

Poppy changed out of her long gown into a knee-length white thin-strapped dress. Darkness fell and candles and hanging globe lights illuminated the picturesque grounds and music played in the background.

Gregory held her close and they swayed to the music for the first dance.

'Are you okay my love?' he asked tenderly, feeling the closeness of her body next to his.

'Oh yes, my darling, it has been the most wonderful day of my life! Although I must admit I'm a little tired but I'm hoping the adrenalin will keep me going!'

He nodded. 'I know what you mean. I feel exactly the same!' he said, and they continued moving gently to the music.

Their glorious day was drawing to a close and guests gave their love and congratulations once more before saying their goodbyes. Finally the newlyweds were alone. 'Happy Mrs Taylor?'

'Deliriously! And you Mr Taylor?'

'Oh yes, I couldn't be happier,' he said, bringing his lips to hers.

They walked arm in arm into the bedroom and made love for the first time as a married couple.

They had three days together opening presents, writing thank you notes and receiving occasional visits or phone calls from well-wishers before flying to the private Fijian island they had booked for two weeks.

Poppy and Gregory cherished every moment of being together and making up for lost time when they were apart. They spent their honeymoon exploring the beaches and diving in the delightful coral reefs surrounding the island, taking care not to touch any of the fragile coral.

They enjoyed making simple meals together. Their evenings were filled with the sound of the ocean and they would gently sway in the hammock with only the light from the candles and stars above. They held each other and planned their future. It was pure bliss to be able to spend all this time together without frantically trying to snatch a weekend in between their schedules.

All too soon they were flying back to the Colorado Rockies so that Gregory could continue with his work but this time Poppy would be staying on location with him. They still couldn't believe that they were fortunate enough to have this time together and each night, after work, they thanked the universe and heavens above for their wonderful life together.

Poppy especially loved watching her husband work. Since she was well-known by everyone working on the set she was allowed to wander around and watch the day's activities. On many occasions, knowing her talents, the director would often ask her advice on a particular scene.

However, she began to feel restless and missed her own creative process. An idea started to formulate and one evening she discussed her thoughts with Gregory. She wanted to pull together all her research and photos from her documentaries and create a series of books covering the different environments she had worked in.

Contribution

Gregory was very enthusiastic about her plans and told her he would do whatever he could to help her vision become a reality.

The next day Poppy contacted her producer Larry and he agreed that it was a good time to write a companion series of books to accompany the documentaries. He told her he would take care of the necessary legalities in order for her to secure the rights for the use of the photos. He also told her that the studio would offer support in making information available to her.

Excited to be embarking on a new project, Poppy spent many hours each day compiling her research and downloading photos onto her laptop.

At the end of the day Gregory and Poppy would talk about their day's work while they prepared a simple meal served with wine in their comfortable studio trailer.

They had got into a good routine and before they knew it six months had quickly passed and they were excitedly packing for the next stage of their journey and once again saying goodbye to friends and colleagues.

They were both looking forward to a month of adventures in India to finish off their honeymoon, even though for Poppy everyday had been a honeymoon! Although Poppy was a little disappointed that she hadn't completely finished her series of books, she knew she could pick it up again and finish it on her return from India.

Chapter 9
India!

The flight from Denver International Airport to India was long and tiring but they were thrilled to be finally arriving in New Delhi.

When they landed at the airport the air was stifling and laden with smoke that burned their eyes. Poppy was disheartened to see so much rubbish floating around in the warm wind. It clung to the wire fences and littered the ground, just as her gran had described to her when she had visited all those years ago.

Gregory and Poppy walked through New Delhi airport and could see a flood of people outside, pressed against the huge windows, hammering their fists on the glass and shouting for the visitors to take their taxi.

Poppy and Gregory located the driver who had been sent from their hotel to collect them. Although it was nearly midnight, they rode through the noisy and bustling streets of New Delhi. In their hot and stuffy taxi they were hit by the stench of sewage and burning fires through the open windows of the car. The driver slowly made his way to the hotel through narrow streets choked with traffic and lined with beggars and homeless people cooking their meagre meals over open, dung-fuelled fires which added to the overall squalor of the oppressive atmosphere.

They arrived at their hotel and the driver agreed to meet them early the next morning to start their journey through northern India. They would be travelling to an area known as 'The Golden Triangle' which included Pushkar, Jaipur and Agra the city of the Taj Mahal.

Their driver's name was Mr Ratan and as the next morning wore on he asked, 'So what do you think of India?'

'It's an amazing place, full of contrasts,' Gregory replied tactfully, noticing some resplendent buildings and wealth next to so much poverty.

'We call it Incredible India!' Mr Ratan beamed proudly.

'I can see why,' Poppy agreed, remembering that was what her gran had told her it was called.

Although Poppy knew that India was an innovative and forward-thinking country with tremendous wealth, she failed to see any prosperity on the hungry faces of many of the people they drove by. She had spent much of her life in third world and developing countries, but this was the first time she had seen so many impoverished people huddled together living on the streets and crowded around camp fires. It was poverty on a mass scale.

'Parts of it haven't changed in hundreds of years – nor will it ever,' Mr Ratan informed them.

The city of New Delhi was a huge, bustling, dirty city with piles of rubbish all over but amazingly enough, nestled amongst all this were magnificent and superb grand forts, monuments and palaces.

The pollution from so many cars and open fire pits had caused a smoky haze to hang over land and buildings and an acrid smell of rotting waste that was almost unbearable. Poppy and Gregory tried to breathe into their scarves and not inhale the pollution when they were outside looking up at the striking architecture. They were hoping that the air quality would improve when they left the huge smoky city and drove through the countryside.

'And what do you think to our roads?' the driver asked, chuckling, driving fast in between rickshaws, cars, lorries, bikes and nearly clipping a horse and cart.

'Manic!' Gregory replied as he watched the driver narrowly miss a small motorbike stacked with two adults and three children.

'Sheer madness but it works!' Mr Ratan agreed and once again grinned with pride!

Poppy and Gregory weren't too sure that it actually worked when they watched nine lanes of traffic converge into four! There were very few cars without bumps or scrapes and the driving was crazy! The unrelenting honking of horns made it nearly impossible to talk. They were sat in the back of the car and Gregory squeezed Poppy's hand while Mr Ratan whisked them away to their next ancient destination.

When Poppy and Gregory arrived they checked into their hotel and said goodnight to Mr Ratan who was staying in a more modest place. They said they would see him early the next morning.

Poppy and Gregory enjoyed a traditional spicy Indian curry and afterwards went to their small room to relax. They discussed what they had seen so far on their journey.

'Isn't it strange that no cleaning seems to get done in restaurants or anywhere else that we've been to for that matter? It's just seems to be different degrees of dirtiness!' Poppy said to Gregory as she changed into her nightie. 'And what really surprises me is that there doesn't seem to have been any progress since Gran and Grandpa Ben's visit all those years ago. To me it sounds exactly the way gran described it!'

'That's sad! I know we've seen poverty before but there seems to be so much more all in one place here on such a large scale! It's no wonder there's so much disease and sickness here, especially with the open sewage near the drinking water! I really hate to see that and I feel like we should do something to help!'

'I agree but there is so much to do where would we begin?'

'Well, we can't do all this by ourselves but maybe with our connections we could enlist more help. So I'm thinking of making another documentary!' he declared.

'Trouble is it's all been done before!' Poppy said.

'Well this time I'm going to try a fresh angle to let people see the human tragedy of it all. We've got to do something!'

'I know.' Poppy loved to see the compassion stirred within Gregory and she too felt a strong need to help.

However, for the moment she lovingly embraced her husband as they turned down the lights…

Early the next morning they had a light breakfast and then met Mr Ratan.

On the rural roads there was even more poverty if that were possible, and many, many people without any shelter and others living in crudely made tents. There were shacks stretching along the straight roads, many used as a kind of makeshift garage with tyres and other mechanical paraphernalia strewn around for the numerous small motor bikes, mopeds and trucks. Buses were overcrowded with people riding on top. The buses often had no brake lights, headlights or bumpers and were rusted or broken and just hanging on by a piece of wire. Men mostly dressed in ragged T-shirts, linen trousers and threadbare sandals or sometimes no clothing at all with the exception of a loincloth. Ironically, the women usually wore brilliantly coloured and beautifully detailed saris and exotic makeup, even to work in the fields or sit on the back of a crowded moped!

They were on their way to the holy place of Lord Brahma in Pushkar as they wanted to visit the Holy Lake they had heard so much about and see the many temples, especially the most famous of all being Lord Brahma's temple.

When they eventually arrived, they once again found it to be a city of contrasts with awe-inspiring buildings and yet bustling with poverty everywhere you looked. It was full of contradictions - holy yet impure; rich yet poor; serene yet energetic; vibrant yet grim; joyful yet depressing. There was a feeling of exhilaration and awareness mixed into a concoction of emotions that assaulted the senses and heightened perception of humanity, including love, happiness, misery and acceptance.

There were outside communal showers and people either stripped down to their underwear or were completely naked, oblivious to the people around them.

'It's a shame to see children running naked through the streets and poverty everywhere, especially in such a holy place,' Poppy said mournfully.

'I know,' Gregory agreed. 'At least here no cars are allowed in the town - only motorbikes, camels and camel carts! But it's still dirty everywhere with lots of rubbish - even cows and pigs roam around eating it and the children play amongst it!'

Poppy nodded. 'I don't think I could ever get used to the smells of sewage and rotting garbage permeating everywhere! But just when I think that, we pass the enticing smells of spices cooking or aromas of exotic perfumes! It really is a place of complete opposites!'

Gregory nodded in agreement, knowing exactly how she felt.

They left Pushkar to continue their journey of the Golden Triangle.

Poppy and Gregory observed that the temples and buildings such as the Taj Mahal of Agra and the Amber Fort near Jaipur were amazing accomplishments and marvellously designed with a wealth of material.

They walked along the walls of the Amber Fort overlooking the city and listened intently to their guide who spoke of its history. They learned that it had taken nearly six hundred years to build the great fort and the double rampart walls that surrounded the city below. They were pleasantly surprised to see the largest black powder cannon in the world still intact and had their photos taken next to it.

When they finished their tour they walked through the city below the fort on their way to the hotel. It seemed as though they were hassled from nearly everyone on the street either trying to sell something or just wanting money.

They finally returned to their hotel and after an enjoyable evening meal they returned to their room. Gregory drew back the heavy drapes in the ornately decorated suite and they looked out to the brilliant golden-lit view of the Amber Fort against the backdrop of the inky black night sky.

'It seems unfair that there is such disparity between the rich and the poor,' Poppy said, feeling guilty from where they were standing and where they knew how people lived just a stone's throw away.

'I know what you mean sweetheart,' Gregory said. 'But there are people suffering in countries all over the world. It's really nothing new,' he said, remembering his time when he did freelance video journalism covering natural disasters and civil wars when he wasn't working on a science fiction movie.

'I know but that doesn't make it okay.'

'That's true,' he agreed, 'but if we really want to make a difference we'll have to think outside the box, do things differently and see how we can improve life for these people. If we do that then the possibilities are endless!'

'I know,' she said thoughtfully, 'at the moment it seems like things are just not working. When we hand out money to so many beggars and disabled people, no matter how much we give, they need more. I try to think what I would do in their situation and I'm not sure I could do things any differently. It makes you realise that it's down to fate where one is born and there but for the Grace of God go I!'

He squeezed her hand and kissed her cheek. He loved the way she was so concerned and tried to put herself in someone else's shoes.

'You know sweetheart, all our lives we are bombarded with TV images of hunger in India, Africa and other places. We are almost to the point of being de-sensitised, but it's not until you visit somewhere like here that you realise that really we have no understanding of the impact and reality of the poverty and despair of these people. It's really heartbreaking.' Gregory said, desperately wanting to help these people.

The following day they continued their journey, driving along the congested rural roads, passing hundreds of stacks of dried dung from cattle and camels. It seemed like most of the rural population still used dung for cooking and wood for heat. 'No wonder there is always a pall of smoke everywhere,' Gregory commented.

Poppy and Gregory were amazed that in this modern age so much of the heavy hauling and work was still being done by camels, oxen and occasionally elephants.

'I'm astounded that so many people live in such abject poverty while so few enjoy a higher standard of living!' Poppy reiterated.

'I know...' he paused, reflecting. 'It's almost as if the sacrifices and life of Mahatma Gandhi seemed to have been forgotten. A country with aspirations to be a great nation should not allow so many millions of its people to suffer!'

'I know,' Poppy sighed. She had always felt she had been able to make a difference in the world but right now she really felt helpless.

Gregory nodded in agreement. 'Those people lucky enough to work often work in harsh conditions.' He remembered seeing men squatting down all day on their haunches, working at grinding gemstones down for tourists, without the use of proper machinery or without any thought for safe working conditions. He observed their gnarled and scarred hands and how their backs were permanently hunched from the toils of their labour. The gemstones they worked with were worth many thousands of dollars yet they considered themselves lucky to be getting paid a pittance by the wealthy owners of the factories and high class shops. Gregory continued, 'It's like the few who have the best in life seem to be living off the backs of the poor. There seems to be no middle class - you either have money or you don't!'

He was dismayed as he thought about some of the beautiful shops tucked away in the back streets, selling silks, rugs, ornate inlaid marble, precious gemstones and jewellery. Most merchants seemed friendly but were often just friendly enough to sell their over-priced goods to tourists.

Poppy agreed and, in an exasperated voice, complained, 'How can people live life comfortably off the labours of so many and have a conscience? At least in the western world, people who work hard have a chance of making a better life for themselves!'

Gregory responded, 'My big regret is that we have put too much money into the hands of people who already have it and not enough into the hands of those who really need it!'

Poppy agreed. 'I know. How about from now on everywhere we go we seek out those really needy people and contribute as much as we can to them and not go into these rich people's shops!'

'It's a good start but I think we can do more! To me it seems that lots of projects get started but never finished,' Gregory noted. He felt sorry for the people here as they seemed disorganised and nothing ever seemed to be done logically or properly, except for the historic monuments.

'So do you have any ideas?'

'I don't know, I was kind of thinking maybe if we were to start on a smaller scale locally and take one of these unfinished buildings and turn it into a safe haven for the homeless. It would have a nice clean bed, bath or shower and soap, towels and a good meal three times a day. Possibly we could find a way to help them become self-sufficient!'

'That sounds like a good idea,' Poppy agreed, liking the concept. 'And maybe they would have to bring a bag of trash they had collected in return for meals and/or accommodation for that day. So that would help clean up the city and empower them, giving back their self-respect as well as giving them the opportunity for food and a good night's sleep,' she enthused, feeling that maybe they had hit on something that would really make a difference.

Gregory agreed. 'Yes and we could also set up a recycling plant, selling recycled paper and glass at a nominal price back to the people so that workers could be paid and help upkeep the recycling plant,' he said, as ideas continued shooting through his head.

'We could then try to encourage this to be done in other areas and hopefully give them the energy to be able to do jobs and things for themselves. So it would be a win, win, win situation,' Poppy concluded, swept along with his enthusiasm.

The next day, still with thoughts of their new plans bouncing around in their heads, Poppy and Gregory sat in awe overlooking the Taj Mahal.

'This is one of the most intricately detailed and amazing places I've ever seen,' Poppy said, almost spellbound.

'I know,' he agreed. 'As everyone says, it's truly majestic and indeed romantic. If I hadn't already married you I think I would have proposed here!' he smiled. He still thought they were true soulmates and would be together for ever. She smiled in return and hugged him.

They finished the day touring other historic buildings in the city of Agra. After having spent most of the day walking around the huge city, needless to say they were exhausted when they got back to their luxurious hotel and slept very soundly that night.

On one of the last days of their month long eye-opening adventure they were travelling down a remote road through the tea fields of India when Gregory saw an opportunity for a unique photograph.

Poppy and Gregory looked out into the field and saw a line of women dressed in striking multi-coloured saris bent over harvesting the tea leaves. The contrast of the colourful dresses of the women against the brilliant green background made for a stunning image.

After Gregory had taken several series of photos he then decided to ride in the front seat of Mr Ratan's car in order to take more photos and capture the stories of people's lives etched in the lines of their weathered faces.

Mr Ratan turned around to Poppy to point out an interesting fact about a roadside memorial but she found it difficult to hear what he was saying and asked him to repeat it. This time he had taken his eyes off the road for a few seconds too long. Poppy looked down the road in front of the car and screamed for Mr Ratan to watch out but in a split second it was too late! He turned abruptly and attempted to steer the car out of trouble but couldn't manage to avoid being sandwiched in between two large trucks loaded with marble slabs.

She felt the car quickly bounce between the massive trucks and could see the huge tyres and metal panels bear down on them.

She heard her own screams, feeling they belonged to someone else as everything suddenly seemed to be in slow motion. She tried to call out Gregory's name and hold his hand but couldn't reach him. Then there was nothing... only complete darkness and silence.

Poppy wasn't aware of the people gathering around, attempting to help them. It had taken emergency workers many long minutes to arrive at this remote location and they did the best they could with the limited tools and equipment they had. They worked for nearly an hour to remove the gravely injured and dead bodies from the mangled wreckage.

A medic frantically tried to stop the loss of blood from Poppy's unconscious, battered and bleeding body as she lay on the hot and dusty road near the wreckage. There was no way for her to know that they had already covered the lifeless bodies of Mr Ratan and her beloved Gregory with white sheets.

The ambulance rushed Poppy to the city and fought through the heavy traffic to a local hospital where she was given the best care they could provide, before being transferred to a major trauma hospital in New Delhi.

Chapter 10
Riding a White Swan!

Poppy lay in a coma in the stark hospital room in New Delhi for three weeks, unaware that her parents had been keeping a bedside vigil. They had wanted to take her back to Costa Rica but at this stage it was felt unsafe to move her.

It broke Toby's heart to see his daughter so mangled up and her body and beautiful face crudely stitched. Her long dark hair had been hacked back to make way for the intrusion of the stitches. He wished he had been there to do the work himself but consoled himself with the fact that he would arrange for her to have reconstructive surgery by the best surgeons in the world at a later date.

Near the end of the third week of her coma Poppy had a wonderful vision that would stay with her the rest of her life.

In that vision she was drawn towards a captivating, intense golden light that beckoned her. It was peaceful and she wanted nothing more than to be engulfed in its magnificence and serenity and she let herself drift into its powerful splendour.

The golden light then turned into a brilliant white light and she looked down and could see herself riding on top of a giant white swan flying higher and higher. She could hear the most tranquil and mesmerising music she had ever heard in her life.

Poppy then turned to her left and Gregory was sat on the other side of the swan cradling a baby. He smiled at her. 'Would you like to hold our son?' he asked, holding the baby out towards her. She gently took the newborn in her arms and embraced the infant.

Gregory moved closer to her so that the baby's head was on his chest and he could put his arms around Poppy.

She looked up at him and smiled. They continued flying higher in the sky. It was the most surreal and wonderful feeling ever. When they looked down they could see people laughing and looking very happy in the lush green fields below. Children below looked up and waved at the young couple and baby riding the majestic white swan. It was a glorious feeling.

Poppy had no idea how much time had passed, only that she knew she wanted this feeling to last for ever.

Then Gregory looked into her eyes with so much love and tenderness. 'You know you have to go back don't you?' he said quietly.

'No! I don't want to!' Poppy said in a panicked voice.

'You have to. It's time,' he continued gently.

'But I want to stay with you and our baby!' she wailed.

He shook his head. 'You can't sweetheart. Not at the moment. You've still so much to do.'

'But what about you and our son?' she tried to reason.

'I'll look after him and I'll watch over you too. You know how much I love you and I'll always be with you in your heart!'

She felt terror overwhelm her and hot tears roll down her cheeks. 'Please honey let me stay with you!'

'You can't my love. I promise I'll be with you. It's time!' he said, and she felt the huge bird tilt and she started to fall. She knew she was slipping away from him. She held out her hand and tried to hold onto him but she could feel herself falling and only just managed to shout that she loved him.

And then the spell was abruptly broken.

The dreamlike scene immediately disappeared from sight and she fell into darkness.

Poppy felt a strange sensation and horror overwhelm her. She knew something wasn't right but she couldn't move – and couldn't do anything about it!

Toby held Poppy's hand and Annabelle stroked their daughter's face, where she could without touching the bruises and bandages covering her cuts.

Poppy's eyes fluttered and Annabelle was startled to see tears flowing down her daughter's swollen face and watched her slowly regain consciousness.

'Hey sweetheart,' Annabelle whispered, choking back tears.

'Mom?' Poppy said, feeling strange and looking around the stark room. The white starched sheets felt rough and alien against her body. She could smell the horrible strong stench of iodine and disinfectant. 'Where am I?'

'You're in a hospital in New Delhi, but you're going to be okay sweetheart.'

'What happened?'

'You were in a car accident,' Annabelle replied flatly.

Memories suddenly came flooding back. 'Gregory! Where is he? I want to see him!'

Annabelle shot Toby a sideways glance, hoping he would be the one to break the terrible news.

Toby interjected, 'Honey... sweetheart... this is so very hard...' He paused, glancing at his wife, unsure if he was doing the right thing, and wondering if he should wait until his daughter was a bit stronger. He continued, 'We are both so very sorry... but he died in the accident...'

Poppy looked confused and then an anguished scream rang out that could be heard all along the corridor. Sobs and hysteria overwhelmed her. Toby and Annabelle held her and stroked her, saying soothing words but nothing calmed her down. Eventually a nurse was summoned who came in and sedated her.

Hours later Poppy woke up. She just stared into space for what seemed an age and then questions started flooding her mind. 'Where is he?' she asked her parents who were still sitting by her side.

'Jim and Nancy came and took his body back to the United States. They were totally devastated but they looked in on you and talked to you but you couldn't hear them. They want you to know they love you and hope you will contact them when you feel up to it.'

'Oh... When is the funeral?'

'I'm sorry sweetheart but they had the funeral just over a week ago.'

'Oh no,' she sobbed, 'I didn't even get to say goodbye!'

'I know sweetheart, but he knew how you felt about him and would understand,' her mother said in a choked voice.

'Did you go?'

'No darling, we were here with you but we sent flowers and cards and have spoken to his parents several times on the phone,' her mother continued in the same hushed voice. Annabelle remembered how she felt so awful for them having lost their only child but grateful, in a guilty kind of way, that their daughter had survived. She could only imagine their loss.

Tears spilled down Poppy's cheeks.

'Did he suffer?'

'No, sweetheart, we understand that it all happened very fast.'

Poppy nodded her head in acknowledgment. 'So how long have I been here?'

'Three weeks honey,' her father replied sadly, as he rubbed her hand.

'Sweetheart...' Annabelle said, 'there's something else we need to tell you.'

'What's that?' What else could there possibly be she wondered? Nothing could be as bad as the news she had just heard, she told herself.

Annabelle couldn't utter any more words so Toby answered for her, 'Sweetheart, we are so sorry, but you also lost the baby.'

'Baby?'

'You didn't know?' her mother asked, shocked, but regaining her composure.

She shook her head, feeling confused. Memories in the back of her mind of her holding a tiny baby next to Gregory and riding a white swan were slowly returning to her.

'You were three months pregnant!'

It all made sense to her now. During her trip in India she had been sick quite a lot but thought it was the food and lack of cleanliness. The thought that she was pregnant hadn't even crossed her mind and now she would never be able to hold their baby.

Tears once again spilled down her cheeks. Poppy was oblivious to her surroundings, her physical pain or her parents uttering words of comfort. The emotional pain she could feel was breaking her heart in two.

She lay in bed for days, totally numb. She heard the nurses and her parents' voices but couldn't answer as people attended to her. She would close her eyes and dream of Gregory and her holding their newborn son, flying higher and higher into the sky. Poppy would then reluctantly wake up feeling like a lead weight was holding her down.

Eventually the doctors determined that Poppy had recovered enough to take the long flight home, although the attending physicians and her parents were worried about her psychological health. They told her she would need to get checked into another hospital as soon as she reached San Jose in Costa Rica. She didn't care what they did, she just wanted to close her eyes and be with Gregory and their baby. She remembered the vision and the lovely feeling of riding the white swan.

The plane journey was long, arduous and painful, even though they had flown first class and the flight attendants had been very attentive. They had managed to cordon off a section with blue curtains and Poppy lay flat in a makeshift bed.

Eventually they touched down in San Jose where an ambulance was waiting to whisk her away to one of the best reconstructive hospitals in the country.

The paparazzi were also waiting and snapping photos.

'Poppy how are you?' one reporter shouted.

Another shouted, 'Everyone misses you and wishes you well!'

'We all hope you soon make a speedy recovery!'

Her parents were angry and wanted to know who had informed the press of their arrival? Poppy just closed her eyes and hoped the world would go away. It didn't matter to her, nothing mattered any more.

At the hospital, plastic surgeons and nurses came into her room, talked to her and carried out a thorough examination. Some were friends and colleagues of her parents. Toby had also called his good friend Winston, from Harvard Medical School, who was now one of the top plastic surgeons in the US. He had agreed to come down to Costa Rica to supervise the surgery. He really just wanted to be there and do whatever he could to help the family cope with their tragedy.

Poppy knew she was receiving the best treatment in the world but didn't care. As far as she was concerned her world had come to an end!

Four weeks later she was released from the hospital and allowed to return home, after her painful but successful reconstructive surgery. However, the physical pain was nothing compared to her emotional pain. She thought her heart would cave in two!

Poppy sat out on her bedroom balcony in a comfortable chair in the shade. She looked at the familiar scenery and out to the ocean, remembering her time with Gregory. It was like a movie, remembering every minute of their time together. They hadn't even had time to find a home together, she thought. It was going to be something they planned to do when they got back from India. Once again tears spilled down her cheeks.

Toby and Annabelle were worried sick about her. Poppy was inconsolable and was in a place neither of them could reach.

After several weeks of her parents taking turns to look after her, they reluctantly returned to Panama. But not before speaking to Sam and asking him to do whatever he could to bring their daughter back to the real world.

Poppy was relieved when her parents left. As much as they had been good to her, she was tired of their fussing around and "walking on eggshells". She just wanted to be left alone with her misery and the comfort of being back in her family home.

Phone calls and well-wishers tapered off over the following weeks when she refused to answer the phone or door. She barely ate or drank and didn't even bother to get dressed. But today was different as the loud hammering on the door continued. 'Poppy let me in!' the muffled voice demanded.

She didn't answer and hoped whoever it was would go away.

'Poppy if you don't let me in I'll break down the door! I mean it!' he shouted through the locked door.

There was silence, some shuffling around and then more silence. She assumed he had gone but jumped and screamed out loud when she saw Sam standing in front of her. He jumped too, shocked at the sight of her.

'How did you get in?' she asked aggressively, shocked at seeing someone standing there.

'I remembered where your gran used to leave the key when we were kids and assumed you probably still left it there and I was right!'

'Go away Sam. I want to be left alone,' she said coldly. She was still in her grubby-looking pyjamas.

'Well I'm not going to leave you like this. Look at the state of you! You're not dressed, haven't brushed your hair for goodness knows how long and look at the state of this place!' he said, pointing to the sink full of dirty dishes. He didn't say she looked almost scary with her wild eyes and unkempt hair that was just starting to grow back after the surgeons had hacked it so they could stitch the deep cuts in her head. The redness of her scars around the sides of her face and neck was still very visible.

'I don't care!'

'Well I do and I'm not going to just let you wallow and rot in here!'

'You've no choice! It's up to me what I do with my life!'

'Well think about Gregory if you can't think about yourself. He wouldn't have wanted you to be like this!'

'I do think about him. I think about him every minute of the day so don't you dare come in here telling me to think about him!' Poppy screamed at Sam, as hysterical sobs spilled out and she was flaying her arms into his chest.

Sam caught her wrists and held them to him as she continued sobbing into his chest. He then gently let go of her wrists and held her in his strong, capable arms, stroking her hair for ages until she finally quietened down. He sat her on the sofa and pulled her to him. They sat still for hours until he broke the silence.

'Poppy,' he said gently, 'everyone is worried about you. It was a terrible tragedy but you can't let your grief overwhelm you to the extent that it destroys you! That's just not right and we both know Gregory wouldn't want this!'

She nodded as tears flowed down her cheeks again.

Sam hated to see her so distraught. 'You know Poppy, we can't control circumstances - only how we react to them!' He paused before continuing gently,

'We all lose someone at some time in our lives. Nothing lasts for ever except for love and I think deep in your heart you know that! That's just the way life is and has always been!' he said softly.

'I know and you're right,' she wailed, 'but it was just too soon and I thought we would have the rest of our lives together!' Poppy gulped back her tears. 'There was so much we still wanted to do and I miss him so much. I didn't even get to say goodbye to him!'

'I know... You didn't get closure,' he said, understanding.

'And I feel so guilty too!'

'Why?'

'Well, if I'd heard what the driver was saying instead of asking him to repeat it the accident would never have happened!'

'You can't say that Poppy!'

'I can... it was me who really wanted to go to India. I wanted to follow in gran's footsteps. And I blame her too!'

'Poppy?'

'If she hadn't brought Gregory into my life at the night of the awards, and if we hadn't gone to the same places in India she had, I wouldn't be feeling such pain now!'

'Poppy you honestly can't look at it like that. That's so unfair!' he said sternly. 'Your gran had nothing but love for you and she was always good to us when we were younger. You can't blame her! I'm not going to let you ruin her memory over this! And surely you don't regret meeting Gregory?'

Poppy buried her head in her scrunched up knees and sobbed. The pain in her heart was overwhelming.

Sam willed her to listen to what he was saying. 'Poppy you can't live your life regretting you ever met him! That just takes away from what you had, and even though it was for such a short time surely that was better than nothing? Some people spend their whole lives looking for what you two had,' he said patiently.

Sam didn't understand how she could try to deny what she had had with Gregory. 'You should be grateful that after you got married you were able to spend so much time with each other and see all those great places together!' He paused, trying to think of the right words. 'It was your choice to follow in your gran's footsteps! She didn't tell you to do it! And you can't just think "what if?".

'I know but I'm so angry she never told me how painful love could be when you lose someone!'

'Poppy you can't put this on your gran! There are just some things in life you have to learn and find out for yourself! Don't you think it was her attitude that helped her through her loss after Ben died?'

Sam remained calm, but he hated to see unfairness and self-pity. He took a deep breath and said in a soft tone, while he gently held her arm, 'It was just Gregory's time and now he's gone home to a better place!'

She nodded and paused, looking for the right words to try to explain how she felt. 'That's what gran would have said. But he was so young – it's so unfair! Twenty-six is far too young to die. We had the rest of our lives to look forward to and I was pregnant too!'

Sam took a sharp intake of breath. 'I didn't know!' He paused, so many thoughts whirling around in his head. 'I am so sorry to hear that.' There was an awkward silence while he tried to think of how to respond. To break the silence he added, 'But I know you will somehow get through this and find a way of making something good come out of this tragedy. Remember all those things your gran used to say to us and what she taught us!' Sam paused again. 'Think of what Gregory would want. Do something for him - make his memory live on,' he tried to persuade.

'Like what?'

'I don't know. The possibilities are endless!'

She nodded and smiled in between sniffles. 'That's what he would have said!'

'Well we both can't be wrong can we?'

'I know. I've been selfish haven't I?'

'No, just distraught and grief-stricken, but you've got to pull yourself out of it and get on with your life in a positive way.'

'I know but I just don't know where to begin!'

'Well, how about a shower, getting dressed and brushing your hair for a start? And while you're doing that I'll clean up down here and fix you a nice healthy meal!' he said, as he briefly kissed her on the top of her head.

'You can't I've hardly anything left in the cupboards!'

'I kind of figured that, so before I came here I did some shopping and brought some food!'

Poppy smiled gratefully at the tall blond she knew so well from her youth. 'Thank you - you're a good friend and I'm sorry for telling you to go away!'

He smiled back. 'That's all right. Besides, you'd do the same for me! And I certainly wasn't going anywhere no matter what you said to me!'

She nodded and kissed him briefly on the cheek before walking up the stairs, feeling comforted by his presence.

The warm shower felt good on her still sore body, and as she washed her hair she thought about Sam's words. He was right, it was time for her to start picking up the pieces and move forward.

Poppy put on a pair of beige shorts and a blue T-shirt and realised she was wearing Gregory's favourite colours which once again brought a stabbing pain to her heart. She brushed her wet hair and sprayed her favourite perfume that Gregory had bought her. The scent evoked painful memories of a wonderful time in the past and she once again struggled to fight back her tears.

When she was ready, she took a deep breath and steeled herself to go back downstairs. Sam had already cleaned up and was cooking chicken and vegetables.

'You look a lot better and smell better too!' He grinned at his childhood love.

'Thank you.' She smiled weakly in return. 'And thank you for everything. You've cleaned up really well and the food smells good too!'

'Well, it's just about ready so if you sit down I'll pour a glass of wine.'

She didn't want to hurt his feelings any further and tell him she didn't feel like eating so she reluctantly did as she was told.

He deftly poured the wine and served the meal.

Poppy didn't want to talk about Gregory at this stage, it was just too painful, so instead she quickly ate the tasty food and was surprised at how hungry she was. They ate in silence until she had devoured it all.

'Wow, you must have been really hungry!' Sam exclaimed.

Poppy nodded. 'I don't think I realised just how hungry I was!'

'Well, I guess that's what happens when you don't eat properly for days on end!'

She thought she'd try to change the subject, so asked him what he had been up to while she'd been away. He told her he'd been making more furniture and sculptures from the driftwood he had found on the beach and, of course, surfing! He and Maria had been getting on really well and she had now moved in with him but he couldn't bear to tell Poppy the news that would further upset her. Poppy was pleased for him and hoped Maria would be in his life a little longer than the rest of his previous girlfriends.

Sam then turned the conversation back to Poppy. 'You know Poppy you need to have something positive to focus on. Wallowing here isn't going to help.'

Poppy nodded. 'I know.'

'Are you still in a lot of pain?'

'Some, but more emotional than physical,' she divulged.

'You need to get back into doing some exercise, even if it's just short walks,' he said gently. 'And meditate too!'

She nodded again. 'I know,' she repeated.

'Will you make a start tomorrow?'

'I guess,' she said reluctantly.

'Good. I can't ask any more than that at this stage!'

She smiled weakly, grateful to him for his concern. 'This is good for me today! You don't know how far I've come in the last couple of hours!'

He nodded. 'Actually I think I do and you know I'm always here for you!'

'I know,' she said gratefully.

Contribution

After they cleared the dishes away, he asked her if she would be all right.

She nodded. 'I will now. I guess I just needed to hear a few home truths and have someone bully me!' Poppy smiled, trying to hold back her tears.

'That's what I'm here for! But I've got a few things I must get done over the next few days and I've also got to go to San Jose. Will you be all right until I get back?'

She nodded.

'And what are you going to do?' He really felt she needed small positive steps to work with.

'I'll take a short walk on the beach tomorrow and afterwards make a few phone calls which I should have done long before now. Then I'm really going to think about what I'm going to do in memory of Gregory and the baby.'

He nodded sympathetically. 'That's a good idea. I'll see you in a few days,' he said, briefly kissing her again on the forehead.

Poppy nodded. 'And thank you Sam, really - thank you!'

'It's the least I can do and, as I said before, you would have done the same for me!' He smiled gently before swiftly closing the door behind him. He leaned against the external door and let out a long deep sigh. He so wanted to help her but at this stage just wasn't sure what he could do and he also knew she would have to help herself too.

That night Poppy lay down on her bed and looked at the three framed photos on her bedside table. She left the one of them together when they got engaged. They were leaning by the bridge in Venice, the sun was shining and they were smiling back at the photographers.

She then picked up the photo of Gregory out on the balcony at their luxury hut in Fiji. Tears rolled down Poppy's face as she studied it. 'Fiji should have been enough,' she said out loud, 'I don't care what Sam says, I really wish we hadn't gone to India then none of this would have happened! I'm so sorry my love,' she whispered.

Poppy put the photo away in the drawer of her bedside table and picked up the framed close-up photo of Gregory smiling back at her. She looked into his soft blue eyes and traced her finger around his handsome face and remembered how she loved to run her fingers through his soft brown curly hair. Poppy sighed, wiped her tears and replaced the photo on top of the table. She closed her eyes and quickly fell into a fitful sleep, dreaming of her love.

The next morning Poppy got dressed, had breakfast on her balcony and, remembering Sam's advice, went for a short walk along the beach. The fresh air and sea breeze were exhilarating as her feet sank into the soft sand. There wasn't another soul around and she felt at one with nature as she watched the waves come crashing down on the rocks. She walked much further than she had originally intended and by the time she got back home she felt invigorated for a short time.

She then rang her parents but only her dad was in. He was relieved to hear that Sam had visited and that she was now up, dressed and had even been out for a nice long walk. Toby and Annabelle had continued to worry about her but their jobs did not leave much spare time and for the hundredth time Toby wished his mother, Jasmine, had still been alive to help them through all this.

Poppy told him that she was going to do something she should have done before now and ring Gregory's parents. Toby was relieved to hear this. 'You know it's going to take a long time to come to terms with this and I know you will but you need take things slowly at first - one step at a time!'

'Yes Dad, I know and I will. I love you and thank you for everything. Mom too!'

'I know sweetheart and we love you too!'

Poppy then made the hardest phone call of her life. Gregory's mother answered the phone and took a sharp intake of breath when she realised who it was.

'Nancy, it's me! I'm so sorry I haven't called sooner but I just couldn't.'

'Oh Poppy I'm just so glad to hear your voice,' Nancy told her in between quietly crying.

Poppy felt guilty for not being in touch sooner as she pictured Gregory's mother at the other end of the line.

'I know,' Poppy said, feeling really bad. After all, they had lost their only son who had been their pride and joy. She wasn't the only one hurting.

'It's okay Poppy, I understand. We've all lost the light of our lives. I only hope he's up there with the angels looking down on us.'

Poppy nodded into the phone, gulping back her tears, almost choking with emotion. 'I know he is,' she continued quietly. Part of her wanted to tell Nancy about her dream of riding a white swan but another part didn't as she didn't want to break the magic or for her mother-in-law to think that she may have lost her mind.

With as much composure as she could muster, Poppy told Nancy that she had some things to sort out over the next few weeks but wondered if she could fly over and visit for a weekend after she had taken care of business. She had some photos of their travels she was sure they would love to have. Gregory's mother was delighted to hear this and tried to tell her so in between tears.

It was the most emotional phone call Poppy had ever made in her life and she felt totally drained. After she ended the phone call she made herself a cup of tea and mulled things over, thinking of what she should do.

Chapter 11
The Road to Recovery!

Poppy continued with her walks over the next few mornings and when Sam stopped by he was delighted to see that she had some colour in her cheeks. He noticed she had also brushed her hair and was wearing a pretty white spotted navy blue dress.

'Good to see you looking much better,' he said cheerfully. 'I like the dress too!'

Poppy looked down and said, 'This is the dress I wore on the day Gregory proposed to me in Venice.' As soon as she said it, she once again felt a stabbing pain and her eyes instantly filled with tears, but she managed to hold them back, and continue explaining, 'At the moment I wear black when I'm out but when I'm indoors I like to wear a colour or garment that connects me to him.'

Sam nodded. 'I understand.' His eyes searched the kitchen as he tried to think of something else to say. 'Here, I got this for you when I was in San Jose,' he said, quickly changing the subject and handing over the small parcel wrapped in brown paper with string holding it together.

'For me... thank you!' Poppy said gratefully, glad of the distraction.

She quickly opened the brown wrapping paper to reveal a book entitled *Do Dead People Watch You Shower?* She looked up at Sam.

'Please read it soon. I'm hoping it will help.'

'I will and thank you for your thoughtfulness,' she said, carefully placing it on the small occasional table.

'You're welcome. By the way, Maria says hi and sends her love.'

'Thank you. Please say the same back. How is she?'

Sam hesitated. 'She's a bit under the weather at the moment but she's fine really.'

'Oh, I'm sorry. Well please tell her I hope she soon feels much better!'

'I will... thanks. Okay, I need to get going, I just really wanted to drop the book off for you and check that you were doing okay. But I'll call around in another couple of days to see how you are doing.'

Poppy nodded. 'Thanks again,' she said, as she placed a brief kiss on his cheek before he left.

It was quiet after Sam left so Poppy picked up the book he'd brought her and started to read it. She quickly became absorbed with its contents and the hours swiftly passed.

A few days later Sam stopped by again but this time Poppy wasn't anywhere to be found. He walked down to the beach where he thought she might be but there was no sign of her. Sam wondered if she would have gone to their special rock at the other end of the beach, where they used to go to when they were teenagers. He walked in that direction and could see her sitting on "their rock". When he reached her, she looked miles away.

'Hey.'

She jumped. 'Oh, I didn't expect to see you!'

'I said I would come by again!'

'Sorry, I forgot.'

'Mind if I join you?'

'Do I have a choice?' She smiled in response.

He smiled back. 'Of course not!'

'It's truly awesome here isn't it? The changing colours, the raw power of the ocean and sea birds gliding gracefully in the air, never ceases to amaze me,' Poppy said, mesmerised by the colours and energy.

'I know what you mean. It's certainly a place where you can feel tranquil and at one with nature.'

They sat in silence for a long time, staring out to the endless horizon, watching the pelicans skim over the tops of the waves and occasionally swooping down to catch a fish. Then Sam quietly asked, 'Did you read the book?'

Poppy nodded.

'What did you think of it?'

'Excellent, thanks.'

'Do you think it helped?'

'Oh yes, without doubt. It gave me a new perspective on life and the afterlife! It did bring me some comfort.'

'Good...' he paused. 'Have you done any meditation?' he asked, already suspecting the answer.

She shook her head.

'Would you like to meditate here with me now for ten minutes?'

'Yes, that would be nice. I can't think of anywhere better.'

'Me neither!' he said, facing her. They both sat cross-legged. He held her hands and they closed their eyes and started to breathe deeply, losing themselves into the energy of their surroundings and the rhythmic sound of the waves. It was a peaceful experience and ten minutes turned into over an hour. Poppy was the first to open her eyes and Sam sensed this and opened his.

'How do you feel?' he asked.

'Refreshed and relaxed,' she replied with a slow smile.

'Good, I was hoping you'd say that. Now you need to do that every day along with your walks,' he instructed.

'Yes boss!' she smiled.

He nodded assertively in response. 'Okay, well I must dash. I'll see you in another couple of days,' he said, bending over to kiss her on the forehead.

A few days later, as promised, Sam came by again.

'Hi,' she smiled up at him.

'Hey, it's good to see you looking a bit brighter and healthier each time I come by. You're looking more like your old self again!'

'Thank you!'

'I guess you've been walking along the beach and meditating.'

'Oh yes, and it is helping, although I struggle with the meditation on my own.'

'I thought you might say that. So I've brought you one of my soothing instrumental CDs that you can borrow and load onto your iPod. You can take it down to the beach to meditate with.'

She smiled, delighted. 'Thank you! You are always anticipating my needs!'

'Well, that's what friends are for!'

She nodded in response.

'So did you come up with any ideas as to what you want to do in memory of Gregory?'

'Well, actually… yes I did.' She smiled and proceeded to tell him about some of her ideas.

'That sounds great. Well, if I can do anything to help, you know you've just got to ask.'

'I know and thank you again. You've helped me a great deal,' she said, smiling into the eyes of her very dear friend.

He nodded in acknowledgement. 'Well, I would like to stay longer but I'm afraid I'm going to have go as I've got some finishing touches to do on my exhibit which will be opening in San Jose this week, but I'll be back again in a few days.'

'That's okay. I'm happy for you and good luck,' she smiled.

'Thanks,' he said and once again kissed her on her forehead before leaving.

After he left, she thought how lucky she was to have such a loving and caring friend. Poppy then went to her computer. Fortunately Gregory had downloaded most of their travel photos before the accident, which had been a good thing as both their cameras had been destroyed in the crash.

Poppy was totally absorbed in the photos and would look at each one for a long time before sorting them into folders. She made a folder for Gregory's parents including the photos she thought they would like most. She would get them printed and put in an album to take to Rhode Island in a few weeks' time, she told herself. It was emotionally exhausting and she heard her dad's wise words coming back to her "one step at a time".

Contribution

'That's what I've got to do - one step at a time - that's the only way I'm going to get through this,' Poppy spoke out loud to herself, to reaffirm the message. 'Don't expect too much of yourself girl!'

Poppy then shut down her computer and suddenly realised just how wet her face was. She hadn't noticed she'd been crying when she was looking at Gregory's handsome, smiling face. She'd been looking at the photos for most of the day, except for when she stopped to make soup, sandwich and a coffee.

The day turned into night and Poppy switched the downstairs lights off and walked up to her bedroom. The evening was warm and sticky as she got ready for bed. She went to the balcony window and looked up to the stars in the black velvet sky, listening to the roar of the ocean. 'I hope you can see me my love and are watching over me. You know how much I love and miss you and our baby, don't you?' she whispered. There was a gust of wind and the floor-length white voiles fluttered in the breeze. She felt sure it was Gregory acknowledging her.

Poppy walked over to her bedside table and picked up the snow globe with the angel that Gregory had given her at Christmas. It was standing next to Gregory's framed photos. She absent-mindedly shook the globe and watched the snow fall over the angel and once again she read the words "Expect Miracles Every Day". Poppy put both her hands over the cool glass of the globe and closed her eyes. 'Well angel I certainly need one now! Please somehow help me get through this!' Poppy said out loud. She then got into bed and fell into a fitful sleep remembering the first magical night she had shared with Gregory in her bedroom.

Her dreams always drifted to when she was with Gregory and the baby. They were flying high in the sky on a huge white swan until she felt herself falling. Then she would suddenly wake up screaming. She had no sheets over her and could feel sweat dripping from her head and over-heated face. She lay in the darkness and once again tears spilled down her face. The loss and huge void of loneliness was overwhelming.

When Sam came by a few days later he knocked on the door and walked in to find Poppy sitting on the floor surrounded by photos and notes.

'Wow what a mess, but at least it's a good mess this time!' he smiled.

She looked up and smiled into his familiar, caring, blue eyes. 'Hi. It's good to see you too and do you always burst into people's homes unannounced?'

'Only to best friends but I will start again. Hi, so how are you today?'

'I'm doing much better thanks. I'm taking one step at a time, just like dad told me to do!'

'Good and I hope you are still taking your walks and meditating!'

She nodded and smiled.

'But what are you actually doing here?' he was curious to know.

Contribution

'I'm gathering my research and photos together to get them published into a series of books accompanying my documentaries. I actually came up with the idea and had done a lot of the work when I was on location with Gregory.' Saying Gregory's name out loud brought a slight gasp. 'But it's a bitter sweet project,' she said, remembering happier times. 'My producer, Larry, always thought it was a good idea and he thinks I should get on with it now and that it would do me good! We're going to use all the profits for setting up projects in the name of Gregory and Baby Gregory.'

'Wow, that's a great idea. Do you have a publisher in mind?'

'Larry knows someone and is going to get in touch with him and get back to me when I've got all this finished.'

'Great stuff; and what else are you going to do?'

'Well, I did think that was enough to be getting on with and it's one step at a time - remember!' She smiled at his persistence.

'Okay!' he agreed, wondering if he might be pushing her too hard too quickly.

'Would you like a coffee?' she asked.

'Sure.'

As Poppy stirred creamer into the coffee, she said 'Sam?'

'Yes,' he said, noticing the change in her tone.

'Can I tell you something strange that I haven't told anyone else?'

'Of course you can!'

'Well it sounds bizarre even to me but when I was in a coma I had a vision that I was flying on a white swan with Gregory and the baby. It felt so real and since then I dream about it most nights!'

'Why didn't you tell me about this before?'

'Because it sounds strange, even to my ears, and I didn't want you or anyone else to think I was going mad... And also I think I didn't want to break the magic spell!'

'Poppy, I wouldn't think you were going mad! I think you had a near death experience and you briefly visited heaven!'

'Seriously?'

'Honestly, I do! There's a book called *Proof of Heaven* by Dr Eben Alexander. I really think you should read it. I'm sure it will help enlighten you on your experience and you won't feel so alone with what happened.'

'Okay, I'll get hold of a copy,' she said, relieved to hear that.

They chatted for a while before Sam left, leaving her to sort out more photos for the books.

The next time Sam called in he was impressed with her progress on sorting out the photos for the documentary books. 'So, what about going back to work on your show?' he asked in a casual voice.

'What, with these scars?' she said in an incredulous voice. 'I'm hardly ready to stand in front of a camera! Besides, I had finished my contract before getting married and travelling and I just don't want to be in the public eye at the moment!'

'I understand, although I think you still look great and the scars will heal eventually! In any event, I'm sure they could easily be covered with a little makeup and you can always start another contract!'

'It's not just that. I've kind of lost my confidence and enthusiasm!'

'They'll return but, in the meantime, I'm sure there are other things you can do, especially with your knowledge and skills. You can always change direction and do something else - maybe something you've always wanted to do and never had the time until now.'

'I don't know. I'll give it some thought!'

'Oh, I nearly forgot to give you this,' he said, delving into his pocket and producing a small exquisite swan he had carved out of wood and painted white. 'I hope this helps remind you that Gregory is watching over you!'

Poppy was almost speechless at his thoughtfulness and her eyes welled up with tears. 'Sam, it's beautiful. I don't know what to say. Thank you so much! I will keep it by my bedside every night,' she said, hugging him tightly.

'You are very welcome,' he said, pleased she liked it so much.

Now that Poppy was improving he felt he could leave his visits a little longer. 'How about I call you in a week's time? But promise me if you need anything before then or you just want to talk you'll call me.'

'I will and thank you again Sam.'

'You're welcome.' With that he kissed her briefly on her forehead and closed the door quietly behind him.

That night Poppy placed the white, wooden swan Sam had given her next to her angel snow globe. She gazed at them both for a long time before eventually falling asleep.

The following week Sam called again. They were falling into an easy routine with her giving him updates of what she'd been doing. He felt it was important to try to keep her focused on projects and that it was the best thing he could do for her.

After several weeks passed, Poppy was boarding a plane back to the United States but not before going into the airport bookstore and buying the book *Proof of Heaven* Sam had recommended. She intended to read it on the plane and hoped she wouldn't be interrupted.

She had wrapped a scarf and large floppy hat around her face and wore dark glasses so that hopefully no-one would recognise her and see her scars, although conversely it seemed to raise more curiosity from

Contribution

passers-by. Thankfully she only had to remove them as she passed through customs. She felt she was treated gently and respectfully. Poppy had dropped the Anderson part of her name and had just used Taylor when booking her flight so that hopefully people wouldn't know it was her. She just wanted to blend in.

Gregory's parents met her off the plane at Providence airport. When she arrived she felt another pang, remembering the first time she had gone to Gregory's home here in Rhode Island. They had spent a wonderful time wandering around his home town, eating, drinking and sailing. She was starting to wonder if this would always be what her life would be like with her going to places and remembering the times she had spent with Gregory and feeling totally overwhelmed.

There were hugs and tears. In the car, on the journey back to Jim and Nancy's home, they kept the conversation light... the real gut-wrenching stuff could wait until later. As Jim drove back to their place, Poppy remembered the first time she had met his parents, and once again felt sadness engulf her.

When they got back to Jim and Nancy's, Jim opened the front door and Misty bounded up to them and, tail wagging, she greeted Poppy, licking her all over. 'Oh my goodness Misty, I didn't think you'd remember me! You miss him so much too don't you?' she said, stroking the lovable golden dog. Poppy felt her hot tears spill over onto the dog's head. Misty looked up with sad, bewildered eyes - she hadn't seen her owner for ages and wanted to know when he was coming back.

Despite their loss and sadness, they all spent a pleasant weekend talking about happier times in between their tears. Gregory's parents were delighted with the album and the larger framed photo of her and Gregory in Fiji when they were on the first part of their honeymoon. They thanked her for her thoughtfulness.

Nancy cleared her throat uncomfortably. 'Poppy... this is probably the hardest thing I will ever have to say... but... well we kept Gregory's ashes so that when you felt up to it we thought the three of us could go out in *Little Annie* and scatter them in the ocean! I feel sure he would have wanted us to do that!' Nancy said, tears rolling down her face.

Poppy took a gulp. She hadn't expected that. Tears uncontrollably slid down her face too. 'Nancy, thank you so much. I really appreciate that, especially as I didn't get to go to the funeral... When do you want to do it?' Poppy asked.

'Well my dear, how about soon? We've waited long enough and, who knows, maybe it will somehow help, although I've got to tell you I will never come to terms with this. A mother should never lose her child. It's quite simply the wrong order!'

Poppy nodded. Once again she realised she wasn't the only one suffering.

Contribution

They made their way to the marina almost in silence, each one lost in their own thoughts and memories. Jim, just like Gregory had done, expertly sailed *Little Annie* out of the marina and away into the deep ocean.

Jim broke the silence. 'Is here okay?'

Both women looked around. They were way out to sea but could still see Gregory's beloved town. 'This would be ideal,' Poppy said, remembering her first time on *Little Annie*. She thought her heart would break in half.

Jim anchored the yacht. He then said a prayer and they each threw a red rose into the water. At the same time, sun rays shone down and they all felt Gregory was watching over them.

They spent some time sitting still… watching… remembering…

Jim was the first to break the spell. 'Come on ladies, it's getting chilly and there's a storm coming.'

They nodded and Jim once again set sail, this time to return home.

During their final evening together they shared food, memories and laughter with tears intermingled. Poppy once again thanked Nancy and Jim for their thoughtfulness and love. 'Do you think we could do this every year on Gregory's anniversary?' Poppy asked them in a tentative voice.

They both nodded. Nancy replied, 'Of course, dear. To be honest we were hoping you would say that. And we want you to know that we consider you our daughter and you are welcome here any time,' Nancy said in a quiet voice before looking at her husband and silently trying to urge him to say the next thing she knew they needed to discuss.

Jim picked up the cue. 'Poppy, there is something else we have to tell you,' Gregory's father said gently.

Poppy looked up at him from where she sat. She had been lost in her own thoughts. 'What's that?'

'While you were in hospital and recovering, we had to sort out Gregory's legal things and, although there is still a long way to go, you need to know that he left everything to you,' Jim said quietly, placing a hand on hers.

She wasn't totally surprised as this had been something they had talked about just before they got married, and she in turn had left everything of hers to him. Although when they made these arrangements with their attorney neither of them had seriously thought something would happen so soon in their lives.

Gregory's father interrupted her thoughts. 'He had saved a lot of money over the years, was a smart investor, and was well insured, especially because of his work and travels.'

She nodded.

'You will be receiving over a million dollars eventually,' Jim said matter-of-factly.

At that point she was totally shocked. She hadn't expected so much. 'Oh no, I don't want it. No amount of money could ever bring him back or ease the pain!'

'I know, but nevertheless it's yours.'

'I really don't want it!' she said stubbornly.

Gregory's father looked at her pleadingly, without saying a word.

She could see the pain in her father-in-law's face and conceded, 'Okay, well what if I do something good with it - in memory of him and the baby?' Poppy added, seeing the anguish in Jim's eyes.

'We thought you'd say that and we both think that's a good idea. Do you have anything in mind?' Jim enquired. It was with a very heavy heart he was having this conversation but he was extremely fond of his daughter-in-law and knew she would use the money wisely.

'I have a few ideas but I'll let you know when I've decided for sure.'

'Well, if we can do anything to help or you need any advice at any time you know where we are,' he said gently. He knew life would never be the same for any of them and he hated all the heartache they shared.

Poppy, Nancy and Jim finished their time together pleasantly before they drove her back to the airport. They said a tearful farewell and hugged each other, promising to keep in touch.

As Poppy was already in the States she thought it would be a good opportunity to fly out to New York and meet the owner of the publishing company her producer Larry had recommended for the book series.

Poppy settled down in the airplane seat and let her thoughts drift back to Gregory and his family. After some time she picked up the book she had bought at the airport in Costa Rica and continued reading *Proof of Heaven*.

Chapter 12
A New Life!

By the time Poppy's plane landed in New York she had finished reading the book and felt sure she too had had a near-death experience and that riding the giant white swan high up in the skies with Gregory and her baby had really happened and that she wasn't completely insane.

Poppy made a mental note that one day she would e-mail Dr Alexander and tell him of her experience. She particularly loved the poem *When Tomorrow Starts Without Me* written by David M. Romano in 1993 which Dr Alexander made reference to in his book and which she took great comfort from and read several times.

Poppy took a taxi from the airport to the hotel and checked into her room at the *Waldorf* which had been reserved for her by the publishing house. She had an early night in preparation for her initial meeting with the owner of the publishing company.

The next morning she quickly got dressed and looked smart and professional in her black suit. She added sunglasses, a large black floppy hat and matching scarf, gloves, handbag and shoes.

The taxi weaved in and out of the traffic, taking her through the busy streets of Manhattan, passing Wall

Street and then onto Publishers Row where she arrived in front of the huge glass building of the publishers. The receptionist took her into the grand oak offices of Stuart Austin Bruce. The tall, white haired, handsome gentleman with vivid blue eyes wearing a tailored blue suit stood up from behind his massive desk to greet her.

'Welcome, Mrs Taylor.'

'Thank you. It's good to be here and please call me Poppy,' she said congenially.

They shook hands and he invited her to sit opposite him at his desk. After their initial introductions, he told her how pleased he was that their mutual friend, Larry, had contacted them.

He cleared his throat uncomfortably. 'I was also very sorry to hear about the accident and for your loss,' he said sympathetically.

Stuart knew how she felt, from his own personal experience, but at least he hadn't had to deal with the media intrusion she had, he thought. It had been reported worldwide in the media that only seven months after the lavish and glamorous wedding of Poppy Anderson and Gregory Taylor that such a tragedy had occurred. The media had reported every little snippet of information they could find.

Poppy nodded. She had heard the same condolences many times now, but it didn't get any easier.

'Before we go any further, would you mind removing your hat, scarf and glasses please,' he said gently.

'I'd rather not!'

'I'm sorry but I can't conduct a meeting with someone I can't see properly.'

'But you don't understand,' she said in a panicked voice.

'Yes I do and I would like you to remove them please,' he said quietly but firmly.

'But I still have some scars!'

'I'm sorry but you can't hide behind a disguise and I want to conduct our meetings eye to eye!'

She turned bright crimson and silently stared at him. She hadn't expected this and it seemed that their first meeting was not starting off well.

He persisted, 'Besides, eventually your scars will fade but in the meantime you have to learn to live with them!'

Poppy wanted to ask, 'How would you know and who the hell do you think you are?' But she didn't say anything. She thought he was being unreasonable. She stubbornly glared at him from behind her dark glasses.

Poppy's first impression of the publishing magnet was that he was an arrogant ass. She seriously considered getting up and walking out of the office. She didn't have to be here she told herself, but then she thought about her long term goals and, after all, Larry had highly recommended him.

After several minutes of uncomfortable silence, she relented. 'All right, please direct me to a bathroom and I'll remove them there,' she replied curtly.

He indicated for her to go through to his personal bathroom adjacent to his office.

Once beyond the heavy oak door Poppy looked around the immaculate masculine bathroom decorated in black granite and oak trim. There was a clean smell of Sandalwood soap and recently sprayed cologne. His comb, shaver and toothbrush were neatly placed next to the washbasin.

She looked in the mirror and slowly removed her sunglasses, scarf and hat to reveal a white face with dark circles underneath her eyes and fading red scars around the edges of her face and neck. She combed her hair which by now had grown to mid-length. She tried to pull some of it forward around her face.

Poppy hated revealing so much of her face and felt very self-conscious when she walked back into his office.

'There!' she said petulantly.

'Thank you,' he replied stiffly and studied her intently. She looked like she had really been through the mill but he would have still known it was her from the photos he had seen, although she had lost the sparkle and vitality she had exhibited on the documentaries that had made her famous. However, she was still a beautiful young woman, he thought.

Contribution

The conversation was stilted as they talked about her ideas and how they were going to format the series of books to link in with the shows. He had already watched hours of her video footage before their meeting. When they finally agreed on the outline he told her he would send her a draft contract for her perusal with the terms and conditions stipulated.

'Are you sure you want all the proceeds to go to non-profit projects?'

'Absolutely, it's something I wholeheartedly believe in. However, I want to make it clear that the book series will be dedicated to my late husband!' She hated saying "late husband" and not for the first time she wondered why people said "late". He wasn't late... he was gone... gone for ever.

'Okay, but how are you going to manage your projects, especially with all your other commitments?'

'I'm not sure yet... I hadn't got that far!'

'Well, if it's any help, I have a friend, Andrew Wilson, who's a genius at creating non-profit organisations. We could have a meeting with him and his lawyer after we get the outline of the books completed, if you wish?'

She brightened and thanked him, pleased that they had overcome their earlier awkwardness.

It was now midday and they called the meeting to a close. She still tired easily and agreed they would have another meeting tomorrow with one of his editors who had been assigned to help pull the material together.

Stuart walked her to the door and said, 'You know Poppy, I really think it's a good idea and should be a great success!'

'Thank you, I hope so!'

She left the building after they said their goodbyes and, because it was such a fresh and sunny day, she decided to walk back to the hotel instead of taking a cab. She was so absorbed with the book ideas and charitable projects floating around her head that she forgot to put her hat and scarf back on. She kept her sunglasses on and blended in among the throng of people in the busy streets of Manhattan.

She had a light lunch in her room and then lay on her bed and took an afternoon nap. When she woke up, she showered, changed and worked a little on her projects before ordering her evening meal from room service, which was to become her routine for the rest of the week.

The next morning Stuart introduced her to Sophie, a dynamic writer and editor in her late thirties. The three of them got on well and worked diligently, sharing ideas and pulling Poppy's notes and photographs together. Stuart didn't normally get quite so involved but he was doing this as a favour to Larry and he really liked Poppy too, despite their chilly start.

They spent the rest of the week with this routine until Sophie was happy that she had everything she needed to make the book series the success they all hoped it would be. They thanked each other and said it was a pleasure working together and that they would keep in touch.

The following week Poppy spent her time in talks with Stuart's friend, Andrew Wilson. He had just turned forty and had spent his entire working life in pursuit of avenues to contribute to those in need.

Andrew was a dynamic man who came from a family of considerable wealth and felt that he should use his connections in an attempt to make the world a better place. He was so good at his job that he was now CEO of one of the largest non-profit organisations in the United States.

During their first meeting, Andrew included his top legal staff. They would help Poppy negotiate the minefield of legalities in order to set up her charitable organisations. It was agreed that they would put all the mechanisms in place to set up the *Gregory Taylor Charitable Trust*, and Andrew would get his human resources manager to find the appropriate staff to work for her newly formed non-profit organisation.

'If it's any help Poppy I know of a large office here in the heart of New York that is owned by a good friend who may be interested in making it available to you at a low cost. It would be an ideal place to start your organisation,' Andrew suggested.

'Oh, wow, I'd really appreciate that. Thank you, I can do with all the help I can get!' she smiled gratefully.

Stuart joined them on their final meeting, which they held at his office, and he was pleased that he was able to bring Andrew and Poppy together, and further help her achieve her goals.

After the meeting finished and Andrew had left, Poppy once again thanked Stuart for all his help. He had certainly made things run more smoothly for her. She looked at the photo on the desk of Stuart and a blonde woman smiling happily at the camera, both looking very much in love. 'Is that your wife? She's beautiful.'

'Yes.' He paused. 'Her name was Amanda. She died three years ago.'

Poppy was shocked. 'Oh, I'm sorry,' she said and felt tears immediately prick her eyes. She hadn't expected to hear that.

He nodded in acknowledgement. 'So now you know I do understand a lot of what you are going through,' he said gently.

Poppy nodded, absorbing the information and seeing a more personal side to Stuart. 'How did you cope? Does it get any easier?' she wanted to know. She had been so caught up in her own loss and misery that she hadn't for one moment thought that anyone else had been in her shoes or was suffering too!

'I don't know. At first I was totally numb and then I was incredibly angry. Why did it happen to us when we were so happy? I threw myself into my work, which is what I still do! The days are fine but it's much harder at night. I guess you kind of learn to live with it and it becomes a part of you. It certainly changes you. I don't normally talk about it but it kind of feels appropriate now.'

She nodded, understanding.

'Do you have any children?'

'No, sadly we don't. We were actually trying for a family but she'd been in a lot of pain. It was then, when she went to the hospital for tests, that we found out that she had ovarian cancer, and it was too far advanced to do anything about it. She died a few months later,' he said emotionally.

'I'm so sorry.'

He coughed lightly, clearing the lump from his throat. 'Thing is, I still look back and feel guilty. Why hadn't I had the sense to send her to the doctor sooner or why couldn't she tell me she felt such pain?'

'But you can't torture yourself like that. She wouldn't want you to!' she said earnestly, remembering Sam's advice to her.

'I know but I can't help it.'

'You know, my very best friend Sam once told me that we can't control circumstances in life - only our reaction to them!'

'And he was right, although it's easier said than done!'

'I know... Can I ask...?' she paused, not wanting to sound crazy or intrusive but she needed to know. 'Do you sometimes feel that Amanda's spirit is with you?'

'Actually it's strange you should ask that but when I'm at my quietest I do still feel she's with me. But I'm not sure whether it's my overactive imagination and just wishful thinking on my part!'

She nodded. 'I feel Gregory's spirit is still with me but I wasn't sure whether it was because it's early days yet.'

'Who knows?'

After their heartfelt conversation Poppy felt they had moved from a working relationship to one of friendship. They agreed they would stay in touch via e-mails when she returned to Costa Rica.

They said their goodbyes and she went back to her hotel to pack her few belongings and catch the next flight back to San Jose, all the while thinking of Gregory, Stuart and Amanda and how sad life was.

Sam called in the following day, excited to hear about her trip to New York. 'So how did it go?'

Poppy poured them a cold drink of coconut milk and they sat cross-legged on the futon in her den, like they used to when they were kids. She enthusiastically told him about her trip and how she eventually liked Stuart after their initial rough start when he insisted that she take off her hat, scarf and sunglasses! Sam liked the sound of him and was glad he'd been able to help her. She also told Sam about Stuart's wife and how this revelation had seemed to move them to a better understanding and indeed a new friendship.

Contribution

'So what now?'

'Why does there always have to be something else with you?' Poppy asked, almost exasperated. She thought she had done well to get this far!

'Because we always have to keep growing and moving forward on our journey of life… and because you always need something to keep your mind occupied to stop you dwelling on what happened!'

'Okay, you got me on that one!' she conceded.

'So what are you going to do now?' he persisted.

'Well, I think the first thing I need to do is to take some flowers to the cemetery tomorrow, and apologise to my gran for the uncharitable thoughts I had!'

'That's a good idea. You two were so close and you always idolised her! It would be a shame to have bad feelings at this stage of your life!' Sam said, remembering all their times together and how shocked he was at Poppy's outburst when she first came back home.

'I know,' she said quietly. 'And I realise how unreasonable I was, which is why I'm going to the cemetery tomorrow to make my peace and ask for her forgiveness.'

He smiled, squeezing her hands, relieved she had come to her senses. 'Well, you're making good strides and I know your gran will forgive you. But maybe you need to also try to forgive yourself too! Feeling guilty that it was you who wanted to follow the route your gran and Ben took, and thinking if you hadn't then the accident wouldn't have happened is not good for you Poppy.'

'I know but I can't help thinking I caused the accident!'

'Poppy you've got stop thinking like this and torturing yourself! Don't you see it could have happened anywhere? It was out of your control! You can't blame yourself. If it hadn't been there then something else could have happened somewhere else. You can't control fate!' he tried to reason. 'And Poppy, you've got to let go of all this hurt and anger otherwise it will destroy you!'

'I know - you're right.' She paused. 'Anyway, enough about me, how are things with you?' she asked, trying to change the subject. 'Is Maria feeling any better?'

'Well...yes...' Sam paused, wondering whether or not he should mention his happy news.

Poppy looked at him quizzically.

'I'm not sure how to say this and I don't want to upset you any further... but Maria's three months pregnant!'

'Oh!' Poppy paused and then added, 'Oh what wonderful news!' she said, trying to put on a brave face and sound happy for them.

However, Sam saw her face pale and wished he hadn't said anything. 'I'm sorry Poppy, I shouldn't have told you yet but I didn't want you finding out from someone else.'

'It's okay,' she said, feeling a stabbing pain in her heart. She knew if her gran had been alive she would have told her to rejoice in others' good fortune, even though at that moment she felt there was nothing left to celebrate in her life.

'I'm happy for you and Maria and I'm glad I heard it from you and not someone else.' She considered things for a moment. 'Are you okay with it?'

'Actually I am and, you know me, I take everything in my stride!'

She knew he would make a good father, knowing how relaxed and easygoing he was with life.

'You know, I think you'll make a wonderful dad!'

'Thank you my dear friend,' he said, pleased with her compliment.

'So when are you getting married?'

'Oh no, that's not on the cards!'

'Really! Why not?'

'For me marriage is only a word… but commitment is in the heart. Maria knows how much I love her and that I'll always look after her and the baby!'

Poppy wasn't really surprised to hear this. In fact she wasn't sure if he'd ever get married!

'Anyway, I need to get going. I have to take Maria for a routine check-up,' he said, getting up from the futon and kissing her on the forehead. 'I'll come by next week if that's okay?'

She nodded. 'As always, thank you again,' she smiled at him, 'and congratulations to you and Maria!'

'Thanks. When Maria is feeling better, we'll both come by.'

'That would be good,' Poppy smiled again.

After Sam left, she made herself a cup of coffee and sat out on her bedroom balcony overlooking the ocean and mulling things over, thinking of her own baby and that of Sam's and how nice it would have been for their babies to have grown up together. Tears slid down her face as her loss once again consumed her.

The next day Poppy cut a pretty bouquet of tropical flowers, including ginger, hibiscus and bird of paradise, from the garden and took the flowers to her gran's place at the cemetery. Poppy spent a quiet hour there praying and making peace with herself and her gran.

The following Wednesday was Poppy's twenty-sixth birthday. She had already opened her cards and e-mail messages. By the time she heard the knock and familiar voice, Sam had already made his way through her living room to the kitchen where she was drinking a glass of water.

'It should be wine today!' he smiled. 'Happy birthday,' he said, kissing her on the cheek and presenting her with an orchid.

'Aww thank you for remembering - that's lovely!'

'Are you having a nice day?' Sam asked, and then immediately regretted the question, realising he had touched a nerve, when he saw sadness swiftly cross her face. He stammered, 'I'm sorry, that was thoughtless of me. I know how hard things are for you, especially at times like this.'

She nodded. 'That's okay,' she said, as she felt unshed tears sting her eyes. 'I can't help but think what we would have done today? What he would have got me? Where we would have gone?'

'I know,' he said quietly.

'Anyway, how's Maria?' she asked, trying to change the subject, but then that thought also brought a stab to her heart.

'She's okay but she's still having a lot of morning sickness and needing a lot of rest.'

'She'll get there. Give her my love.'

'I will. So did you get to the cemetery last week?'

'Yes, I took gran some flowers.'

'And you made your peace?'

'Yes! And before you ask, yes I feel better for doing it!'

He smiled in response. 'So what are you going to do next?'

'Well I was thinking of doing something that helps babies and their families… possibly building a specialised unit at a hospital that needs a new baby unit for premature babies in San Jose. I could either donate a lump sum or set up a fund with Andrew Wilson's people in New York. I was thinking of calling it *Baby Gregory's Neonatal Unit*.

Poppy hadn't officially known whether her baby had been a boy or a girl. But when she had her dreams of riding a white swan and holding him she always saw him as a boy. She could imagine a gorgeous little version of her husband and in her mind's eye she could see Gregory looking after their baby so she had decided to call him Baby Gregory.

'I like the sound of that,' Sam enthused. 'Good on you!'

She smiled, knowing there could well be a lot of work ahead.

'And how's the book series going?'

'I'm waiting for the proofs to come back and the legal work to be put into place before we can start the next stage.'

'That's great. I'm so proud of you and you know Gregory would have been too?'

She nodded, once again feeling tears sting her eyes, more so today. Poppy wished with all her heart she had woken up to Gregory's kisses and birthday presents and just being able to spend the day together, walking hand-in-hand along the beach.

Sam noticed, once again, grief crossing her face. 'Always remember Poppy that your spirit is far more resilient and powerful than you think and you will somehow get through this. Keep being positive and doing the good things you are doing for other people and your outlook on life will change. You will learn to live with this and one day you will be able to think of all the special memories you shared without this piercing pain in your heart!'

She nodded, trying to choke back her tears. 'So how did you get so wise?'

'I guess I was just born that way!' He smiled and kissed her on the forehead before once again leaving.

After he closed the door behind him, Poppy climbed the stairs and, suddenly feeling tired, she lay down on her bed and remembered her last birthday and how she shared it with Gregory. And she wondered what they would have done today and what he would have given her but none of that mattered any more. All she wanted was to wake up in his strong arms and taste his kisses, feel his caresses and just hear him wish her happy birthday and hold her.

She quietly cried and had nearly drifted off to sleep when she suddenly felt Gregory was beside her. She could smell his distinctive Armani cologne and hear him say in his soft voice, "Happy birthday my darling, you know how much I love you! I'm here with you always!"

She smiled, feeling warmed and comforted before drifting off to sleep, dreaming of being in his arms and of happier times.

When Poppy woke up she felt refreshed and started her research into which hospital she wanted to donate money to for *Baby Gregory's Neonatal Unit*. This was to be the first of many projects she had in mind.

Chapter 13
Poppy's Projects!

Poppy rang her parents first and told them of her plans. They were delighted she was doing something positive and said they would talk to a few people they knew in San Jose and find out where a new neonatal unit was needed the most. They hadn't told Poppy, but they too had been devastated at not only losing their son-in-law but also their grandchild.

Toby quickly came back with the name of the director at the hospital he knew in San Jose.

The next day Poppy drove up to meet the esteemed acquaintance of her father to discuss her wishes.

It was an easy matter of donating an extremely sizeable sum and signing papers. They already had a section of the building that had been underused so it was just a question of buying all the specialised equipment needed to provide state-of-the-art infant care for premature babies and hiring the necessary specialists to run the new unit.

Poppy made several trips to the hospital in San Jose to check the progress of the remodelling project. She spent many hours with the project manager and the new staff that had been hired but there wasn't as much work in creating *Baby Gregory's Neonatal Unit* as she first thought. However, two months did pass quickly and she was glad of the project to help keep her mind occupied.

The neonatal unit was well received by the city's community, especially as there were areas for parents to stay over with their babies.

Poppy stood in the sunshine, looking smart in her little black jacket and black cotton dress, waiting to give a short speech on the opening of the unit. Amongst a lot of publicity, she was soon cutting the blue ribbon to formally open the much needed baby unit which was painted in bright colours.

Choking back tears she looked at the name *Baby Gregory's Neonatal Unit* engraved in stone above the exterior door entrance to the unit. Baby Gregory's name was also etched on a bronze plaque in the foyer dedicated to his memory.

The hospital had installed the latest technology and equipment, and the team had made inviting, comfortable family rooms for anxious parents while their babies were being cared for.

In addition Poppy put in place a monthly payment schedule to help pay for the administration and upkeep of the unit. She had assigned one of the staff at the *Gregory Taylor Charitable Trust* to also set up a foundation to constantly help raise money for *Baby Gregory's Neonatal Unit* to help keep it running and to keep up-to-date with modern technology, ensuring his name was never forgotten.

Several days after the completion of the neonatal unit she received an e-mail from Stuart telling her that he'd seen an article showing her opening the new unit. He wrote that he thought it was a great idea and was very proud of her. He also told her that Sophie had finished the mock-ups of the books and asked if she would like to come back to New York to look at them and give her final approval.

Poppy thanked him and thought perhaps it would be good to have Larry's input too. Stuart agreed that it was a good idea and he would arrange a time when they could all meet.

Poppy booked a flight back to New York within a matter of days and checked into the *Waldorf Hotel* again. She wanted to keep herself as busy as possible and to feel the positive energy it inspired.

Early next morning Poppy arrived at Stuart's office. He greeted her with a gentle clasp of the hand and a brief kiss on the side of her cheek. 'It's good to see you Poppy. You look great. The tropical sun must be good for you!' he said, noticing her hair had grown back and she had acquired a slight tan, helping mask her scars which were now nearly healed.

'Thank you, although I guess I couldn't have looked much worse!' she said, smiling ruefully.

'Oh I'm sorry, I hope I haven't spoken out of turn!'

She smiled. 'No, it's okay. I know I wasn't at my best!'

Stuart smiled a gracious smile.

Poppy hadn't noticed Larry sitting on the comfortable leather sofa at the other end of the office watching and listening to the warm exchange between his good friends. He coughed slightly and Poppy turned, surprised to see her producer and dear friend getting up to greet her. Larry hugged her and told her how good it was to see her.

After their greetings, Stuart said, 'Let me bring Sophie in and she can show you what she's done. I'm very pleased with it - I hope you will be too!'

Sophie entered the large, luxurious, masculine office and she proudly showed Poppy and Larry the completed work and hoped she had done it justice.

Both Poppy and Larry were delighted with the final outcome and told Sophie that she had anticipated everything well and couldn't think how she could improve it. They were all looking forward to it being published.

After discussing the current project Larry was working on, he excused himself and said goodbye to everyone so that he could catch an early flight back to San Francisco where they were currently filming.

Poppy had a sudden pang of regret when she kissed Larry goodbye, remembering that not too long ago she would have been the one returning to filming in an exciting and interesting location. She was glad it had been a man who had replaced her as the main anchor on the show, which had already changed slightly in format.

Stuart saw the fleeting look of regret and after Larry left he asked, 'Do you miss it?'

Poppy let out a deep sigh. 'Yes, sometimes. I had a great time there but I've changed and I wouldn't want to go back to it now. At least now I'm able to do other things that I want to do and wouldn't have had time for!'

At that point, Sophie told them she needed to get back to her office so that she could schedule a series of press releases, interviews and book signings for Poppy to generate publicity and get the ball rolling.

Stuart noticed Poppy immediately tensing up.

'I can't do it.'

'Can't do what?' Stuart asked.

'I can't do the interviews.'

'Why not?'

'It's too soon!'

'Poppy you have to, it's the best way for you to help sell the books and generate the funding you need for your other projects.'

'Can't I just do the book signings?'

'Unfortunately you need to do the interviews too.' He'd seen her do interviews many times before when she was promoting her shows and she had always done a great job. But he saw her briefly touch the side of her face and understood her reluctance.

'I'm sorry, Poppy.' He paused briefly. 'I kind of got used to seeing the scars and had forgotten about them, especially as they hardly show now.' He paused again before continuing, 'I know it's probably a bit soon after the accident but I don't understand what the difference is between meeting the public and doing an interview? In fact an interview will probably be easier because makeup and camerawork will hide anything you don't want anyone to see!' Stuart was starting to feel uncomfortable, thinking maybe he was being tactless and pushing her too hard too soon, but the success of the book series rested on her personal appearances.

Poppy was silent as she looked around the room, trying to think of the best way to explain how she was feeling.

He tried a different tack. 'Poppy, you have many fans out there who want to see you and you've always been able to influence people. I really think it would be beneficial for you to do the interviews.'

'I know. It's just that I feel nervous about it. I've been out of the limelight for a while now and I'm frightened about what they might ask me,' she tried to explain. Poppy had been well aware of the press coverage after the accident and the media still took a great deal of interest in her. However, she was mostly worried that if they asked her anything about Gregory she wouldn't be able to keep her composure.

'Okay, I understand. What if we set the ground rules in advance, stating which questions they are allowed to ask? And I'll be standing at the sidelines on your first interview.'

Contribution

Reluctantly, and against her better judgment, Poppy agreed.

Stuart was relieved. Convincing her had been much harder than he thought it was going to be. He told her that he would start getting her booked into radio and TV shows but that it would be at least a few months down the road anyway.

Poppy was glad she had some time ahead of her. This would give her more time for her scars to heal and she also had another project she wanted to work on and told him all about it. Stuart was once again impressed with her tenacity and loyalty to her husband.

Poppy returned to Costa Rica and quickly started her next project. She e-mailed Gregory's best friend, John, who had been the best man at their wedding. Gregory and John had worked together for over five years and had done great work on many projects. Poppy told John of her plans and wondered if he could help.

John was pleased to hear from her and e-mailed her back telling her once again how very sorry he was about Gregory. He was still stunned at the loss of his best friend and told her that he would do whatever he could to help. He was also sorry he hadn't managed to visit her yet but the memories were still too raw, although he knew it was time for him to move forward and helping in a project in his best friend's name would be a good start.

John was on location in Chile and made arrangements to fly to San Jose in a week's time to meet her. This would give Poppy enough time to finish sifting through the videos and photographs Gregory had taken when he was in India, and unpublished footage of human suffering he had taken in different parts of the world. She would then hand over her chosen footage and photos so that John could do the necessary editing.

Going through the old videos, and especially the videos of India, was a double-edged sword. She took comfort from seeing all of Gregory's work but at the same time the ache deep inside her was almost unbearable. At times she would suddenly realise her face was soaking wet from tears she hadn't known she was shedding.

By the end of the week she was drained with having selected so much work but she knew she had the best footage for John to turn into two documentary films. One about world disasters and the other about worldwide poverty and homelessness, especially focusing on India.

John had taken a few days off work to fly from Chile to Costa Rica. Poppy met him at San Jose airport. It was only a relatively short flight and he felt refreshed enough to start work but was taken aback when he realised the last time he'd been at this airport was for their wedding.

John kissed Poppy briefly on the cheek when she greeted him, and he once again apologised for not being in touch sooner. He was troubled to see her look so sad and gaunt. The Poppy he knew had lost her spark and vitality and her black outfit was a constant reminder of their loss.

Contribution

John and Poppy chatted while she drove him through the busy city traffic to a nearby hotel. She told him all about the book series she had been working on in New York and told him she couldn't wait to see the series published. She also told him about *Baby Gregory's Neonatal Unit* and the *Gregory Taylor Charitable Trust* she had set up.

'That's great Poppy. I know Greg would have been very proud of you.'

Poppy gave a deep sigh. 'Thank you. But I'm just trying to keep as busy as possible and my mind occupied, and at the same time not letting Gregory be forgotten.'

'Well I think that's very commendable,' John said in admiration. He had found it extremely hard coping with the loss of his best friend and couldn't imagine being in Poppy's shoes.

When they arrived at the hotel, they found a quiet corner in the lounge area of the foyer. She spread all the videos, photographs and notes on the coffee table. They sat opposite on the sofas and he wrote reminders of what she wanted as they bounced ideas off each other.

Poppy made it clear that she wanted the profits from the world disasters documentary to go into a fund to be used for worldwide emergency relief. Then the profits from the poverty and homeless documentary to go to impoverished people in India.

Poppy was grateful to John and his team for their help with editing the footage. She thought John should be paid appropriately but he wouldn't hear of it and said he wanted his time to be donated in memory of his dear friend, but reluctantly agreed that his staff could be paid. However, he felt sure when he discussed it with them they would feel the same way he did, knowing Gregory had been a highly respected member of their team.

Poppy thanked him and told him that in any event Andrew Wilson, from her charity trust, would be in touch at the necessary time to put everything in place.

Poppy also told him there were five people working for her at the *Gregory Taylor Charitable Trust*, one of whom was handling the *Baby Gregory Neonatal Unit* fundraising efforts. Nevertheless, they were all now so busy that she had decided to employ two more staff to organise channelling the funding from the documentaries to the appropriate places. John thought it was a good idea.

Poppy asked John to make sure that at the end of each documentary it clearly showed that it was released in memory of Gregory. She wanted everyone to know what he had done to try to make a difference. John agreed to do everything in his power to make it happen.

'Thank you,' she said earnestly.

'Poppy, you know I'll be more than happy to do this and that it would be an honour,' he said sincerely, looking steadily at her. 'It's the least I can do for such a great guy. I really don't think I'll ever get over losing him!'

Contribution

'I know,' she said, reaching out to squeeze his hand, realising once again that it wasn't just her who was suffering. She smiled and continued, 'John, you know Gregory thought the world of you and I have complete confidence that you will do this incredibly well.'

He nodded, as he sipped his coffee. 'Thank you, I appreciate you saying that.'

Poppy was pleased with their meeting and the way her work was going to help other people. By the end of the day they had everything sorted and both were feeling mentally exhausted.

Poppy and John decided to have a quick bite to eat before going to their respective rooms. They wanted to mull things over and meet up again in the morning at breakfast to make any changes either of them felt necessary before he returned to work in Chile.

Poppy, feeling drained, quickly got ready for bed and fell into a restless sleep thinking of Gregory and all that he had done and what she knew he wanted to achieve.

The next morning after breakfast Poppy and John discussed some minor changes but on the whole it seemed the project was ready to move forward. Poppy then drove John back to the airport so he could catch his return flight to Chile. Before he proceeded to check-in, John looked earnestly at Poppy and said, 'Poppy, once again I want you to know that I will carry out your wishes to the best of my ability. After all, it's the least I can do for you and Gregory,' he told her with heartfelt sincerity. He still couldn't believe that it wasn't even a year since they were all celebrating the wedding.

Hearing Gregory and her referred to as a couple again made her heart skip a beat but she managed to thank John for everything and told him she knew he was the man for the job. They hugged and briefly kissed each other on the cheek. John told her he would e-mail her with progress.

Poppy had been on the go so much and had so many projects milling around her head she was exhausted when she finally arrived home. She went straight to bed to lie down for a short while, her thoughts, as always, full of Gregory.

For the next few weeks Poppy returned to her routine of long walks along the beach and meditation, but she couldn't clear her head and her thoughts drifted to Gregory and her projects. At times she found it challenging to try to quiet her restless mind.

As usual Sam popped in on occasions and gave her words of encouragement and inspiration.

Christmas was fast approaching and Poppy was dreading it. Sam and Maria had invited her over to their house but Poppy declined their kind offer. She really wanted to spend it on her own but Toby and Annabelle insisted that she spend it with someone and not be alone. Finally Poppy relented and said she would visit her parents in Panama hoping that Christmas would be very low key. Her parents felt the same way and agreed that they would just treat it as a couple of days' quality time together and get through it the best they could.

Chapter 14
Trials and Tribulations!

A few weeks after Christmas Poppy got an e-mail from Stuart telling her that he had received a lot of interest in the book series, had already generated some good PR coverage and had arranged for her to go on a talk show.

She wrote back telling him she still wasn't ready.

An hour later, the phone rang and she was surprised to hear Stuart's voice.

After the usual pleasantries, he said, 'Poppy, this is a real catch so soon in the game. We're very lucky that a guest cancelled and an opening has become available on such a popular morning show!'

There was a long silence.

'It's too good an opportunity to pass up and if it makes you feel any better I'll go to the studios with you. It will be fine - I promise!' Stuart said in a calm and assuring voice, gently persuading her to accept the invitation on the national network in two weeks' time.

In the end Poppy relented. 'You can be very persuasive when you want Mr Bruce!' she smiled timidly into the phone. 'I just hope I'm doing the right thing!'

'I know and you are! Honestly, it will be fine - you'll see!' he replied gratefully and told her he would arrange for someone to pick her up from JFK the day before the interview.

In the meantime, Poppy knew what her next project would be and kept busy by putting in place all the things she knew she needed to get started. She would use Gregory's insurance money as the seed money to start his dream of a place for the homeless in India, just the way they had discussed before he died.

It was Stuart who met Poppy off the plane at JFK. He greeted her with a brief hug before taking her to her hotel. They shared an evening meal in the restaurant at the hotel and caught up on their news. Stuart told her the schedule, starting with a radio interview in the morning and then a pre-recorded interview on the talk show they had previously discussed.

After they finished their meal, Poppy told him she needed an early night as she was tired from her flight and she still hadn't fully regained all her energy yet.

'That's fine, I understand,' he said empathetically. He was just grateful he had managed to persuade her to come to New York for the interviews.

The next morning Poppy finished getting ready and felt more nervous than she thought she would have.

'Come on girl get a grip,' she told herself sternly, as she looked in the mirror. 'Just because it's been a while since you were on TV doesn't mean you've lost it! You used to do this kind of thing all the time!' But she knew deep down it wasn't the time that had elapsed but the awful foreboding feeling she couldn't shake. Poppy brushed her hair forward, trying to make her fringe and the sides of her hair cover as much of her face as possible. She smoothed down her black wool knee-length dress, which accentuated her slim figure, and clasped the silver chain with a single diamond that Gregory had given her on their first and only Christmas together. Not wanting to waste any more time she then collected the rest of her things to go.

As promised, Stuart was waiting with his car and took her to the radio station.

The interview went very well. She confidently answered the questions the radio host asked, and began to relax and enjoy it.

Stuart looked on through the glass of the soundproof room and gave her a thumbs-up.

After the interview, Stuart smiled charmingly, 'See, it wasn't so bad after all, was it?'

'I guess not,' she conceded, smiling in return.

When Poppy and Stuart arrived at the network studios they were escorted to the makeup artist. The pretty young woman with her long blonde hair tied back into a pony tail welcomed her.

Contribution

Poppy sat down in the chair and looked into the mirror at the reflection of herself. Her hair had almost fully grown back but was now shaped around her face. She felt it was her but not her. She almost didn't know herself any more but then she guessed that was hardly surprising when she thought about all the changes in her life over the last year. She took a deep breath before asking the makeup artist to disguise her scars as best as possible.

'Don't worry, by the time I finish I assure you no-one will ever know. Besides, you can hardly see them now anyway!' the young woman declared and was true to her word.

Stuart excused himself to get coffees for them both. When he returned Poppy was getting out of the chair and once again smoothing down her plain black wool dress.

'Wow, you look great,' he said appraising her, feeling she still needed that extra boost to her confidence.

She smiled, pleased with his compliment. She thanked him for the coffee but didn't want to drink it and spoil her makeup so she gave it to the makeup artist instead.

Just then an assistant came in to take them to their next destination. The three of them made polite conversation while walking through the maze of corridors. They were then ushered into a studio to start taping the interview. Poppy was now feeling a little more confident and it was almost like the old days.

The interviewer looked impeccable, wearing an electric blue suit, having the polished looked of a woman used to being in the limelight. She was pleasant, although she did have a reputation of being a tough interviewer, and liked to get straight to the point with optimum impact.

The interview started well with the host showing photos from Poppy's series of books on the overhead screen while making comments and asking questions. Poppy was actually starting to relax and enjoy it until towards the end.

Stuart realised the change of tempo a minute too late when the host flashed up a wedding photograph and then swiftly a photograph of the scene of the accident with two bodies wrapped in white sheets amidst the chaos.

'No, don't let her do this. She promised!' Stuart shouted at the crew, listening to the presenter breaking her word that they wouldn't discuss the accident.

It was the first time Poppy had seen the photo. It was the one that had hit the front page of every newspaper worldwide and which had been the one her family had hidden from her. She knew one of the bodies was her beloved Gregory. She was transfixed and shocked. Dazed, she heard the woman's voice saying, 'Nearly twelve months since the wedding and six months since the accident...' and the word 'scars'... before, seemingly in slow motion, Poppy looked at the woman and back at the screen. Then standing up, Poppy forcefully tore the mike from the neckline of her dress.

'How could you? You were told not to mention Gregory or the accident!' she screamed, running off the set crying.

She ran towards Stuart who caught her and held her. 'Poppy I'm so sorry!'

'How could you let her do that? You promised!' she wailed, breaking free from his grip.

Stuart felt as betrayed as she did. He ran after her and caught up with her again before quickly leading her out of the studio through the throng of people rallying around. He shouted back to the crew that there would be repercussions!

Inside his car her sobs finally abated and she quietly said, 'Please take me back to my hotel.'

'Poppy...'

She cut him off before he had chance to say any more. 'I want to go home. I'll catch the next flight back to San Jose. You'll have to do the rest of your PR work without me. And this time I mean it and I don't care about any contract!' Poppy asserted stubbornly.

He nodded. He knew how he would have felt if they had done that to him. He had let her down and berated himself for being too trusting.

'Poppy I'm so very sorry... if I had thought for one moment...'

'I did tell you I was worried this would happen!' she snapped. 'I know only too well that the media can be a great tool but they can also be heartless - anything to make a story!'

'I know, I know, truly I'm very sorry,' he said morosely, but he knew it had fallen on deaf ears.

Stuart drove Poppy back in silence, until he reached the hotel entrance and said goodbye. He told her he would be in touch at a later date. He was about to tell her again how sorry he was but she curtly said goodbye and quickly made her way through the front door of the hotel.

Once Poppy entered the hotel bedroom she flung herself on the big bed and sobbed. She must have fallen asleep because some time later she woke up with a heavy heart and looked around the room, remembering what had happened.

Poppy got up, washed her face and packed her few belongings before checking out and making her way to the airport. She had rung ahead to see if she could change her flight and was grateful they could squeeze her in on the next one.

When Poppy finally arrived home, she rang Sam and told him all about it. He called around straight away and held her as she sobbed once more.

'Well, it's done now. There's nothing you can do about it,' he said gently.

'I know. I just feel let down and I'm annoyed with myself, more so because I should have listened to that nagging feeling that told me not to do it!'

'I know, but you're going to have to let it go!' he continued in a gentle voice, still holding her close.

She nodded.

'Come on, let me make you an iced tea,' he said, helping himself in the familiar kitchen.

They sat on the deck, overlooking the ocean and sipped the tea he had made.

'So what are you going to do next?' he asked when she had calmed down.

'You're still bugging me for the next thing?' Poppy smiled, wiping her tear-stained face and blowing her nose, grateful for his persistence, friendship and loyalty.

'Of course! So what are you going to do?'

'I'm going to run away and hide for ever!'

'Not an option. So let's try again!'

She sighed, knowing he wouldn't let it rest.

He continued. 'I've got to make sure you're still pushing yourself forward! Besides, you've got to do things which will help open up your heart again: to give love and receive love. I'm not going to let you close down, no matter how much you may want to!'

'You're a stubborn man but a good friend Sam!' she said, resigning herself to the fact that she had to keep going but wondering if she had enough energy left to do so. What would she ever do without him? She continued to wonder.

He raised an eyebrow in anticipation of an answer.

'Okay! First I'm going to spend a couple of days with Jim and Nancy in Rhode Island and go out in

Little Annie. I somehow feel closest to Gregory when I'm there. And then I was thinking of going back to India!'

Sam raised an eyebrow again, surprised she was thinking of returning to India.

Poppy continued to tell him of her plans. 'I just hope I have enough inner strength to carry this one through!'

'I'm sure it will be challenging to take on such a large project, especially there but I think it would be a marvellous thing for you to do. I can give you the details of my good friend Akbar who lives there. He would be a great help. As you know, I got to know him a few years ago when I was wandering the world. He's a really great guy - very spiritual and has a lot of connections.'

Poppy smiled, relieved to know that he knew of someone trustworthy to help her get started. 'That would be great, thanks. Anyway enough about me, how's Maria and the baby doing?' Poppy enquired, eager to know how they were getting along.

The baby had been born prematurely and remarkably he had been one of the first preemies to be treated at the new *Baby Gregory Neonatal Unit*. Sam and Maria had been grateful that Poppy had created such a life-saving and much needed medical facility. After a worrying time for everyone the baby had quickly put on the pounds and became a healthy and thriving little boy. Poppy was elated that her project had been successful so close to home and especially for her dear friends. She had sent her congratulations and a gift but felt it too soon for her to go and visit and hold the baby in her arms.

'They're great thanks,' he said, proudly showing her a photograph of Maria and their baby boy. Then he looked at her a little unsure. 'Poppy, there's something else I'd like to tell you,' he said.

'Go on,' she said, unsure of what he was about to say.

'Maria's pregnant again!' he said, unable to hold back his excitement. 'It's early days yet and we've only just got the results!'

'Oh gosh, and so soon!' she said, still feeling a pang every time she heard that someone was pregnant, thinking that she would never have a family of her own. She missed Gregory and her baby with every beat of her heart.

'She got pregnant almost straight after having Daniel,' Sam said, aware of the momentary shadow that crossed Poppy's face.

'Well, congratulations to you and Maria and thank you for telling me. So how do you feel about it?' she asked, trying to regain her composure and be happy for them.

'Good actually. We're hoping for a girl and hopefully it will be easier and no preemies this time! Then we're done!' Both Sam and Poppy smiled. 'It will be good in many respects having them so close together in age but we know it's also going to be a lot of hard work!'

'That's for sure!' she said, trying to sound more cheerful. 'So are you going to get married?' she asked, suspecting the answer, knowing he was such a free spirit.

'No, I don't think so. We're doing just fine as we are!' he smiled. 'Anyway, I guess it's about time I was going and seeing how they are doing,' he said, changing the subject. 'I also want to try and get some surfing done before the sun goes down! Will you be all right? I do worry about you Poppy.'

'I will now thanks. Let me know when you've been in touch with your friend in India.'

'I will,' he said, finishing with his usual brief kiss on her forehead before leaving.

The next morning there was a knock at the door and a delivery man held a huge beautiful bouquet. Poppy thanked him and took the flowers inside. They were from Stuart with a note saying he was truly sorry for the way things had turned out and asking if she could find it in her heart to forgive him. He hoped the flowers would help brighten her day. She knew by the size of the colourful bouquet that it must have cost a fortune.

She immediately rang him and thanked him, letting him know all was forgiven.

'You know they weren't necessary but I'm absolutely delighted with them!' Poppy gushed.

Contribution

Stuart smiled to himself, picturing the beautiful young woman arranging them in a vase. 'I'm glad you like them and that I'm forgiven!' He was relieved. He truly hadn't wanted to lose her trust or friendship and it was so good to hear her lovely soft voice again.

'But that doesn't mean I've changed my mind about doing any more PR work!' she told him firmly as an afterthought and rather guardedly.

'No, I know and, believe me, I fully understand. Just to let you know though, the television network did write a letter of apology. And as it was pre-recorded they cut out the last part so only those people who were there were aware of it. They also reprimanded the interviewer for breaking her word!'

'Thank you Stuart and I also want you to know I don't blame you! I know it was completely out of your control and she betrayed us both. Besides, it's also down to me as to how I handle things and I've got to say I don't think I handled it too well!'

'Well to be honest Poppy, I think most people would have done the same but thank you for making me feel a little better about it.'

Poppy then went on to tell him she was going to India soon to carry out another project but this time it would be a huge undertaking and she would probably be away for at least a year.

He took a sharp intake of breath and told her he was sorry she would be gone so long and that he would miss her. She was startled to hear him say that.

Stuart then continued, 'I know when you make up your mind to do something it's almost impossible to change it. Anyhow, I want you to know I'll make sure the book series continues to run smoothly at this end and you don't need to worry about anything here!'

'Thank you, I appreciate that,' she said sincerely, and grateful for his thoughtfulness and concern.

'And Poppy!'

'Yes?'

'Please take care and e-mail me to let me know how you are doing,' he said earnestly.

'I will. You too!' she said, touched at his tenderness.

After she put the phone down she thought about the silver-haired, sensitive and kind man who had quickly become her close friend and confidant. She guessed it was because they had both lost loved ones so young in life and thus shared a common bond.

Poppy packed a small suitcase to return to Rhode Island for a couple of days to spend time with Jim and Nancy before she left for India.

Her time in Rhode Island was sad and very similar to the last time she was there. Except this time Nancy mentioned that no-one had been back to Gregory's condo. 'Everything is still the same as it was dear,' Nancy said quietly. 'And we were wondering if you felt up to going and sorting out what you want.'

Contribution

Poppy paled at the thought of returning to his place. She knew she wasn't ready. 'I don't know... I don't think I can yet,' Poppy said, almost apologetically.

Nancy patted her arm. 'No worries dear, when the time is right that's when you'll be ready.'

Poppy nodded, grateful she didn't have to deal with it right now.

'Let's go and have dinner,' Jim said, trying to lighten the conversation.

The next morning the three of them went down to the marina and once again Jim sailed *Little Annie* out into the ocean. Nancy and Poppy cried. Jim tried to put on a brave face but the void was still as huge as ever. However, they all took comfort in each other's presence and spending time out on the ocean in Gregory's small yacht. Somehow it always made it seem as though they were closer to Gregory even though in reality he was rarely far from their thoughts.

Their time together swiftly came to an end and Jim and Nancy drove Poppy back to the airport so that she could return to Costa Rica to make the final preparations before embarking on her long visit in India. Her in-laws were concerned about her returning there. 'Are you sure about going back?' Nancy asked in a gentle voice. 'I know it will be hard to do and will bring back awful memories.'

'I know but I feel I've just got to do it!'

'Well please take care,' Nancy said. Her stomach was in knots at the thought of her daughter-in-law going back.

'I will and please don't worry,' Poppy tried to reassure them.

Chapter 15
Returning to India!

Sam arranged for his dear friend Akbar to meet Poppy at New Delhi airport.

The slender shy family man held up the sign he had made with Poppy's name written in bold green lettering. She walked through the crowded terminal and could see the brightly painted sign and smiled cordially at Akbar.

Akbar greeted Poppy with a broad smile when she came through arrivals and made her way towards him.

After their initial introductions Akbar enquired politely, 'How are you Poppy? I'm sure you must be very tired after such a long flight!'

'I am but I'm okay thanks,' she replied warmly, relieved to have arrived after the long journey. She admitted to herself that she was getting tired of making so many flights, especially between Costa Rica and America and was quite relieved at the thought of not flying again for at least another year.

'I brought you some water,' he said genially, passing her the unopened bottle.

'Thank you, that's very thoughtful of you,' Poppy said, taking the small bottle from him and opening it, grateful for the refreshment.

Akbar politely ushered Poppy out of the airport and they made their way to his beaten-up old car. The passenger door creaked as Poppy got into the damaged vehicle that had seen better days.

Akbar skilfully drove through the busy streets to his house where she would be staying with him, his wife, four young children and his parents. It was the Indian way to share their homes with their families and guests.

'So how's my dear friend Sam?' Akbar asked, before continuing, 'It is quite a while since we last saw each other but we do keep in touch by e-mail fairly regularly.'

Poppy smiled at him and could see why Sam liked Akbar's deferential manner. 'He's fine thanks and doing well. You know Maria's expecting another baby?'

'Ah yes, that's right. I'm sure he is a wonderful father to little Daniel,' he said, remembering his good friend whom he had met when they were on their spiritual pilgrimage and how thay had quickly become firm friends.

'Oh he is,' Poppy agreed.

Akbar cleared his throat and quietly said, 'Poppy, I wanted to say how very sorry both my wife and I were to hear of your loss. Obviously Sam told me all about it.'

Poppy nodded before he continued, 'I know, from what Sam said and from what I sense from you, that you have a very strong spirit and purpose in life and will get through this painful period,' he said empathetically.

'Thank you,' she sighed. 'I've got to say though, some days are harder than others.'

'I'm sure,' he agreed, pausing. 'I'm sure Sam has been very supportive. He is a very wise man!'

'Oh yes. To be honest I don't know where I would be right now if it wasn't for him!'

There was a slight awkward silence before Poppy asked Akbar to tell her more about his family and his career as a teacher of philosophy at the small university near where he lived.

Akbar stated that the university had just closed for the holidays and therefore he would be able to spend some time introducing her to the people she needed to meet and help her find the property she desired to get the project off the ground. He was particularly delighted to be of assistance and felt it was such a good cause for the people of his country.

They finally pulled up outside his home. As soon as Poppy got out of the car, the sights and strong smells brought back recollections of her last trip to India so vividly that her knees almost buckled beneath her and she felt sick to her stomach. She wanted to turn around and go back to the safety and security of her home in Costa Rica but she knew she had to somehow get through this and make the project work for the sake of Gregory's memory.

Akbar noticed she had suddenly turned very pale. 'Are you okay?' he asked, concerned that the long trip may have been too much for her.

She nodded, taking a sip from the nearly finished bottle of water.

'Come on, let's get you inside the house and sit you down. It's much cooler in there!'

Akbar escorted her into his dark home and guided her to the nearest chair. His family rushed to her and fussed around her as he introduced each of them.

Akbar, his wife and two eldest children spoke English well but the rest of the family spoke only a smattering of English. However, they all greeted her genially.

Akbar's home was humble but she felt honoured to be there and to be welcomed so kindly. The family had made a makeshift sleeping area with a curtained screen and a cot for her in the corner of the room next to the children.

Akbar's family made her feel comfortable and she quickly felt a great connection with them all.

Although it was dark and dank on the cold concrete floors there was an array of delicious homemade food on the table in honour of their guest and Poppy thanked them many times for their kindness and hospitality.

That night, after Poppy said goodnight to everyone and got changed behind the screen, she lay down on the hard cot and pulled the threadbare sheet over her. Eventually her eyes became accustomed to the dark night and the voices quietened as everyone fell asleep. She thought about the lovely family she had just met and the harsh conditions they lived in, which were

Contribution

considered much better than a lot of people's in the area.

Even though she was tired from her long trip, she couldn't get to sleep and once again she wondered where the journey of life was going to take her now that Gregory wasn't with her. It still felt strange for her to be without him, especially here, and yet just before she fell asleep she sensed he was with her.

Over the next few days Poppy was once again mesmerised by everyone's amazing resilience and ability to pray so fervently early in the morning and at various intervals throughout the day and evening.

At her insistence, Poppy pitched in and helped with the chores and cooking, and all the women laughed and joked as they attended to their tasks.

Poppy and Akbar quickly got into a routine of getting up at the crack of dawn and, after he finished praying, they worked until early in the evening, only stopping for much needed refreshments of water and food.

After dinner and prayers Poppy and Akbar would spend hours talking about their progress and planning the following day's work.

Poppy was so exhausted by the end of the evening that when she finally fell into bed she barely had time to think about her bleak surroundings, but would always have a fleeting image of Gregory watching over her just before she fell asleep.

As the weeks wore on, Akbar's wife, Rahat, was worried that Poppy was working too hard and reminded Poppy to meditate. Poppy agreed that was a good idea. She now found during meditation, when she emptied her mind of busy thoughts, that the answer to a particular problem would come to her and a feeling of calmness would wash over her.

The weeks and months flew by and Akbar continued to introduce Poppy to all the right people willing to help her get the project underway.

Akbar helped her find workmen to renovate the dilapidated building that she had purchased to turn into a retreat. He also assisted in interviewing people to find the right personnel to operate the retreat once it was up and running. He was always very respectful and mindful and thought she was an amazing woman who was totally driven in making her project succeed.

The retreat was going to be a safe haven with twenty bedrooms, usually with two people to a room, two communal living areas - one for quiet contemplation and the other for socialising.

There would be a kitchen, offices, a creative room to encourage people to work on projects of their choice and an educational area where people would learn to read and write and learn how to use computers.

There was also going to be a room where they could pray at any time they wished. They were going to call it *The House of Gregory*. Poppy knew only too well that this was a small start to such a seemingly overwhelming problem but she hoped that this would be the beginning of an idea that would spread across the nation.

Akbar introduced her to Mr Khan who owned a small recycling plant and they discussed how Poppy could help expand his business by getting people to collect rubbish to recycle in return for them having a free bed for the night at the retreat. This had the effect of helping clean up the city and giving people a chance of a roof over their head for the night.

Also in return for a free night's accommodation and a good meal, people could do other jobs such as cleaning, cooking and maintenance of the building in the communal areas in an attempt to empower them, making them self-sufficient and giving them back their pride. Poppy wanted to bring comfort, hope, inspiration and joy to as many people as possible.

She regularly kept in touch with Sam and Stuart via e-mails, letting them know of her progress. Poppy told them, it was constant hard work and a barrage of questions and meetings but that she felt motivated and energised. However, Poppy didn't tell them that with working so many long hours and being on the go so much she had lost a considerable amount of weight from her already slim body.

Sam and Stuart in turn e-mailed her saying what they had been doing and how they both missed her.

Poppy was delighted when the project was completed and she had the right staff in place to oversee that everything was done in accordance with her wishes.

The project had generated a lot of interest and the *New Delhi Times* constantly reported, both in English and Hindi, on their progress, culminating with a full front page and following two pages dedicated to the grand opening of the project.

Poppy cut the purple ribbon and stood back, looking at the front entrance with the name *The House of Gregory* painted in colourful letters on the wooden plaque. She was once again pleased that Gregory's name lived on and she knew he would have approved of the huge undertaking.

Twelve months had passed rapidly and the time had come for Poppy to leave India. She hugged and tearfully thanked each member of Akbar's family for their love and hospitality. They had become family to her and she knew she would miss them dearly, but she was more than ready to return home. She had done what she had set out to.

Before leaving, Poppy arranged, out of her own savings, that some of her construction crew would build an extension onto Akbar's overcrowded home as a thank you for all he and his family had done.

She also told Akbar that she would pay for the plane tickets for his family, including his parents, to come and stay for a few weeks at her home in Costa Rica whenever was convenient to him.

'Poppy that is very kind of you but you really don't need to do all this. It was a great pleasure having you stay with us and do what you did for my country!' Akbar said graciously.

Poppy nodded and put her hand on Akbar's arm, 'It's the very least I can do. Besides, wouldn't you like to see Sam again and come and visit our country?'

Akbar nodded and smiled, with a faraway look in his eyes. 'I certainly would,' he agreed. 'You can be very persuasive when you want Miss Poppy!' he said, having been witness to this many times when she was negotiating. He didn't think anyone could ever say no to her!

'Now I guess I'd better take you to the airport otherwise you're not going to catch that plane back home!' he said reluctantly. 'But I would like you to think of here as your second home and come back and visit us whenever you can!'

'Thank you Akbar. You are a very dear friend and I really appreciate that,' she said with sincerity.

At the airport they hugged each other and Akbar told her to take care and give his best to Sam.

Akbar watched her walk through the airport doors and let out a sigh. He and his family would certainly miss her. She had become part of their family and had been a breath of fresh air and a true inspiration to them.

Chapter 16
One Step at a Time!

Sam met Poppy off the plane at San Jose and was surprised to see how thin she looked, but was nevertheless excited to see her and was encouraged by her enthusiasm.

On the way back home Sam said, 'I'm glad you found the experience worthwhile and that you liked Akbar and his family. He's a good man!'

Poppy smiled in return. 'I know. He and his family were wonderful hosts and I feel like they're my family now too! They really are salt of the earth.'

Sam nodded, already knowing that.

'And guess what?'

'What?' He turned to momentarily look at her.

'I'm flying them out to Costa Rica next year to stay at my house!' she told him excitedly.

'What?' He grinned.

Poppy nodded and smiled. 'Yes, the whole family will be staying for a few weeks!'

'Poppy that's marvellous. I was saying to Maria only this morning that when the kids are older I would love to take them to India to meet them!'

'Well, now you don't have to wait that long! But it's a great idea to take them there when they're older so they can see all the wonders of India and the many facets of human nature that we don't always see here. It's very humbling.'

'I know and thank you!' Sam said, referring to her comment that she would bring Akbar and his family here. He thought for a few seconds and turned, briefly putting his hand on hers. 'You are very special, you know!'

She blushed. 'No, I'm not! I'm just doing what I feel is right!' Poppy smiled, pleased at his compliment. 'And, of course, you are very special too and thank you again for everything you've done for me! It really is the least I can do for you and Akbar!'

Sam and Poppy continued their journey catching up on everything in between companionable moments of silence, both lost in their own thoughts.

They finally arrived back at Sam's house where Maria had a meal of fish, rice and beans followed by fresh tropical fruit waiting for them.

Poppy enjoyed catching up with her friends and spending time with their little boy, Daniel, and new baby girl, Mia, who had been born while Poppy was in India, and thankfully this time, without any complications.

Although Poppy was delighted to be a part of Sam's ever-expanding family she once again felt a pang shoot right through her when she thought about what she was missing with Gregory and her baby.

Sam noticed she had been pale and quiet when he introduced the latest addition to his family. He still worried about her emotional well-being.

Poppy said she was tired and that it was time she was going back home. Shortly after that Sam dropped Poppy off at her home.

'Will you be all right?' Sam asked, as she started to get out of the car.

'Of course, I'm just tired that's all!'

'Okay, well I'll call tomorrow if that's okay?'

Poppy nodded and once again thanked him before he drove off.

Poppy let out a deep sigh. She looked around her home and opened the long drapes and huge windows to let some fresh air into the musty-smelling rooms.

'It's been far too long,' Poppy said out loud, relieved to be back in the comfort and familiarity of her own home.

She ran a bath and inhaled the scent from the floral bubble bath she had hastily poured in. It seemed so long since she had the luxury of lying in a big tub. Then she felt guilty knowing that her friends and many people in the world never experienced such delights that she took for granted.

After her long soak she stepped onto the marble floor and picked up one of the large, soft towels and patted herself dry, lost in her thoughts. She found her

Contribution

favourite thin white nightdress and pulled it over her head.

Poppy walked out onto her bedroom balcony and breathed in the evening's heady cologne of tropical flowers. She stared out to the ocean, knowing she quite simply loved this place and all the happy memories it held for her. It was home.

Poppy returned to her bedroom, turned down the cool white sheets and relaxed in the comfortable bed. She looked at the photos of Gregory on her bedside table and brought one of them to her lips and kissed it. 'I love you my darling,' she said to the familiar smiling face.

Poppy then thought how different her bedroom was to the hard uncomfortable cot on the stark concrete floor she had spent the last year sleeping on. She knew how lucky she was to have been born here and how different things could have been just by chance. Poppy said a grateful prayer of thanks to the universe for the opportunities she had been given in life.

Poppy, tired from her travels, then quickly fell asleep.

The next morning Poppy got up early and made breakfast before turning on her computer. Gregory's handsome face smiled back at her on her screensaver. She took a deep breath. Everywhere there were photos of him. She was starting to wonder whether that was such a good thing, especially as she hadn't had the same intense reminders when she was staying at Akbar's.

She was startled by the knock on the door and Sam coming through, interrupting her thoughts. 'Morning!' he said in a cheerful voice.

'Morning.' She tried smiling back but he saw the sadness etched across her face.

'Are you okay?'

She sighed deeply and tears quietly slid down her face.

'Come here,' he said, as she turned into his chest. 'I'm sorry.'

'No it's me who's sorry. I always seem to be crying when I'm back here and yet I love it here,' Poppy sniffed.

'I understand,' he said soothingly, stroking her hair and holding her tightly.

'I guess you've once again caught me at a low moment,' Poppy said, wiping her tears away. 'It's probably jetlag catching up with me and the relief of being home…'

'I know, I know,' Sam said quietly. 'And it's all right to cry too you know!'

Poppy nodded. 'I have to admit it was a lot of hard work out there and I know I'm exhausted. At first everyday reminded me of Gregory and our last days together. But then it seemed to get easier, especially when I was so busy I barely had time to think. But coming home and seeing all of his photos just affected me so deeply!'

Contribution

'It's okay,' he said gently, totally understanding.

'I can't believe it's now over eighteen months since the accident and how quickly time passes and that life has actually gone on!' she said morosely, blowing her nose.

'I know Poppy, but you've been doing the right thing. Keeping yourself so busy helps it go faster. And the things you've been doing for the benefit of others have been amazing!' Sam paused. 'I have to tell you I'm very proud of you and I know Gregory is too!' Sam said, looking up to the ceiling.

'Thank you.' She smiled up at him, once again grateful for his concern and comforting words. 'I forgot to mention, next week I'm going back to Rhode Island to spend a couple of days with Nancy and Jim.'

Sam nodded, understanding her need to be close to Gregory's parents. 'That's nice, but Poppy I've got to tell you, I still worry about you. You need to look after yourself... and eat! Gregory wouldn't have wanted you to work yourself into the ground, even though it's great you are getting involved with all these projects. And all this travelling backwards and forwards isn't good for you either! You should take as much time off as you need until you feel rested and ready. Maybe spend longer than just a few days with Jim and Nancy. You still need to have a balance in life by taking care of yourself!'

She nodded. 'You're right but I really need to get going on some more things. After I leave Rhode Island I'm going back to New York to check on the GTCT.'

Poppy referred to the Gregory Taylor Charitable Trust which was now affectionately abbreviated to GTCT, and which was now their logo and brand name. She also wanted to employ another six people to help continually raise funds for the *House of Gregory* and help out in other ways in India. 'Then I'll take a week off after that. And I'll start eating healthier, exercising and generally looking after myself more! How's that?'

'You should be doing that now not putting it off until another day!' he scolded.

'Okay, okay, as from tomorrow I'll start exercising again and eating better!'

'Good!'

'I'll just about agree to anything to stop you from nagging me!' She smiled, knowing he was only trying to help and was once again grateful for his concern. But she really didn't want to have more time to herself and rest more – that was when too many memories came flooding back. She wanted to try to keep herself as busy as possible.

'Well, I need to get going. Let me know if you need anything,' he said amiably, getting up and briefly kissing her on her forehead in his usual way.

'Say hi to Maria and the kids for me. And thanks again Sam.'

'I will! That's what friends are for!' He smiled affectionately at his lifelong friend.

Poppy nodded and smiled back.

Contribution

After Sam left, Poppy returned to her computer and e-mailed Akbar to tell him she had arrived home safely and thanked him once again. She also told Akbar how delighted Sam was that he and his family were coming to stay at her house next year.

Poppy then e-mailed Stuart to tell him she had arrived home after a successful but tiring time in India.

A few hours later the telephone rang and she was pleased to hear Stuart's voice. He told her he hoped she didn't mind him phoning but he found it quicker and easier to ring rather than e-mail. He didn't say how much he just wanted to hear her voice.

Stuart went on to tell her that his PR department had done a good job and sales of the books were going really well. But he thought a couple of book signing days at some New York bookstores would be beneficial if she felt up to it.

Poppy was unsure but told him she would think about it and let him know in a few days' time.

Stuart hoped Poppy would agree to the book signings but more importantly, he thought to himself, he was looking forward to seeing her again.

After Poppy put the phone down she admitted to herself, albeit with a twinge of guilt, that it was good to hear Stuart's voice and that she had missed his friendship over the last year.

A few days later Poppy rang Stuart back and told him she had given the matter a great deal of thought and after visiting her in-laws in Rhode Island she would be coming to New York to check on the GTCT. She agreed she would then follow on with a couple of book signings.

Stuart was relieved to hear this and told her he would deal with everything to make her stay in New York run as smoothly as possible.

The following week, Poppy once again packed her case and said goodbye to Sam and Maria and was on her way to Rhode Island.

Jim and Nancy met her at Providence airport and took her back to their home. They were eager to hear all about her stay in India. They hadn't wanted to admit to Poppy that they had been worried sick about her being there on her own. It had also brought back painful memories for them too... not that they ever really went away.

Poppy's time with her in-laws was pleasant and once again it was a struggle when they went out sailing in *Little Annie* but equally they drew comfort from it. They guessed it would always be this way.

Poppy still couldn't go back to Gregory's apartment. His parents understood... after all, that was exactly how they felt. Even Misty had lost the bounce and sparkle she once had, but they acknowledged that their faithful dog was also getting old.

Their time together drew to a close and it was another tearful goodbye. They all hugged each other at the airport and Poppy promised she would be back.

Contribution

Poppy boarded the plane heading for New York and breathed a sigh of relief as she thought of returning there. She loved her in-laws dearly but these days it was always depressing and she knew, for her own sake, she had to somehow lift her own spirits. New York was the one place that didn't hold any memories of Gregory for her. She felt it was almost like a fresh start when she worked there and she looked forward to her return.

Stuart met Poppy at JFK and greeted her with a hug and told her it was good to see her. She told him the same and politely enquired as to how things were going. As they left the airport and amiably chatted, she told him all about her trip to India. He listened intently on their way to one of Stuart's preferred restaurants for lunch. When she had finished telling him all about it, he said, 'I'm so glad to hear you got the project up and running but I've got to tell you I'm really glad you're back safe and sound. I missed you!'

Poppy blushed and felt uncomfortable.

As soon as he said it he wished he hadn't. 'I mean I kind of got used to you being around and I enjoyed our meetings,' he said, not wanting to frighten her off.

'Thank you,' she smiled. 'Me too!'

They finished their lunch and he dropped her off at her hotel so she could rest for her first book signing tomorrow.

Stuart collected Poppy from her hotel the next morning and thought how sophisticated she looked in a mauve and grey suit with a string of pearls accentuating her neckline. He liked how she had moved from wearing black all the time to lighter colours. He told her he would collect her at the end of the day and take her back to her hotel. She thanked him for looking after her while she was in New York.

'My pleasure,' he smiled amiably.

The day passed quickly and Poppy was pleased that the book signings had gone well. She enjoyed meeting people and taking the time to talk to them. She repeated this to Stuart when he collected her, weaving his way through the heavy rush-hour traffic back to her hotel.

'Would you like to go out for dinner tonight?' he asked in a casual voice, not wanting to pressure her.

She sighed and looked at him kindly. 'Thank you but I'm so tired after all that, I think I'll just have dinner in my room and have an early night tonight.'

'Okay, I understand. Well, I'll pick you up tomorrow morning, if that's okay?'

'Thank you, but you know you really don't have to. I can make my own way there!'

'I know but I want to. It's the least I can do, especially as I know you didn't really want to do this in the first place.'

She smiled back at him, grateful that he seemed to understand her.

'Okay, well thank you. I'll see you in the morning then.'

Poppy watched the News and ate a light meal in her hotel room. Afterwards she got ready for bed, propped the pillows up and read until she fell asleep.

The next morning she wore a light grey trouser suit with white blouse underneath and her customary pearl necklace and waited patiently in the lobby for Stuart to collect her.

He bounded up the steps and she was pleased to see the man who had become her good friend. They exchanged pleasantries and made their way towards his car and he was soon driving her through the busy traffic.

When they arrived at the book store he told her he would collect her at the end of the day. Poppy was grateful for the company.

The day drew to an end and the crowds disappeared. Just when she was about to leave, a young girl and her mother came up to Poppy. The young girl smiled shyly and asked Poppy to sign her well-thumbed book. 'You know I would really love to do what you do!' the girl almost whispered.

'Then why don't you?' Poppy asked cheerfully.

'Oh, my family could never afford to send me to college,' the girl replied matter-of-factly.

Poppy stopped writing and looked up at her, before continuing writing a message of hope and inspiration in the book. 'You know, anything's possible if you think it, feel it, believe it and, of course, work towards it!' Poppy encouraged. 'Things have a way of working out!'

Poppy saw the look of doubt on the girl's face so she started to write on the back of one of her business cards, 'Let me have your name and e-mail address!'

'Really?' Emily was elated that her idol wanted to stay in touch.

Poppy smiled in return at the young girl's delight as she thanked Poppy over and over again before she left.

Poppy watched the young girl and her mother walk away.

Poppy then cleared the desk that had been allocated to her and thanked one of the staff, telling her she would be in touch. Poppy made her way towards the book store entrance to wait for Stuart to collect her. And as she did so an idea started to formulate in her mind.

That was when Poppy's grandmother's words suddenly came to mind: "people come into your life for a reason… whether it's for a short time or a long time but however long you can be sure it's to help you along on your journey or to help you with a lesson in life you are here to learn!"

Contribution

Poppy was startled, not so much because her grandmother's words came to mind but because Gregory had preoccupied so much of her thoughts she realised she hadn't thought about her grandmother much in a long time. She hadn't even really thought about her parents that much either.

Poppy considered the people she loved and had lost but also the people she loved who were still here and whom she hadn't paid so much attention to. It was with a mixture of grief, loss, love and understanding that she vowed to herself that from now on she would start paying more attention to the living. She made a mental note to ring her parents and arrange to go out to Panama to see them as soon as possible.

While Poppy continued waiting for Stuart, ideas popped into her head at lightning speed and she started to formulate a plan.

It was at that point Stuart walked up the steps to the store.

'Hi, how did it go?' he asked, smiling brightly.

'Good thanks. Once again I met lots of lovely people but in particular a young girl who has got me thinking about another project!'

'Oh really? Well I'd love to hear all about it. How about joining me for dinner and you can tell me about it then?' He was about to say, 'And I won't take no for an answer this time!' But she beat him to it and looked up smiling, 'That would be lovely!'

Stuart nearly did a double-take and looked at Poppy more closely, wondering what the girl could have said to have brought about such a change in her.

When they arrived at the restaurant they were ushered to a secluded corner. After the waiter had taken their order and returned with the requested bottle of red wine, Stuart encouraged Poppy to tell him all about the new project she had in mind.

'You're sounding more and more like Sam!' she teased.

'Sorry, I didn't mean to push, it's just that it's always interesting hearing about your latest project and you somehow seemed different at the book store!'

'Mmm, well the young girl at the book signing got me thinking. She also made me remember something my grandmother used to say which reminded me that I need to start paying more attention to the living!'

'That's good - go on,' Stuart encouraged, intrigued to find out more.

'The young girl said she wanted to do what I do but would never be able to afford to go to college. So I wondered what I could do to help young people right here and I'm now contemplating setting up an environmental studies high school for gifted and talented inner city kids who wouldn't normally have the resources for further education. They would be able to study marine biology, conservation and environmental issues and at the same time learn a foreign language. They would also have the

Contribution

opportunity of a six-week student exchange programme with other young people in Costa Rica and as they approach graduation we could help with financial aid for college tuition or locating scholarships.'

'That's a really great idea Poppy but how are you going to fund it?'

'Well, there is still some funding left at GTCT but I would certainly have to raise a lot more through charitable efforts.'

Stuart nodded, mulling it over.

Poppy continued, 'However, it will mean staying in New York for at least the next year. And I must admit I'm ready for the change and challenge. But I will have to return to Costa Rica every now and again for at least a week to catch up on things back home. I'm hoping my time in New York will give me the opportunity to make it happen!'

He was delighted to hear that she would be staying that long. 'You could also do some more book signings!' he grinned.

She smiled. 'I thought you might say that!'

'So where are you going to stay?' he enquired.

'I haven't figured that out yet. I'll probably look for somewhere to rent here in the city.'

Stuart pondered for a moment and said hesitatingly, 'Well, I do have a suggestion. I hope you don't think it's too forward of me but you could stay at my house, at least until you find a suitable apartment! I have three spare bedrooms and I mostly stay at the office during the week anyway. And even when I'm home on a weekend I'm usually working or out riding my bike, so you'd have it pretty much to yourself.' He didn't like to say he could barely face being there since Amanda died. He had been meaning to sell it but hadn't been able to muster up the energy to do so yet.

'Oh I couldn't possibly…'

'Of course you could. The house needs to be lived in again. You may as well. Just come and go as you please. Where else are you going to go?' he asked in a persuasive voice, liking the idea of her being close to him.

She thought about it for a moment or two. 'Well, if you're sure?' It would save her the time of finding somewhere to live, she thought.

'Absolutely!'

Poppy was relieved that she could just concentrate on finding a location for her school. She didn't like to admit it to herself but she also liked the idea of being near Stuart.

The next few weeks were again very busy for Poppy. She moved a few of her belongings into Stuart's large, well-kept home and began to search high and low for a property that would fulfil her vision.

Poppy barely saw Stuart and when she did, it was a comfortable friendship.

One Friday, just as she was starting to feel she would never find what she wanted, she found an old high school that had been closed many years ago during financial hard times for the city and it never reopened. She knew with some serious refurbishment she could make it into the building of her dreams.

Poppy negotiated with the agent and met with the School District to pitch her idea for her school and, because it would not cost the School District any money, they readily agreed to sell the property to Poppy at a greatly reduced price. Her agent then made arrangements to close the deal on the purchase of the property.

Stuart returned home later that evening, after a day of meetings and stressful negotiations for his latest block-buster publishing deal. While undoing his tie, he commented, 'You know, Poppy, you don't have to cook for me, although don't get me wrong, I'm very grateful!' he said, smelling the delicious aromas.

Poppy replied, smiling, while serving the beef in red wine sauce with creamy mashed potatoes and green beans, 'It's the least I can do and a way of thanking you for everything. Besides I've got some great news I want to share with you!'

They sat down to dinner and she excitedly told him all about finding the old school, the story behind it, and her negotiations.

'That's great news Poppy, I think this calls for a celebration!'

After they finished their meal Stuart got up and went to the fridge, removing the bottle of champagne he had been keeping for a special occasion. He popped the cork and swiftly poured the golden bubbles into two crystal champagne flutes. 'Here's to my talented and very caring friend!' Stuart beamed.

'Thank you,' she smiled back.

'I have to say, I'm very proud of you. When you get an idea you really go for it!'

Poppy smiled back, 'I think it's called tenacity!'

'Well, whatever it's called, it works! And it helps others too!' But more than anything, he liked that it was helping her.

They spent the remainder of the evening talking about her future plans for the building.

The next morning, Poppy looked in the mirror and realised that after her hectic schedule of the last month, she was looking tired and her normally olive skin was quite pale. She knew she needed to bring a healthier routine into her life and she remembered her promise to Sam that she would start looking after herself. She had got out of the habit of eating at least five fruit and vegetables a day, lots of fish, traditional dishes of brown rice and beans and drinking plenty of water.

As well as improving her diet, Poppy also started a morning regime of alternating between stretching exercises, running and using Stuart's gym in the basement downstairs. These were inspirational times for Poppy and would bring her clarity so she could think of what she needed to do to make her latest project work.

Poppy also wanted to continue with the yoga Rahat had taught her when she was in India, so she enrolled in classes once a week and really enjoyed them. She was also starting to make new friends. She was especially pleased about that, since for the past couple of years she barely saw Andrea, Bev or her other friends, other than Sam, any more.

In addition, she extended her morning meditation to twenty minutes and visited a shiatsu practitioner once a month. All this gave her time and space for quiet contemplation and examination of her soul. She listened to the wisdom deep within her and considered her purpose in life and she knew, without doubt, she was doing the right thing in educating and inspiring young people to make the world a better place.

She was starting to feel better in herself and had already healed physically. The anger and injustice of having Gregory snatched away from her so suddenly and brutally was slowly starting to dissipate and her vitality was gradually returning. She was starting to come to terms with the accident and feel an inner peace and tranquillity that had been buried deep after the accident.

Poppy was looking healthier, happier and more relaxed with each passing day and Stuart noticed how vibrant and beautiful she was looking. He couldn't take his eyes off her. He was immensely proud of her and knew he had fallen deeply in love.

Chapter 17
Team Work!

Her *Team Charity*, as Poppy now called them, continued to expand. It was a happy environment with the entire organisation working towards a common goal of global good. Without exception everyone felt that their knowledge, skills and talents were doing something worthwhile, which of course they were, and they felt satisfied with their achievements. They were all positive people and very hard working.

Even though they were working for Poppy's different charities they were still under the same umbrella of the Gregory Taylor Charitable Trust and everyone co-operated and worked together, sharing ideas and good practice. As a result, everything ran like clockwork.

Poppy played her part in using her fame and connections with the rich and famous to open many doors to get huge donations from people she knew, or knew of, to help with the projects. She found that people usually wanted to help, but very often would tell her not to let others know that they had donated, wanting their gifts to be kept anonymous, especially those who were donating larger sums. It was almost a knock-on effect as one success lead to another.

Poppy had a natural knack for making people feel needed and appreciated and, even though she was their boss, her employees were always relaxed and happy when she was around. She talked to everyone and made sure that they were all content in what they were doing. The open office was, therefore, one of friendliness and harmony and she enjoyed her weekly visits to check that everything was going well and finding out if there was anything anyone needed.

The planning of Poppy's educational facility for gifted and talented children in inner city areas now occupied most of her time. However, she was even thinking further ahead and contemplating doing the same in other large cities such as Detroit and London. However, to pull all this off she knew she needed her inner strength and confidence to motivate others on the biggest project that she had carried out.

By now she had received planning permission to renovate the building and was pleased with the plans her architect had drawn.

Poppy needed to find more staff if she was to achieve her dreams. She consulted with her colleagues and interviewed the best and brightest young people who were motivated to want to make a difference and she knew she would have to call on all her intuition more than ever to find the right people with open hearts and minds, who dared to push boundaries to come up with the most innovative designs and concepts in order to make this the most outstanding interactive

Contribution

learning environment that both educated young people and helped all her causes.

Poppy reminded herself that whatever you give attention to can only grow and come to fruition. With this in mind she found the perfect people for her project. She was lucky enough to have employed the best who agreed to give their services at a reduced salary as it was such a worthwhile endeavour.

Even though things were moving along well, Poppy wished they would move even faster. Once again she had to remind herself that everything happens in perfect timing and she had to accept that it would take its own course.

Now that Poppy had created such a large organisation she realised she now needed to have directors for each division of her enterprise and would have to have formal meetings once a week - not just informal chats, as had been the case - so that everyone could hear what she had to say.

Poppy therefore wanted to hold the meetings in a venue with comfortable seating so that everyone could be updated on progress and also exchange ideas in a relaxed environment. She would provide cakes, sandwiches and coffee so that people could have a break. As they exchanged information Poppy would write the ideas on the large white board with excitement and enthusiasm.

She had installed a fully-equipped gym next to the offices in the corporate headquarters building so that if her staff were feeling mentally fatigued or needed some creative stimuli they could work out for half an hour or so to feel better. She also had a discount service at the nearby salon for employee pamper days as she felt that happier and healthier staff would be a more productive and innovative workforce.

Even though Poppy had the money from Gregory's insurance for her charity work, her own savings and the grants, lottery money and fund-raising events that her team had generated she knew that she needed even more money to make this project work.

Poppy considered what she could do to further raise money and remembered the beautiful photos that Grandpa Ben had created. So, after giving the matter a lot of thought, she embarked on organising two huge fund-raising events in New York and London.

Poppy worked long and hard throughout the day and sometimes late into the evening, although she always tried to get back to Stuart's home on a night, often feeling exhausted but exhilarated.

Stuart had also started coming back home on an evening, arriving back about the same time. He worried about Poppy being alone on an evening. Besides, he really enjoyed her company and together they would prepare a light meal with a glass of wine and talk about their day and share their ups and downs. It had grown into quite a companionable routine and he was always interested to hear how her projects were going. Stuart thought she was extremely brave to take on such a huge task, and worked far too hard, but couldn't say anything because he knew he'd been the same when Amanda had died and he too had thrown himself into work and to a certain extent still did!

For the fund-raising events in London and New York, Poppy downloaded Ben's landscape and wildlife photographs and wrote a brief description with the story behind each one, which she knew so well from the stories her grandmother had told her.

Poppy then contacted Ben's children, who were a lot older than her parents. She told them she had created a glossy book of Ben's photos with descriptions and would like to sell the books with the profits going towards the education facility if they were happy for her to do this. They all agreed it was a great idea. They also decided she could sell the last of Ben's large original signed and framed photographs at the fund-raising events and get the best possible price for them. They didn't mind her selling these as they all had their favourite ones displayed in their own homes and each of them had digital copies of the whole collection anyway. They were honoured that it was all in aid of a good cause and that it enabled their father's memory to live on through his work.

Stuart undertook the publishing of the photographic books which were large sleek creations of Ben's best work and would be sold on-line, in main street stores and at charitable events.

With the help of her staff, Poppy set about organising the first auction of Ben's signed photographs in New York at the fund-raising dinner. They charged a hefty price for tickets to the event and then bidding started after the meal. By this time everyone had been drinking and people were more than generous with their bids.

Poppy did the same two weeks later in London. Both events were a great success and widely reported in the media. Poppy sold all the photos in Ben's collection and raised over 3 million dollars towards the project. Her team were delighted, particularly as sales of Ben's books were also going very well too.

Meanwhile, the remodelling of the school building started to take shape, utilising products made from recycled materials. They also installed solar powered panels to make the building energy efficient. Poppy wanted it to be a sunny building with lots of glass windows. She also instructed that all paints and other such materials should be non-toxic throughout. Her aim was to make the building as environmentally friendly as possible and for all products to have their names clearly seen to encourage other people to use them.

Poppy was already generating interest in the project, particularly as she wanted it to be a stimulating learning environment. Comfortable chairs were placed in the auditorium where students would have a virtual reality tour of rainforests with birds and animals, showing a total eco-system. The scenery would then change to the ocean with coral reefs, changing from light to darkness and stars shining above. The lecturer would give information as 3-D birds flew past and objects and words floated in the air giving an out-of-this-world experience.

The large lecture theatre would also have a hi-tech screen at the front and a podium for lecturers educating students on an issue that would either help people or the environment. Again the theatre would be lined with comfortable seats. Videos would be shown highlighting environmental and humanitarian issues.

Although classrooms would be large, the number of students in each would be smaller than in a regular school. Students would be assigned their own workstation and each given a laptop. They would sit at large desks on comfortable seats and the learning environment would be a comfortable one where students would want to be and thus enable the very best learning to take place where students would excel.

There would also be a fine arts and craft area where students would have opportunities to pursue their creative talents and create art in well-equipped workshops taught by working artists.

Each classroom would have an innovative teacher to facilitate ideas and learning in all the environmental subjects offered and, of course, the usual core subjects of English, mathematics and science.

The school would even have friendly roaming robotic trash cans to collect waste material for recycling.

The final area of the school would be a language lab where students would learn a foreign language. In particular Spanish would be encouraged to aid in the exchange programme in Costa Rica.

Next to this would be a huge gymnasium and swimming pool where students would learn water safety, how to swim and other fun and challenging water activities such as scuba diving and kayaking.

Poppy had been told that it was do-able but it would be difficult and costly. However, she liked the idea of a hi-tech, comfortable learning environment and it was her dream to make it happen.

Poppy was thrilled that the brightest brains were coming up with innovative and fascinating ideas that would engage a student's curiosity, hold their interest and educate them to want to discover things and instil in them a sense of excitement to look after our world and make it a better place.

One night as they were preparing dinner, Poppy told Stuart that she wanted to start promoting Gregory's documentaries and Ben's photographic books on television and participate in the interview circuit again, to further help raise funds.

Stuart was surprised to hear this and took a sharp intake of breath. 'Are you sure about this Poppy, particularly after last time?'

'Well, to be honest I do feel somewhat nervous but having said that I now feel more in control of things.' She knew her passion for wanting to make the project a success spurred her on. 'I think this time I'll make sure I'm more prepared for any questions they could ask. You once said that time was a great healer and I'm now starting to think you were right as somewhere along the way I think I've finally started to come to terms with what happened or at least I'm certainly learning to live with it anyway.'

He nodded. 'But only do it if you're absolutely sure this time,' he said after giving it some thought, remembering the last time and still feeling guilty about how upset she'd been.

Poppy took her time in choosing the right person for her talk show interview and this time the interviewer was friendly and much more understanding. 'So tell me Poppy, what made you come up with the idea of an almost virtual reality school for inner city children?' he asked in a gentle voice. 'I've got to say the focus on mainly environmental studies in this type of setting is unusual to say the least!'

'I guess I wanted something that would immediately engage students' interest, in a modern hi-tech way and to help disadvantaged children get an opportunity they might not otherwise have. When I was growing up in Costa Rica I was lucky enough to be able to play amongst and appreciate the wildlife and flora of the stunning rainforests. And I wanted to share that with young people who may not get to experience it first-hand and also educate them on preserving this for generations to come.'

The interviewer turned and referred to the photographs on the overhead screen showing pictures of rainforests, eco-systems and various stages of the school being completed as Poppy explained the story behind each picture.

'So have you decided on a name for the school?'

'Yes, we're going to call it *One World School of Environmental Studies*!'

'I like it. So what made you decide to call it that?' the interviewer asked.

'Basically because we all share this planet and I wanted to make it a global theme. I think it's a way to teach children that philosophy so that the beauty of the world will be here for future generations.'

'Well, congratulations on your achievement Poppy. I wish you success with your endeavours and I hope that our viewers feel inspired to donate to this very worthwhile cause! And I also hope that one day I will be interviewing graduates from your programme!'

'Thank you,' Poppy smiled in return, 'now that would be nice!'

It was felt by all that the interview had gone very well and was a great success. Sure enough shortly after her TV appearance donations began to roll in, some as small as a dollar from schoolchildren and others in larger amounts. The City of New York donated time and labour to acquire parking and infrastructure for the school.

Poppy was elated when the school was finally finished and the hi-tech equipment installed. Stuart was beside her as she cut the green ribbon and finally declared it open, to a frenzy of photographers and reporters. She received flowers and notes from many well-wishers and Stuart suggested that they should go out for dinner that night to celebrate.

Seated at the small table at the luxurious and intimate restaurant Stuart ordered champagne. 'Let's make a toast to the beautiful and talented Poppy Anderson Taylor,' he said, raising a glass to her, 'and, of course, your amazing school,' he smiled.

Poppy blushed at his compliments. No-one had referred to her as being beautiful since the accident, she suspected, mindful that they didn't want to dredge up memories of her life before then. It left mixed feelings, and something long forgotten began to stir within her.

'And don't forget the GTCT too!' She smiled, trying to stay on track.

'Of course,' he declared, 'you and your team deserve all the success that I know is coming your way,' he beamed, then leaned over and kissed her softly and longingly on the lips.

Poppy pulled away abruptly to study the menu, again unsure of that long forgotten feeling that had suddenly returned and which she tried to quell.

'Sorry, I shouldn't have done that,' he apologised.

Poppy shook her head. 'It's okay. We just got carried away with the excitement of the evening!' she said softly, trying to analyse her feelings.

For the remainder of the evening Stuart and Poppy kept the conversation light, both keenly aware that their friendship seemed to be changing, almost of its own volition. When they got back to his house, Poppy felt awkward so briefly kissed Stuart on the cheek, telling him she was tired and wanted an early night. He looked unsure so she quickly thanked him for a lovely evening.

Poppy lay in bed, feeling confused, and for the first time she didn't just think of Gregory before falling asleep but thoughts of Stuart crept into her mind. She had a restless night as she tossed and turned, dreaming of them both.

Chapter 18
Mixed Feelings!

The next morning Poppy got dressed and noticed dark circles under her eyes, and quickly concealed these with makeup.

She went downstairs. The coffee was already made and next to the coffee pot was a note from Stuart telling her he had left for the office early. He also scribbled that he would stay at the office for the rest of the week. They both probably needed some time to sort out their feelings and he was sorry if he caused her any distress last night.

Poppy didn't know what she expected, but she was surprised that she felt disappointed that he had gone and wouldn't be returning until the weekend.

She let out a deep sigh and thought that it was perhaps for the best. So she gathered her purse and coat and left for the offices of GTCT.

Once there she opened her mail and was pleased to receive a letter stating that in recognition for all her charity work, especially her work in India and her new school, Poppy had been nominated for a prestigious award from an international humanitarian organisation. She announced the news to her team and thanked them all, telling them she couldn't have done it without them. After sharing the news they all got back to work and as usual the day was very busy.

When Poppy got back to Stuart's that evening the house felt cold and empty without him and she realised she missed him more than she would have liked to have admitted. She explored her feelings and acknowledged that they had become very good friends but she was confused that their feelings were seemingly changing. She hoped she hadn't inadvertently done anything to give him the wrong impression and she certainly didn't want them to do something that would spoil their friendship. She knew she still wasn't over Gregory yet and the thought of an awards ceremony made her remember that first magical night she met Gregory. It brought a lump to her throat. The awards ceremony wouldn't be for a while and she started to think that perhaps she should spend some time away from Stuart and maybe go back to Costa Rica to sort out her conflicting emotions. After all, she could do a lot of her work over the internet.

Over the next few days Poppy ensured that she had done everything she could at the offices of GTCT and that she had enough work to do on the internet to keep her busy when she returned to Costa Rica. She also booked her flight.

That evening she made the difficult phone call she'd been putting off.

'Hi!'

'Hi,' Stuart was surprised but delighted to hear from her and rushed in, 'I'm sorry about the other night,' he said earnestly, 'but I think you realise I have feelings for you although I know it's early days for you and I certainly don't want to spoil our friendship!'

'That's okay. I know, and I don't want to spoil our friendship either, that's why I think I need to return to Costa Rica for a while to sort out my feelings!'

She heard the slight intake of breath.

'I'm sorry I shouldn't have frightened you off!'

Poppy wanted to be honest with him. 'It's not just that… well…' Poppy was wondering how to be upfront with him without hurting his feelings. 'Stuart, I'm so grateful for everything you've done for me and you know I think the world of you… but I'm really not over Gregory yet. I'm not sure I ever will be, but whatever, I really think we need some space here.' The silence on the other end of the line was almost deafening. She tried to lessen the hurt she was sure he was feeling by adding, 'For the moment anyway.'

He nodded into the phone. 'I know and I do understand. I'm sorry for rushing you!' He had had a lot longer to recover from the loss of Amanda and he knew he would have been in the same place she was right now. He chided himself for pushing her too soon, as he of all people should have known better. He continued silently berating himself. 'Just promise me if you ever need anything you will let me know!'

She nodded. 'Thank you for your understanding.'

He too nodded. 'So when will you leave?'

'Tomorrow, if that's okay with you?'

It wasn't, he wanted her to stay for ever, but if she didn't want to stay he at least wanted to make sure they remained friends. So once again he just nodded into the phone and simply added, 'Let me take you to the airport.'.

'Thank you but I couldn't have you come all the way out here and back again. I'll take a cab.'

'Well at least let me meet you at the airport. I don't want you going without saying goodbye face to face.'

'Okay and I want to say goodbye too.' She was starting to feel a little guilty about leaving.

She told him what time she would be at the airport and after they said goodnight she brushed away her tears and finished off packing.

The next day Poppy arrived at the airport and found Stuart already waiting for her. He looked sad and when she walked up to him he gently touched her arm.

'Poppy, I'm so sorry I frightened you off,' he said miserably.

'It's not you, it's me. I think I still need more time.'

'I understand,' he said, still annoyed with himself. 'But you will at least keep in touch?' he implored.

She smiled. 'Of course, I will. You have become a very dear friend and I really don't want to lose our friendship... and once again thank you for everything you've done for me.'

'You're welcome – it was the least I could do. I'll miss you though!' he said forlornly.

They hugged each other tightly. She then walked to the check-in counter, turned and they both waved a sad farewell before Stuart left the airport, hoping that this was not the last time he would see her.

On the plane, Poppy wondered if she had done the right thing and finally fell into an uncomfortable and fitful sleep. She hadn't told anyone she was returning and felt miserable when there was no-one there to meet her at arrivals.

She took a cab back home and felt desperately lonely as she unlocked the empty house. She turned on some soft music and opened the windows but was restless so went for a walk along the beach, but that didn't clear her mind either. When she returned home she made a few phone calls and then set about keeping herself busy over the next few days with cleaning the house and checking on her projects.

After a few days, back in Costa Rica, Sam knocked on her door and this time waited for her to answer.

She smiled, 'Hey!'

'Hey, I heard you were back.'

'Come on in. What's this? You've given up on barging your way through my home?'

He grinned. 'Well I happen to think you've come a long way since then and perhaps I should start behaving like a normal visitor!'

She smiled in return. 'Thank you. Would you like a coffee?'

'Of course!' Costa Rican coffee was something they missed when they were away. They both considered it the best in the world, which was why in recent years Poppy had got into the habit of packing some in her luggage wherever she went. But it still wasn't the same as drinking it at home!

They sat out on the deck, overlooking the ocean, and Sam looked steadily at her. 'So what's brought you running back?'

'What makes you think I'm running back?'

He raised his eyebrows. 'This is me you're talking to, your best friend, and I'd like to think the person who knows you better than anyone else!'

'Okay, if you're that good then you'll know!' she retorted sharply, which was unlike her.

He weighed her up. 'Okay, I'm guessing it's something to do with Stuart?'

She looked surprised. 'How did you guess?'

'Well you two do spend a lot of time together!'

'I thought he'd just been helpful that's all,' she said sullenly.

He raised his eyebrows again. 'I think someone's not being honest with herself!'

She threw him a "don't push it look".

'You know it's okay to have feelings for someone else. You're not being disloyal to Gregory and you are human after all! I know he wouldn't have wanted you to stay alone for the rest of your life!' Sam said in a quiet and understanding tone.

'I know, but it's too soon!'

'Poppy, it's been nearly three years now! And from what you've told me, Stuart seems like a very good man.'

'I know and he is… but I just can't seem to let go of Gregory…' She let the words drift as she became lost in her thoughts.

Sam sat and tried to think of what he could say to help her as he watched the shadows of sadness cross her face. 'You know there is enough room in your life to have your memories of Gregory and to make a life with someone else,' Sam said softly and sympathetically.

Poppy nodded. 'I know. I guess I'm just not ready yet,' she agreed.

'Well, when the time is right you will be. Do you remember your gran always used to say everything happens in perfect timing and I think she was right!'

Poppy smiled ruefully, 'You always resort to something my gran would have said when you're trying to persuade me to do something!'

'I know – that's because it works! You know I miss her. I spent so much time here when we were kids she was like my gran too!'

'I know and I miss her too!' Poppy smiled in agreement.

'And do you remember Aunt Millie?' Sam prompted.

'Of course, I remember her! How could I not? She was gran's best friend and when those two got together there was nothing but laughter!' Poppy smiled, remembering.

'I know.' Sam also smiled at the memories. 'She was such a character!'

Poppy nodded in agreement. 'Gran used to tell me stories of when they were younger and the adventures they had!'

Sam and Poppy beamed at their recollections. They sat quietly for a few minutes before catching up on the rest of their news. Sam told her that Maria and the little ones were doing well and that they would love for her to visit.

'I'll come and visit soon,' Poppy said, but they both knew she wouldn't. It was still too painful for her to be in close proximity to babies and small children. And every time she was an overwhelming ache would burn through her as her thoughts returned to baby Gregory and her loss. Sometimes it still felt like yesterday.

Soon after that Sam said goodbye, feeling that she needed to be alone.

During the next four weeks Poppy kept busy, making phone calls and writing e-mails, checking on how all her projects were going and ironing out any problems.

Once or twice a week Sam would stop by for a short while just to check in. Although she had read it before, Poppy picked up her copy of *Proof of Heaven*. It gave her comfort and helped her in understanding life beyond and the start of real emotional healing.

No matter how busy she kept herself, images of Stuart would creep into her mind and she found herself missing him and feeling lonely. She was a little disappointed she hadn't heard from him but knew he was giving her the space she had asked for.

Poppy began to think that perhaps Sam may have been right and it was now time to let someone else into her life.

Stuart had gone back to spending week nights at the office. He hated being alone in the house after so many enjoyable evenings chatting with Poppy. It felt empty without her and his mind would overflow with images of her and the things they had done together. There were so many times he would pick up the phone to call her but each time he changed his mind before dialling. He kept to his word and gave Poppy the time and space she said she wanted.

Chapter 19
When Friendship Isn't Enough!

During her time back home in Costa Rica, Poppy managed to catch up with everything she had wanted to do and today she was at a loose end. She ran herself hard along the beach, came home and had a shower. She poured herself a coffee and sat out on the deck and watched the waves rolling up to the shoreline in the bright sunshine. Her mind drifted to Gregory and then to Stuart. She particularly missed the evenings with Stuart when they would prepare meals together and sit down with a glass of wine and talk about their day.

Stuart was a very kind, thoughtful and handsome man and good company too! She missed him more than she cared to admit. Poppy remembered Sam telling her that she shouldn't feel guilty about having feelings for Stuart and that there was enough love to go around to include her memory of Gregory and to have someone else in her life. Besides, Gregory would have wanted her to find love again and not put her life on hold, Sam reminded her.

Finally, with some hesitation, Poppy tentatively pulled her cellphone off the table and rang Stuart. She could tell he was surprised but delighted to hear from her. They talked about what each of them had been doing and relaxed into the warmth of their friendship.

'So when are you coming back?' he ventured to ask. He paused, before continuing, 'I've missed you.' He didn't want to frighten her off again but he also wanted to be honest with her.

'I've missed you too!' Poppy said quietly.

He was delighted to hear this and smiled to himself. 'Well, what about doing something about it?'

'I guess it's time,' she said timidly, knowing the huge leap she was about to take. 'When would you like me back?'

'Yesterday!'

She laughed. 'Okay, I'll book the first flight out!'

When Poppy arrived at the airport, Stuart pulled her close to him and briefly kissed her on the lips. He carried her case and told her she looked well and that the sunshine and being back home had done her good.

In the car, on the way back to his home, they chatted excitedly and Poppy began to see him in a way she hadn't before. She finally realised that she felt a strong attraction to this quietly charismatic gentle man.

When they arrived back at Stuart's house she immediately noticed the flowers he had arranged in vases throughout the downstairs living area.

'Wow, they're beautiful,' she announced, 'I'm assuming they're for my return!'

'Of course,' he beamed.

'Thank you!' she said, appreciative of his thoughtfulness.

'Well, I know how much you like flowers!'

'I do indeed!' she glowed.

'And I've made you your favourite Italian pasta for later,' he said proudly.

'I could get used to this!' Poppy smiled, watching him pour a glass of wine.

'Good! That's what I'm planning on!' he smiled warmly at her. 'To celebrate,' he said, raising a glass. 'Welcome home!'

'Thank you, it's good to be back! I've missed our time together,' she said honestly.

'Me too!' Stuart held her gaze steadily.

After their delicious Italian dinner and a few glasses of wine, Poppy helped him clear away the dishes. They were relaxed and laughing and she nearly collided into him as she put the last dish away. The attraction was almost palpable.

They looked steadily into each other's eyes. Before she had time to turn away he kissed her fully on the mouth. He stirred a passion deep within her that had been long buried and she returned his kisses with equal passion and tenderness.

He looked deep into her eyes and into her soul. Then held her hand and gently guided her up to his bedroom.

Stuart passionately kissed her again and they quickly undressed each other. He laid her gently on the bed and in between kisses asked if this was okay?

He didn't want to rush her but the fire deep within them was burning too fervently for either of them to stop now. She simply nodded and returned his kisses with the same passion and abandonment. Their lovemaking was urgent and sensual as their long held passion was unleashed and their compelling friendship turned into love.

Afterwards, Poppy lay motionless in Stuart's arms. He felt warm tears spill onto his bare chest. 'Are you okay Poppy?' he asked in a concerned voice.

She nodded. So much emotion had erupted from her with memories of Gregory mingled with the presence of Stuart. He held her tightly, realising she was smiling in between her tears and he understood. He understood their losses, their journeys and the start of something incredibly special together.

'I love you so much Poppy. You know I would never do anything to hurt you!'

She nodded, wiping her tears. 'And I love you too!'

His heart skipped a beat and he beamed broadly. 'Really? Did you say you love me too?'

Poppy looked up at him and grinned at his boyish enthusiasm.

'Poppy I can't tell you how happy you've made me!'

She snuggled up to him and continued smiling. 'Thank you for sticking by me all this time and not giving up on me!'

'Well, what else could I do? I think I fell in love with you the day you walked into my office and into my life!'

Poppy smiled at him again. 'You hopeless romantic!'

He smiled and kissed her forehead. They lay contentedly in each other's arms and that night slept peacefully, holding each other.

When they woke the next morning they looked at each other and smiled.

'Good morning, my love.'

'Good morning,' she replied, looking into his clear blue eyes full of love.

'Are you okay?' Stuart asked.

She nodded, smiling, 'Absolutely!'

'Good. Me too! So what shall we do today?' Stuart wanted to know. He left his arm wrapped around her shoulders.

'Are you not at work today?'

He shook his head. 'No, I've taken a few days off so we can spend some time together and have some fun!'

Poppy beamed. 'That's great! I don't know. Surprise me!'

'Okay, I will!'

After showering, Stuart found one of his robes and put it around her soft bare shoulders. They relaxed into each other's arms and then went downstairs to make a leisurely breakfast.

Later they dressed and Stuart took Poppy into the city so they could go shopping. They enjoyed browsing through the department stores and Poppy found a lot of stylish clothes including an elegant black cocktail dress that she could wear on an evening out.

They ate a late lunch and afterwards Stuart suggested a walk in Central Park and to her delight a horse drawn carriage awaited them. Stuart helped her into the carriage and the driver took them around the park. They admired the beautiful landscaping and watched people enjoying the afternoon sun.

The carriage ride came to an end all too soon and the driver returned them to Stuart's car. They both thanked him for his time and Poppy noticed Stuart discreetly handing him a note and large tip.

When they got back to his house Stuart told Poppy that he was pleased she had bought the new dress and he hoped she would wear it on their first official date this evening at his favourite restaurant and then to the theatre afterwards.

'You really are spoiling me!' Poppy told him delightedly, wrapping her arms around his neck while his strong arms encircled her waist.

'Nothing less than you deserve my love,' he acknowledged, then tenderly kissed her.

After their romantic and intimate dinner that evening, Poppy was surprised to see the same horse drawn carriage and driver waiting for them outside the restaurant. They greeted each other amiably before he whisked them off to the theatre for an enjoyable evening of music and laughter. It was a truly magical day and evening and a time Poppy was sure she would never forget.

Afterwards Stuart asked, 'Did you enjoy today?'

'Absolutely, thank you for such a wonderful time!' But more than anything she enjoyed being part of a couple again.

The following day they drove out to a place in the countryside Stuart liked to visit for peace, quiet contemplation and solitude. They strolled hand in hand. In between companionable silences they chatted and laughed in the summer sunshine. Then to her delight Stuart produced a small but delicious picnic with a bottle of chilled white wine.

Amazed, she asked, 'When did you do this?'

He smiled, pleased with himself. 'When you were sleeping. I got up early this morning and then came back to bed!'

She beamed, 'I can see I'm going to have to watch you Mr Bruce!'

He smiled in return. Poppy melted into his embrace and they kissed each other tenderly.

Poppy enjoyed being with Stuart, he was great company and always warm and loving. She also knew that somewhere along the line she had fallen deeply in love with him too. It was a love that had grown from respect, empathy, admiration and friendship into a gentle kind of love and she knew that she wanted to spend the rest of her life with him.

Chapter 20
Opinions!

Poppy and Stuart fell into a very pleasant routine, with both of them going out to work through the day and coming home on an evening to fix dinner together, or go out to a restaurant, and talk about their day.

Weekends were spent hiking, bike riding and generally just having fun. They both believed in working hard but also creating a balance in life and giving themselves time to enjoy nature, outdoor activities, keeping fit and giving time to themselves, including reading, listening to music and meditation. Neither of them could believe how they were both always on the same page and how enjoyable life had become.

Finally the awards ceremony arrived and Poppy and Stuart excitedly got ready for the evening ahead.

Poppy couldn't help but remember other award ceremonies she had attended, especially on the night she first met Gregory. However, this evening was different. She almost felt like she had grown up and as a consequence become a different person.

Contribution

It was good to receive the award, not just for her efforts but for her team and for keeping Gregory's name in the limelight. She was happy, knowing Stuart was in the audience watching proudly.

Poppy walked up to the stage to receive her award and heard the host describe her as, 'One of the most respected young women of our time... I would like to honour the charismatic and dynamic Poppy Anderson Taylor! She is a modern visionary, genuine and honest... a compassionate woman who facilitates the dreams of others and makes the world a better place!'

There was loud applause and a standing ovation from the audience. The energy in the room was so tangible it was almost electrifying.

Poppy went up to the podium and glimpsed photographs being exhibited on the big screen behind her. There was a photo of her with doctors and nurses at *Baby Gregory's Neonatal Unit*, several photos of her working in India and one of her opening the new school. Then finally the display ended with a photo of a smiling Gregory, which she knew about in advance and was pleased to have displayed. She still wanted people to always remember him.

'Thank you for everything,' she said with heartfelt sincerity. 'I receive this award graciously but not without sadness. However, it is this sadness that spurred me on to give willingly and to try to help make a difference in the world and to keep Gregory's name alive... But I honestly couldn't have done it without the support of the general public and all the efforts and kindness of so many people, especially my best friends

Stuart and Sam, and in particular my team at the *Gregory Taylor Charitable Trust* - they are the true champions and I am accepting this award for them. Thank you!'

Poppy returned to her seat next to Stuart to the sound of loud applause. He squeezed her hand encouragingly. She was grateful he was by her side and for his unwavering love and friendship. He had become her rock, the person who always listened to her trials and tribulations, encouraged her and introduced her to people who could help her. They smiled a contented and loving smile at each other.

After the ceremony they went out for supper and Stuart told her again how proud he was of her and commented on how far she had come during the last few years.

'Thank you,' Poppy smiled gratefully, 'but it's like I said, I really couldn't have done it without you, Sam and my team! But I especially appreciate your continued love, loyalty and support.'

'No need to thank me. That's what you do for people you love!'

'I know and I truly love you too,' Poppy smiled, leaning over to briefly kiss him. Both were unaware that other diners were sneaking admiring glances at the striking couple sat at the small round table in the corner of the dimly lit restaurant.

Contribution

The next morning Poppy and Stuart sat at their kitchen table eating the fresh continental breakfast they had prepared together. They scanned the Sunday newspapers which had been delivered to them.

Poppy paused at the double page featuring the awards ceremony with photographs and snippets of information about the recipients. She was dismayed to read underneath her photo a small piece undermining her. It said that if it hadn't have been for her fame and fortune, none of her charitable accomplishments would have come to fruition.

Outraged, she told Stuart she would have no alternative but to write to the newspaper.

'Don't take it to heart, sweetheart. You know the media like to put a downer on things!'

'Why can't they accept people as they are instead of looking for something negative or sinister?'

'That wouldn't be newsworthy for them!' Stuart smiled ironically. He sighed deeply and continued, 'I think also you're so used to being the darling of the media that when someone says something derogatory you don't like it!'

'I know but this seems unfair! It's not me I'm thinking of here but the others involved who work so hard every day without ever being noticed or recognised!'

'I know,' he said in a sympathetic tone.

They finished off their breakfast and perused the papers in silence, both preoccupied with their own thoughts.

Poppy got up to clear the table and Stuart helped her. 'So what do you want to do today my love?' Stuart asked, putting an arm around her.

She looked up lovingly at him. 'The weather's nice so how about a long walk? But first I want to write to the editor!'

'I thought you might say that and I'm probably not going to change your mind but if it's okay with you I'd like to read what you've written before you send it. You know I don't think anything should ever be written in anger!'

'I know and I understand. I would value your comments anyway,' she said, briefly kissing him before going to the study to compose her letter.

She sat down at her laptop and began:

Dear Editor, for the first time in my career I am writing in response to an article printed about me!

It was in today's Sunday newspaper and I have to say I think your reporter was unfair to have said what she did when covering the awards ceremony.

Yes, I can see how people may think that my fame and fortune have enabled the charity work to happen. And I admit that it has helped open many doors!

However, without doubt, it is mainly the efforts and hard work of my team and other people because of the love they have for the world and the people in it that has made things happen!

Contribution

There are many people all over the world who do charitable work every day, without recognition, fame or fortune, and these ripples all have an effect and make a difference! They are the ones who attract the true riches of life and as a result life is abundant! They have so much love to give and do whatever they can - from a smile, to giving a helping hand to a neighbour, to helping build a church, a school, a park and housing for people in need.

Yes, I threw myself into good causes because of my grief but I hope everyone who has supported my charities can see the genuine love and need to help others that spurred me on!

Each and every one of us can make a difference by taking small steps each day and doing whatever we can to give a helping hand.

There are those people who want to help but are put off doing something until a later day thinking they need to save more money, get a particular qualification or retire so they have more time. But we can all start by doing something small "today - not tomorrow", from visiting a child in hospital or an elderly person in a nursing home or helping raise funds in some way or taking a bottle of water and a sandwich to a homeless person and telling them you care and bringing a smile to their face! Anything to brighten someone's day! To me that's what life is all about! Growing to become the best we can, fulfilling our dreams and along the road helping others wherever possible!

Giving is one of the most precious gifts we have for creating a purpose and feeling a sense of achievement, and we can all do it - one small step at a time. To say that it is easy for someone like me is insulting and detracts from the amazing things that so many people do every day of their lives without acknowledgement from others!

You, the media, could play your part too! You love to report negative events - you always focus on bad incidents and sensationalise these! Just think how much nicer it would be if you also focused on the good things too and reported someone doing something beneficial for someone else for no other reason than they wanted to! Emphasising something positive and reporting on the good that someone has done would inspire others to do the same or more! It would help lift peoples' collective spirits and consciousness and stop the world feeling such negative vibes all the time.

Please try writing more positive articles and giving the benefit of the doubt! Trust me, the world will be a happier, healthier and better place for it!

Yours sincerely, Poppy Anderson Taylor

Poppy only hoped her response would make a difference, although she wasn't sure at this stage. She showed Stuart the letter and he agreed with her reply.

'So what are you going to do now?' Stuart asked when they walked arm in arm in the bright sunshine around the large lake near their home.

'I'm not sure. I think just continue overseeing all my projects and I've got to get back to India at least once a year. So I think all that should keep me out of mischief for a while!' She smiled up at him and he smiled back, wanting to broach something he had been thinking about recently but then deciding not to say anything yet.

Contribution

Poppy wasn't surprised when she received a standard reply a few days later saying they get so much correspondence that it would be some considerable time before anyone could get back to her. Not surprisingly, she didn't hear any more.

Chapter 21
Unexpected Gifts!

A couple of weeks later, Poppy and Stuart sat down to dinner at their favourite table tucked away in the quiet corner of the dimly lit restaurant. Stuart took hold of Poppy's hand and clearing his throat, asked quietly, 'Poppy do you ever think about settling down and starting a family?'

Poppy looked shocked. She certainly hadn't expected that question!

'Sorry, I shouldn't have asked. I didn't mean to pry but I just wondered if one day you might want to have children?' He saw the shadow and sadness cross her face and he almost regretted saying anything but he had to know. Every night he went to bed wondering if there could be more of a life together for them.

'I did but I guess that's out of the question now!'

'It doesn't have to be,' he said softly.

She looked at him, unsure of what to say.

'Poppy I love our life together, talking to you and sharing any spare time we have. You know how much I love you, don't you?'

She nodded, gazing into his clear blue eyes.

Contribution

He observed her uneasy look but before she could say anything else, he rushed in with the question that had been preying on his mind for so long, 'Poppy will you marry me?'

Poppy looked shocked.

'I'm sorry I don't want to frighten you off again. But I think we've both been alone long enough now. Let's not waste any more time without each other. And I think we'd both really like to have children. I can't imagine having a family with anyone but you!'

She had already done so much with her life, but she knew more than anything that she wanted a family of her own. She also knew Stuart would be a wonderful husband and father.

At one time she thought she would never love again after Gregory but had been surprised to find she had fallen in love with Stuart too. She now realised her heart was open and big enough to embrace life fully again.

At that moment she couldn't think of what to say other than, 'I know you're a wonderful man, and I love you too! It's just been a shock that's all. I really hadn't been expecting this!' Poppy said, her face slowly beaming with love and a long forgotten feeling of excitement for the future.

'I know but we've already spent such a lot of time working together and we're practically living together anyway!' Stuart said persuasively.

Her head was spinning with many thoughts and she was lost for words but she looked at him with love.

Poppy knew she was capable of managing on her own but didn't like the prospect of living alone for the rest of her life and especially didn't want to be without this wonderful caring man.

'I know it's been a shock Poppy, but I do love and adore you. Please marry me Poppy!'

Poppy could no longer find a reason to say no and with tears in her eyes she nodded. She didn't know how she could have got so lucky - twice! 'Yes, I would be honoured!'

Stuart smiled broadly. 'You've made me the happiest man alive!' he declared, turning around to the nearest waiter, and totally out of character, saying, 'She's going to marry me!'

The waiter grinned. 'May I be the first to offer my congratulations?' he said graciously. 'Would a bottle of champagne be in order sir?'

'I certainly think so!'

The next day Poppy rang her parents, who were delighted, and then Sam to share her news.

'So what's the problem?'

'Why do you think there's a problem?'

'I can hear the "but" in your voice! I'm guessing you've got mixed feelings because of Gregory.'

'Well it's all happened very fast and I must admit I do feel a little guilty.'

Contribution

'Poppy we've already had this conversation,' Sam said, almost exasperatedly. 'You know Gregory wouldn't want you to spend the rest of your life alone. He'd want you to be happy and Stuart is a really great guy and good for you too. But are you in love with him?'

'I know he's good for me and yes I'm in love with him! I honestly didn't think it would be possible to love this way again!'

'Then there's nothing for you to feel guilty about. And you know what I think about guilt,' he continued, 'it's a wasted emotion!'

'I know.'

'Just be happy. That's all you need to be! Live in the "now" and enjoy the moment!'

'Okay, I will!' She was glad she'd phoned him. He always had a way of putting things back into perspective and making her feel better.

That night an image of Gregory came to her in her sleep. He told her he was happy she would be marrying Stuart. He would always love her and watch over her. She deserved to be happy.

The next morning Poppy woke up refreshed and joyful, feeling she had Gregory's blessing.

Over the next six weeks Poppy and Stuart busily prepared for their wedding. It would be an intimate occasion with just Stuart's elderly mother and younger sister Julie flying in from their home town in Connecticut, his father having passed away several years earlier.

Poppy's parents, a few colleagues from the publishing company and GTCT would attend as well as Sam, Maria and their children. She just wanted a small wedding after the fanfare of her first wedding with all the paparazzi. Stuart was more than happy to oblige; he too wanted it to be kept to a minimum.

Finally, their special day arrived. Poppy entered the room and Stuart smiled broadly at his bride-to-be, watching her walk towards him in the large traditional room dedicated for weddings in one of the city's mansions overlooking Central Park.

Poppy held his smiling gaze with one of her own, as she approached him. Stuart whispered, 'My darling you look so beautiful and radiant!'

She was wearing a knee-length, slim fitting pale blue dress with high heeled pale blue sandals. Her dark hair was piled up on top of her head with blue forget-me-knots weaved into the back of her hair.

Stuart looked distinguished in his tailored dark blue suit which matched his blue eyes and silver grey hair.

Poppy continued smiling at him and whispered in return, 'Thank you my love!'

Contribution

The ceremony was brief. After they exchanged vows there was loud applause and cheers by the small gathering before they all entered the room next door to enjoy an exquisite five-course meal and fine wine to celebrate.

The wedding guests were staying the night at the city mansion. Stuart and Poppy also spent their first night there together as man and wife as they wanted to spend as much time as possible with their close family and friends before the guests returned to their homes and daily lives the next day.

Late into the evening they said goodnight to their guests and told them they would see them at breakfast in the morning.

When they were alone in their room, Stuart asked Poppy in a slightly tentative voice, 'Happy Mrs Bruce?' He still wasn't sure if he had pushed her too soon.

'Oh yes, how about you?'

'Definitely!'

Poppy had a mischievous twinkle in her eyes and added, 'You've made me very happy and I can't wait to have miniature versions of you!'

Stuart raised an eyebrow in mock surprise and grinned. 'Well my darling, maybe we'd better get to work on that!' he said, taking her in his arms and kissing her longingly and tenderly.

'Mmmm, I was just thinking the same,' she said, melting into his arms.

The next morning Poppy and Stuart had a long leisurely breakfast in the dining room with their guests. They all hugged each other as each guest reluctantly left to go back to their daily lives, all having enjoyed the union of two of their favourite people. Stuart and Poppy also had a flight to catch to the UK later on in the day.

There was just a small byline in the *New York Times* informing readers of the wedding between the eminent publishing magnet Stuart Austin Bruce and the famous Poppy Anderson Taylor. It was in complete contrast to the double page spread that had dominated many glossy magazines and newspapers when she married Gregory.

For their honeymoon they visited Stuart's ancestral home in Scotland for two weeks. Although chilly, the sun shone brightly and they were blissfully happy. They spent many hours walking arm in arm amongst the rolling, heather-clad hills, taking photographs and talking of their plans for the future. Their nights were filled with warmth and passion as they lay intertwined in front of the roaring fire.

A housekeeper and two assistants opened up Stuart's family home and cooked delicious traditional meals served with good quality wines in the oak panelled rooms with heavy tartan drapes covering the huge leaded windows. Fine oil paintings and old photographs were strategically placed around the large dark rooms.

Contribution

Poppy looked across at her husband who was enjoying sipping an exceptional single malt Scotch whisky. He was sitting in one of the high-backed brown leather chairs beside the roaring fire. 'You look very contented there my dear,' Poppy observed.

He smiled back and sighed in confirmation. 'That's because I am!'

'Are you enjoying being back here in your old family home?'

Stuart nodded in affirmation. 'And I'm enjoying showing you around here too! We used to visit fairly often when I was a boy and my grandparents were still alive but I must admit I haven't been here for quite a few years.'

Poppy nodded. 'Well I'm glad you brought me here to share in a piece of your family's past.'

'Me too!'

When they returned to New York they continued happily with their busy schedules and started to look for a home together that would house the family they both craved for.

They put Stuart's house on the market and very soon found a buyer who offered what they wanted. All they had to do now was find another home that would suit their needs, which turned out to be easier said than done! There were many apartments available but they had their hearts set on a family home in its own grounds.

After sifting through countless properties on the internet, they narrowed it down to looking at just a few. On their final showing they found the home of their dreams. The modern, spacious home with room for a growing family was fifteen minutes from Manhattan's upper west side and was everything they had hoped for. It cost a fortune and was more than they originally wanted to pay but they put in an offer which, happily for them, was accepted.

Poppy and Stuart looked forward to the move and the weeks swiftly passed while all the legal formalities were put in place.

On the day of the closing, the movers packed the last of Stuart's furniture and belongings. Poppy turned to see him looking back at the house.

'Are you okay?' Poppy asked in a gentle voice.

He gave a deep sigh and put his arms around his loving wife. 'Yes, thank you sweetheart. I was just looking back one last time and remembering a previous life with Amanda.'

'I know, I understand.' Poppy said empathetically.

'But as one door closes, another opens! Right?'

Poppy nodded in agreement.

'And I was just silently saying goodbye and letting go with love,' Stuart said, before turning to start their new life together.

Holding hands they walked down the path of his old house one last time, moving forward to a bright new future.

Contribution

They arrived at their new home and Stuart deftly picked Poppy up in his arms, carrying her across the threshold. She squealed and laughed with delight in his strong arms.

Stuart placed her down once inside the house. 'Welcome to your new home Mrs Bruce. I hope you will be very happy here,' he smiled at her.

'Thank you! I'm sure I will!' She smiled in return, looking around and then back to him. 'And welcome to your new home Mr Bruce and likewise I hope you will be very happy here too!'

'I'm pretty sure I will,' he agreed amiably. 'Now I guess we'd better start turning the house into our home!'

Poppy and Stuart spent several happy days unpacking boxes and moving furniture to complete the home of their dreams. In between unpacking boxes they snatched coffee and snacks whenever they could but Poppy kept feeling queasy and being sick. Finally Stuart insisted that she visit the doctor.

The doctor confirmed their suspicions and they were both truly delighted.

Poppy had been worried that after losing Baby Gregory it might take some time to conceive but happily she had got pregnant almost straight away. They didn't want to take any chances and agreed that Poppy should cut back on her working hours, which they thought was probably the right time as her staff now had everything running the way she wanted.

Poppy learned to relax more and enjoyed not working quite as much while her stomach grew bigger. They furnished the house the way they wanted and had already painted the nursery.

Stuart made sure he came home earlier on an evening and they would spend quality time just talking, walking, reading and listening to music, excitedly looking forward to the birth of their first baby.

Months later a beautiful baby girl was born. They named the tiny bundle of joy Karina. They were thrilled and very proud, doting parents. They would cradle her and look at her with love and awe, amazed they had created such perfection. Both families visited shortly after the birth and helped in looking after Poppy and the baby.

They took their baby everywhere possible and showed her off to all their friends.

Over the months and years Karina grew from a baby into a curious toddler, always smiling and bringing them joy. She had her father's blue eyes and once fair hair, and her mother's features.

Their happiness was complete after two years when their second child was born, a gorgeous baby boy. They named him Joshua. Karina loved having a baby brother and she would cuddle and play with him every waking moment.

Poppy was learning how to juggle family life and still oversee her projects, which now usually ran like clockwork.

By now Stuart also wanted to be more involved with philanthropic work. Poppy was immensely proud of him for setting up a scholarship fund for gifted and talented young writers from third-world countries.

With the help of several well-known authors whose works were published by Stuart's publishing company, they began working with young people to improve the quality of their writing skills. They would encourage the young adults to write about their lives and submit articles and stories either on-line or through the post. Their stories would then be published in a monthly magazine, for which the youngsters would get paid.

At the end of each year a panel of authors would vote on the best articles of the year. The winner would be awarded a full scholarship to a university of journalism. The idea was derived to inspire young people to bring about positive change in the world through their stories and articles.

Another two years later, Sonia, their third child, was born and they were thrilled to have one more beautiful, healthy baby. They were elated with their young family and everyday brought laughter and new challenges as they embraced family life. Despite all of Poppy's and

Stuart's successes, the children were their greatest joy and their home was always filled with love, learning, fun and laughter.

Every day was a delight and a wonder with the children as they eagerly learned as much as they could. The days, weeks and months flew by. Those were the times that made Poppy feel most fulfilled and happy. The pain and heartache from her younger days became a distant memory and she felt incredibly blessed.

The Bruce family had a housekeeper, gardener and nanny on a morning so that Poppy could continue to work on her projects during that time and then have quality time with the children in the afternoons. These were very special times for Poppy as she played with their children and taught them how to talk, colour and eventually read and write.

Poppy wanted to teach them everything she could. She would remember her own childhood and would tell the children stories of her life growing up with Gran Jasmine and wandering the tropical rainforests with Sam.

Poppy and the children would stick paper together, draw, create cards and all sorts of craft things. She encouraged her children to use their imagination as well as work things out logically for themselves. All three children were enrolled into music classes on a weekend. They wanted their children to have as much of a balanced life as possible.

Stuart loved to play games and sports. He taught them everything he knew, including how to sail when

Contribution

they got older. Very quickly they were becoming well-rounded young people.

Joshua was the opposite to his eldest sister, who was fair and blue eyed, whereas he had his mother's dark hair and eyes but his father's features. Sonia was a complete mini-version of her mother, not only did she have her mother's dark hair and eyes but also her features.

Poppy loved to braid both of her daughters' long hair or brush their hair back into ponytails, Karina's fair hair contrasting with Sonia's dark.

Joshua was cute with his mischievous little ways and loved playing pranks on his sisters but they were all good friends.

The girls in turn enjoyed writing plays. Sam, on a visit with Maria and their two children, once made them a stage for their puppets and the girls spent hours making stringed figurines talk and move. Friends and family had to be the audience and would roar with laughter at the puppets' antics.

All three children were talented and extremely good students. The house began to rapidly fill with trophies, awards and photos of the children making their mark in the world. Once a year Poppy, Stuart and their children had a professional photo taken of them smiling back at the camera. They always looked a happy and content family.

Stuart and Poppy loved spending Christmas in New York with their children. They particularly loved the snow, although Poppy always said she didn't think she would ever get used to the cold, but she adored its fresh crispness and watching the children play in it and listen to them squealing with laughter. They enjoyed shopping in the city with the bright Christmas lights and they adored all the traditions associated with this special time of year especially decorating the tree and singing traditional Christmas songs together.

Poppy and Stuart didn't mind what their children did when they grew up as long as they were doing their best and were happy. Both parents were always mindful that their children were made aware that no matter how much, or how little, they had that they should appreciate nature and the natural wonders of life, and have the philosophy of giving back to people.

Karina, in particular, loved reading and had a flair for writing her own short stories.

Joshua loved numbers and was always working out maths solutions.

Sonia loved playing nurse with her dolls and friends and if anyone was ever slightly hurt she was always the first to rush and try to help.

Poppy was immensely grateful she had such a loving family, great friends and that she had found immense joy and happiness in her life. Each night she would snuggle up to Stuart and before falling asleep she would appreciatively recount to herself every encounter of the day and give thanks to the angels and the universe for her wonderful life.

Chapter 22
Family Life!

At the end of the day, after the children had gone to bed, Stuart and Poppy would pour themselves a glass of red wine and relax on the large comfortable sofa, rejoicing in their children's endeavours and celebrating the joy they had brought into their lives.

Sometimes they had to pinch themselves and were always thankful that this opportunity hadn't passed them by, as it so easily could have, knowing how lonely they would have been if they hadn't taken the paths that had brought them to this point.

Poppy and Stuart listened to each other with interest while they told each other about their day and Poppy would snuggle up next to him on the sofa. They had a good life and she was always grateful for the bliss Stuart and the children had brought into her life so unexpectedly.

Poppy and Stuart also made sure they returned to her family home in Costa Rica at least once a year. At the same time Poppy's parents would take their annual vacation, from their still hectic schedules, and join them there. They loved being grandparents and having the chance to be with their daughter and son-in-law back in the family home. It was a happy family time.

They would always meet up with Sam and his family and other friends too. They all played games, ate, and enjoyed the beach and ocean together.

One winter's evening, Poppy snuggled up to Stuart on the sofa and said, 'You know honey, I was thinking I might like to start another arm of the Foundation.'

Stuart put his newspaper down and looked above the rim of his glasses. 'What have you got up your sleeve this time my darling?'

'Well, I was thinking about trying to find ways to help disabled people to give them their independence and at the same time enhance the care they receive.'

'Sounds like a good idea. What were you thinking?

'I know there are plenty of suitable ground floor apartments and bungalows for physically handicapped people. But I don't think there has been enough money ploughed in to staff going into their homes to provide therapy, exercises and especially hobbies. I'm sure this would help stop people from becoming so bored. So I was thinking we need to fund professional staff prepared to offer gentle exercises, and create home-made crafts, draw and use interactive computer aids etc with patients.'

'That's a great idea,' he encouraged, smiling at her.

'So I need to get *Team Charity* to help raise funds and set up an organisation to go in and help people in this way.'

'What are you going to call it?'

'I was thinking *The No Obstacles Group*.

'I like the sound of that...it should work!'

'That's what I thought so I'm going to start getting it off the ground!'

Over the following weeks and months Poppy contacted her team and they spent many hours bouncing ideas around and getting the project up and running.

Poppy and Stuart's love deepened even more over the years, if that were possible. They were totally devoted to each other but still very busy with work and their charitable organisations, which included a considerable amount of time travelling to different countries.

Occasionally, they would have to travel alone but usually Poppy and Stuart managed to travel together and wherever possible would take the children. They both felt it important that, as well as spending time together, the children should have an insight into how people live in Third World countries and understand their parents' vision of the world and their hopes and dreams for a better future.

Sonia, in particular, would play with children in remote villages and wanted to contribute whatever she could. Every time she returned home she would gather some of her toys and sell them to send money back to help. Poppy and Stuart would then add a sizeable sum to whatever Sonia had raised.

One rainy afternoon, when Poppy was at home looking after the children, she realised everything had gone quiet upstairs so she tiptoed up to the second floor but all the children's rooms were empty. With an unsettled feeling she went back down to the first floor level and started shouting their names. She came to her bedroom and could see that her walk-in dressing area door had been left open and could see through to the room beyond. The door was slightly ajar which was strange so she quietly walked towards it and saw her three children sprawled on the floor surrounded by open magazines and books.

Sonia looked up. She was now nine. 'Wow Mommy, is this you? You look so beautiful!' she exclaimed in wonderment.

Before Poppy had a chance to reply, Karina looked up at her and, with a look of accusation and self-righteousness that only a thirteen-year-old could muster, declared, 'I don't believe this! You had another life and were married to someone else?' She got up to run out of the room, tears streaming down her face.

'Let me explain,' Poppy pleaded.

'No, I don't want to hear. Everything about our lives is a lie!' Karina screamed, running past Poppy through the bathroom and upstairs to her own room. Poppy heard the door slam and sighed. She looked at her other two children. She thought she would leave

Karina to calm down and talk to her other two children about it first. She guessed it was time, although she hadn't wanted them to find out like this.

'Firstly, I want to know, how did you guys get in here?'

Joshua, a handsome boy at the age of eleven with dark hair and eyes, looked up rather sheepishly. He was holding the handmade swan Sam had carved all those years ago, now with a lot of the white paint chipped off. 'Sorry Mom, we knew where the key was and we've all been curious for a long time. I was the one who climbed up and got it down from the shelves!'

Poppy tried to give him a disapproving look. 'Well at least you're honest and have owned up to it!'

'So I'm not going to get grounded?'

'Not this time. Besides, maybe it's time for me to tell you about my life when I was a famous marine biologist and about Gregory, my first husband. Come here... both of you,' she said, sitting on the sofa and holding her arms out for each of the children to sit on either side of her. She kissed the tops of their foreheads. 'You know how very much I love you all don't you and I wouldn't change a thing about our lives?'

They looked up and nodded, knowing she was going to tell them something important that they hadn't known about. 'And you know how very much I love your father too?'

They nodded again, eagerly anticipating the information she was about to divulge. 'But a long time ago my life was very different...'

She went on to tell them about her conservation work and how she became famous, about meeting Gregory and marrying him. And the sad story of how he and her unborn baby died in a car accident in India and how devastated she was. She went on to tell them how Sam helped her move on with her life and how she met and fell in love with their wonderful father.

After she finished her story, she asked, 'Are you two okay with this?'

Sonia eagerly stated that it was like a fairy tale!

Joshua said he thought his mother was beautiful, brave and caring, which brought a lump to her throat. She could barely speak so she simply kissed her children once again on the tops of their heads and then told them how much she loved them.

Poppy gently untangled herself from her youngest children. 'Right, well I'd better go and see your sister. What do you two want to do? You can stay in here if you'd like and look at some more magazines.'

They both said that's what they wanted to do. Poppy was relieved to hear this. She noticed that Joshua was still holding the swan. 'Would you like to keep it with you?'

He nodded. 'For a while, if that's all right?' Joshua loved the simplicity of the wooden bird but, now knowing the story behind it, the carving had taken on a whole new meaning to him.

'Of course,' Poppy said, once again heartened by her children's maturity and sensitivity.

Poppy made her way to Karina's bedroom, knowing this conversation would be a lot harder. She gently knocked on her door. 'Karina, sweetheart, can I come in?'

'I guess,' she replied sullenly.

Poppy walked up to her. Karina was lying on her bed and Poppy brushed her daughter's fair hair back from her eyes and could see she'd been crying.

'Why are you so upset sweetheart?' she asked her eldest daughter gently.

'Because I always thought I knew everything about you and daddy and our family and now I feel I don't know anything at all!'

'I understand, and you do know most things about us, but maybe I owe you an explanation,' Poppy said quietly. 'However, first I want you to know how much I love you all and daddy too!'

Karina nodded and sniffed, waiting to hear her mother's story.

'A long time ago when I was much younger my life was very different...' Poppy said softly and went onto to give the same account she had just given to Joshua and Sonia.

Karina listened intently without interrupting. When Poppy finished she asked her daughter, 'So now do you understand?'

Karina nodded. 'I'm sorry Mom that you had such a terrible accident and you lost Gregory and the baby.'

'Thank you, sweetheart. But it's okay. Gregory is in heaven with your baby brother and I feel they are always with us, watching over us all. Their names live on and I went on to meet a lovely man whom I love very much and have had three wonderful children with and one day we'll all be together again. I truly can't ask for anything more!'

'And it made you do things you wouldn't have if it hadn't been for the accident,' Karina said, and Poppy was taken aback by her daughter's maturity and understanding.

'That's true. I feel I grew as a person in many different ways. I'm not saying it was easy or that I didn't wish things could have been different when I was younger. But tragedies happen to many people at different times in their lives and we all have to somehow learn to live with them!' Poppy answered, proud knowing her daughter was a compassionate soul.

Karina nodded.

'That's why I disappear once a year for the weekend and leave you three with daddy.'

'What do you do?' Karina asked inquisitively.

'I go to Rhode Island to spend the weekend with Gregory's parents. We always go out in Gregory's boat to scatter roses on the ocean and think about him.'

'That sounds nice. Can we go too?'

Poppy took a deep breath. 'That's a really nice thought sweetheart but I'm not sure it's a good idea.'

'Why not?'

'Well, it's always kind of sad and I think you would find it a little depressing. Plus, I think Gregory's parents might find it difficult being surrounded by you all.'

'Because they would wish we'd been Gregory's children?'

Again Poppy was pleasantly surprised with Karina's understanding at such a young age. Poppy took a deep breath and nodded. 'Possibly. And they're getting older! Nancy, Gregory's mom, said last time they didn't know how much longer they would take the boat out but that I would always be welcome to visit.'

'Do they know about us?'

'Oh yes, I've always sent photos of you all each Christmas and they always ask about you.'

'Gosh, Mom, it's like you have two separate lives!'

'I can see how it looks that way, but to me it's not. You three children and daddy are the most important people in the world to me but I guess I still hold onto the past and I kind of feel it helps Nancy and Jim when I visit.'

'Does daddy mind?'

'No, he understands.' Poppy paused. 'Daddy was also married long before he met me to a lovely lady called Amanda and he still visits her graveside once a year.'

'Really?' Karina was astonished at this latest piece of information. 'What happened?'

'Sadly she had cancer and died very young.'

Not for the first time that day, Karina looked stunned. 'So does he have another family too?'

'Not really. Daddy didn't keep in touch with Amanda's family the way I did with Gregory's. I think he found it too hard. I guess we all have different ways of dealing with loss and grief.'

Karina couldn't think of any more questions.

'Come on, why don't we go downstairs and watch a movie? I'll make some popcorn!' Poppy suggested, trying to lighten the conversation.

Karina thought that was a good idea. They went downstairs together, feeling that today Karina had reached a milestone in her life and had grown up considerably. Poppy shouted for Joshua and Sonia to join them downstairs.

She listened for her two younger children, hearing them lock the door and come running downstairs.

Poppy put on one of their favourite *Disney* movies and then prepared popcorn.

She went back to the living and all three children had their throws wrapped around them and were avidly watching the show. She sat in the middle of them and they all snuggled up together.

Later Stuart arrived home to find his beloved family all huddled together on the sofa, with their arms wrapped around each other.

'Is everyone all right?' he asked, placing his leather briefcase down and undoing his tie, sensing something different and wondering if one of the children was ill.

'We are now!' Poppy said and mouthing, 'I'll tell you later!'

Stuart came over to Poppy and briefly kissed her on the cheek followed by a hug and kiss for each of his children as they kept one eye on the movie!

'Well, while you guys are watching the movie I'll just go and have a shower!' he responded. 'What's for dinner?'

Poppy looked at him apologetically. 'I didn't have time to prepare anything this afternoon so I thought maybe we could get a takeaway pizza tonight for a change?' There was a loud cheer from the children as they didn't often get the chance to have their favourite meal.

'Sounds good to me and you kids are obviously in agreement!'

Later that evening, when the children had gone to bed, Stuart poured them both a glass of wine. 'So what's been going on?'

'Oh… they let themselves into the archive room…' Poppy sighed. 'Joshua and Sonia were curious more than anything but Karina was very upset. She felt we hadn't been honest with her and she didn't know who we were!'

'I see… Is she all right now?'

'Yes, once I explained all about Gregory and the baby. I also told her about Amanda too.'

Stuart looked surprised. 'How did she take it?'

'I think she was shocked at first. She said she always thought she knew everything about us but was stunned that she didn't. Then she seemed to understand with remarkable maturity.'

Stuart nodded. He wasn't surprised. He always thought Karina was mature well beyond her years. 'What about Joshua and Sonia? How did they take it?'

'They were fine – they seemed to take it all in their stride. I guess it was time. I just hadn't wanted them to find out like that!'

'No, me neither but… well, I guess it's done now! We'll just keep a close eye on them, especially Karina. You know what teenage girls are like and it was obviously a shock for her. I tell you what, as it's Saturday tomorrow why don't I take Joshua and Sonia out for a bike ride and give you some more time with Karina?'

'That's a good idea. Thank you sweetheart,' she said, tenderly kissing him.

The next day, the house was finally quiet and Karina and Poppy were left alone. Poppy asked Karina if she was all right and if she would like to look through the archive room with her? Karina said she would love to and be able to spend some time with her mother without her kid brother and sister butting in!

After some time, Poppy noticed her daughter had a faraway look in her eyes. 'Would you like to be alone with this sweetheart?'

'I'm okay, thanks Mom,' she replied, before returning to reading the newspaper clippings.

They had a pleasant morning and both were glad they had this time alone together.

When Stuart and the children returned from their bike ride he found Poppy in the kitchen, Karina having gone back to her own room. Stuart asked about Karina and Poppy's morning. Poppy told him she thought it had gone pretty well and had been a good bonding time for them. Stuart in turn told her he had enjoyed the bike ride with their two younger children and they had lots of fun, although he was feeling very tired.

Throughout the week, on an evening, Karina would come and ask her mother if she could spend an hour or two on her own in the archive room, which Poppy let her do.

'I'm just worried that she's been so quiet and spending so much time in there!' Poppy told Stuart one night as they were getting ready for bed.

'I think she's just trying to assimilate everything in her mind. Give her time, she'll get used to the situation.'

Nothing more was said about it until a few weeks later when it was Poppy's birthday. Stuart had asked the children what they wanted to buy for their mother's birthday. They told him it was a surprise and that Karina was in charge of organising it. So he left them to their own devices. He, on the other hand, had arranged theatre tickets, a meal at their favourite restaurant, a gorgeous bouquet of flowers and a bottle of her favourite perfume.

Poppy's birthday fell on a Sunday this year so she had a lovely long lie-in. When she came down for breakfast Stuart and the children had set the table with orange juice and croissants. After breakfast Stuart produced her presents. She excitedly opened them and then Karina, Joshua and Sonia stood in line.

'This is for you Mom, we hope you like it,' Karina whispered, almost reverently, holding out the large envelope to her.

Intrigued, Poppy took the envelope from her, thanking them all and quickly opening it. She looked inside the card and gasped.

Contribution

The children held their breath, watching tears fill their mother's eyes. Karina was starting to think maybe she shouldn't have done it but had thought it was a good idea at the time.

Tears spilled down Poppy's cheeks. 'Oh, my... I really don't know what to say!' she cried.

Stuart peered over her shoulders, reading the card, wondering what on earth it could be.

'Mom, are you okay?' Karina asked tentatively.

Poppy nodded, trying to stem her tears.

'Maybe we shouldn't have done it?'

Poppy shook her head. 'No... no sweetheart, it's wonderful... and so thoughtful... I just never expected anything like this!' Poppy re-read the two certificates identifying the star names and stellar coordinates locating where they were in the sky. Poppy gently caressed the two silver stars, enclosed in the card, engraved with the names Gregory and Baby Gregory on each one.

Karina let out a sigh of relief, thankful she hadn't done the wrong thing. 'We thought it would be nice to have two stars next to each other named after Gregory and the baby so they could look down on us and be a part of our family too! And maybe one day we'll all have stars next to each other and all be together again!' The children didn't say, but they also planned to do the same for their father's birthday and name a star Amanda next to Gregory's and the baby's.

Poppy was touched at their thoughtfulness. Tears continued to flow down her cheeks, and even Stuart had a tear in his eye.

'It's lovely, thank you! Come here,' she said to Karina, hugging her daughter tightly. She then turned to her younger children and Stuart. 'Time for a big group hug!'

Afterwards, when they were alone, Poppy told Stuart, 'I can't believe they did that! It was so thoughtful and so accepting of our past lives - mine in particular!'

'I know. They're great kids. I'm delighted they're caring, talented and smart. And I know they're really proud of what you achieved!'

'Thank you!' She snuggled into Stuart's chest. 'How did we get so lucky?' Poppy asked her husband.

'I think I have to give their mother credit for that!'

She smiled up to him and shook her head. 'No, I think it's their father who should take credit! You are always so patient. You listen and encourage them in whatever they want to do and spend as much time as possible with them!'

'So do you my love,' he smiled. 'You've led by example with all the things you've done in your life!'

As the children got older, of course, there were all the usual growing pains throughout their teens with boyfriends, girlfriends and school work. But Stuart and Poppy tried to give them opportunities to see the world and keep them focussed and on an even keel.

The years wore on and Poppy and Stuart continued to be extremely happy. They stood as proud parents watching each of their children graduate from high school.

All three children had been brought up to be independent so it didn't surprise either of them when the young adults left home early to start college.

Poppy in particular found it hard when each child said goodbye to continue his or her education away from home. But they would regularly ring or e-mail and often returned home on a weekend and holidays.

Not surprisingly, Karina majored in modern literature, Joshua in financial accounting and Sonia in medicine. They had all gone into professions they had shown a flair for when they were younger.

Poppy and Stuart were always delighted when their children visited, often all at the same time. They still carried on the family tradition of staying at the family vacation home in Costa Rica at least once a year.

They were especially delighted when Karina, Joshua and Sonia surprised them with a party to celebrate their twenty-fifth wedding anniversary. 'Where have the years gone to my love?' Poppy asked her husband, looking up to him.

'I really don't know, all I know is they are going by far too quickly!'

The visits from the children were always special times for Poppy and Stuart but they enjoyed being alone, settling down into their old routine before the children were born. On an evening they would cuddle up into each other's arms and catch up on their day over a glass of wine and read or watch TV together.

However, Poppy was becoming increasingly worried that Stuart always looked tired and thin and lacked energy these days. He didn't have the same appetite he used to and when she suggested he should visit the doctor he said he was just working too hard, that was all and not to worry.

Meanwhile Poppy's parents retired from their hectic schedules in Panama and had moved back to the family home in Costa Rica. They were using this as a base while they travelled to countries they hadn't had time to visit when they were working. Toby and Annabelle enjoyed their retirement and having the opportunity to spend more time together.

Without warning, Poppy's parents suddenly died within a short time of each other. Poppy was devastated when she heard the heart-breaking news. Annabelle had been the first to die of a heart attack, followed

Contribution

quickly by Toby. Although Poppy felt her father's was more of a broken heart after losing his childhood sweetheart.

Poppy consoled herself that at least they had enjoyed some years of retirement together after their lifelong dedication to the medical profession but regretted that she hadn't spent more time with them. The whole family returned to Costa Rica for the funerals within a short time of each other. It was a sad and distressing time for all, but they consoled each other in their time of sorrow.

Poppy was grateful that at least her parents had seen her receive the accolades for a lifetime of contribution towards good causes and had watched her own children grow into fine young adults.

After her parents' passing, Poppy kept herself busy with a series of interviews. Generally the interviewer asked what she intended to do next and she always replied that she just wanted to continue to educate people on conservation and the wonderful world in which we live, help people, travel and, of course, be there for her family. Stuart always stood next to the camera crew and watched her proudly.

Poppy was sorry to hear that Sam and Maria had gone their separate ways after their children had grown up and left for college but she wasn't totally surprised, nor was Maria.

Like Sam had always said, he needed his freedom and Maria knew he had to walk his chosen path alone. In all honesty both Poppy and Maria had been amazed that Sam had managed to commit to her and the children for as long as he did. But Maria understood his spirit well and she let him go with love. She felt it was the kindest thing to do for all their sakes and Poppy loved this wonderful woman more than ever for her compassion and understanding.

It had been a difficult year after losing her parents and Poppy still worried about Stuart, especially when she saw him holding his stomach and grimacing or noticing him disappear to the bathroom for a long time.

'Honey, I really think you should see a doctor.'

'I'm okay, honestly, it's nothing to worry about. It's probably just an upset stomach.'

'But sweetheart you've always got an upset stomach these days!'

'I know - oh the joys of getting older!'

She raised an eyebrow and let it go for the moment.

Chapter 23
The Twists and Turns of Life!

Poppy's and Stuart's lives carried on as always with their busy schedules until one fateful Tuesday. Poppy thought it strange that Stuart hadn't come down for breakfast. She went back up to their bedroom and was startled to see him lying on the bed.

'Honey, what's the matter?'

'I don't know, but I've got a really bad stomach-ache and I just don't feel well.'

'Right, I'm going to call the doctor. We should have done this a long time ago!' Poppy said assertively.

Their doctor asked many questions and Stuart reluctantly admitted that he'd had constant stomach pain and lately had noticed some rectal bleeding. The doctor scolded Stuart for not coming to see him sooner but told him to take it easy. In the meantime he would book Stuart in at the hospital for tests.

Poppy accompanied Stuart to the hospital for the series of tests. They then spent the next several weeks anxiously waiting for the results while Stuart's health continued to deteriorate.

After the doctor received the results he sat Stuart and Poppy down in his office and gently confirmed

Poppy's worst fears: Stuart had cancer and would need to start chemotherapy almost immediately.

Numb with shock, Poppy drove Stuart back to the house almost in silence. When they arrived home they both broke down and cried, holding onto each other tightly.

'Honey, I wish you'd gone to the doctor sooner. You must have been in a lot of pain for a long time.'

'I was. I'm sorry.'

'So why didn't you go?' Poppy wailed.

'I thought if I didn't think about it, it would go away. I guess I was scared. I think deep down I knew, especially as I had some of the symptoms dad had. He died so young!' Stuart felt guilty for Poppy's emotional pain, remembering how he felt and having said the same to Amanda after her diagnosis.

Poppy nodded, understanding how he felt. However, it was with a heavy heart and feeling of regret that she hadn't been more forceful and insisted he visit the doctor sooner. Poppy took a deep breath and said, 'Well whatever, we're going to fight this together and come through it! Okay?'

Stuart nodded and pulled her close to him again, burrowing his head into her hair and shoulders, trying to shut out a million thoughts that were bombarding his mind.

That night Poppy lay awake in bed worrying into the small hours of the morning. She thought about all the things Gran Jasmine had told her years ago. Poppy knew she would have to put her faith in the universe and be as positive and optimistic as possible to help them through this awful time.

Distraught, Poppy put her work on hold and left it to her staff to handle the busy schedule. Stuart had already passed down responsibility to Karina, even though she was still very young, but he knew she was capable and mature enough to take over the publishing company and she was good at it too.

Poppy spent her days accompanying Stuart to his chemotherapy treatments. It tore Poppy apart to see her beloved husband so ill from the effects of the treatment.

Later, when they returned home, she would try to make him as comfortable as possible. She would often read to him or give him updates from Karina about what was happening at work.

Much of Stuart's time was spent sleeping from the effects of the pain medication. It broke Poppy's heart to see the once strong and vivacious man she loved so much lying in bed weak and pale.

The weeks passed and their hopes that the treatments would halt the spread of the cancer began to fade. Unfortunately it was now spreading rapidly throughout his body.

Stuart's doctor often called in to check on him and offer moral support. One afternoon he took Poppy aside and told her he wasn't sure how much time Stuart had left. It could be days, weeks or even months – but not many, of that he was sure. After the doctor left, Poppy sat alone at the kitchen table and broke down and sobbed until there were no tears left.

Some weeks later, they finally got the news she was dreading: there was now no hope of remission. The death sentence hanging over them was unbearable. Poppy tried to put on a brave face for Stuart's sake but when alone her sobs were uncontrollable.

It was Stuart's decision to spend the remainder of his time at home with Poppy attending to him. In addition, they arranged for nurses to visit on a regular basis to administer his pain medication.

Poppy and Stuart spent their last few weeks together talking, holding hands and spending as much time as possible with their family who all visited frequently.

They were already a close family but it was as if knowing the time they had left made every little thing they did together that much more precious and poignant. It was both a happy and sad time, and in a way almost surreal. Poppy did everything she could possibly think of to make Stuart's life as pleasant as possible.

Stuart's and Poppy's love for each other deepened even more so. Poppy would do whatever she could to attend to his needs, try to lessen his pain and make him comfortable. They would listen to his favourite music as he lay in bed overlooking their picturesque, well-tended garden. Knowing how much Stuart loved flowers and plants Poppy brought many potted plants into the downstairs room that had now become their bedroom. She would open up the double French doors so that he could breathe in the fresh spring air.

Stuart told her again and again how much he loved her. He thanked her for all she had given him and the wonderful children and life they had shared together. Although she had heard these words from him many times over the years, now they always filled her with sadness, knowing their time together was coming to an end.

Poppy in turn would tell him how much she loved him. She too thanked him for the wonderful life and children he had given her. They would hold onto each other through love, pain, tears and smiles.

Even though they thought they were prepared for it, they were still shocked the day Stuart's health worsened. The two assigned nurses attended to his pain and Poppy lay next to him on top of their bed, cradling his head in her hands and listening to his laboured breathing. Stuart opened his eyes and weakly asked to see the children.

After the children had all been in to say their final goodbyes he then asked to be alone with Poppy. The family and nurses left the room, quietly closing the heavy oak door behind them.

'My love,' he breathed deeply and whispered, 'I know you think we've covered everything.'

Poppy looked at Stuart with love and tenderness in her eyes and nodded, agreeing.

'But there's something else I want you to do.'

She looked at him puzzled, not wanting to interrupt as she knew how painful it was for him to talk now.

'Let Sam look after you!'

'What? No!'

'Please!'

'Honey, it's you who's the love of my life!'

'I know but you're too young and vibrant to spend the rest of your life alone!' Stuart weakly tried to convince her that life would go on and that she should have someone there for her. 'Please Poppy. I know he loves you!'

Poppy didn't want to think about anything other than "the now" and her love for Stuart. 'Darling it's you I love and want to be with! I really can't bear the thought of being without you!'

He continued, 'I know, but if you and Sam are together it won't take away from the life we've shared! We've always loved each other but there's room in your life for someone else too!' Stuart took a deep breath as he struggled to say what he knew he must. 'Eventually, when you've had time to grieve properly, let him be there for you. Please! And for goodness sake don't hang onto your grief for me like you did with Gregory!'

'Honey please don't, I can't bear it!' Poppy cried hysterically, unable to get any more words out.

Stuart could only manage to gently squeeze her hand and utter the words, 'I love you!'

'I love you too!' she said, watching him close his eyes one final time.

Stuart could see two rows of angels cloaked in white waiting for him. They then parted to make way for Amanda floating in between them, wearing a long white gown, a crown of flowers adorning her long golden hair flowing over her shoulders. She looked beautiful and youthful. She smiled, holding out her graceful hand to him. He could feel himself reaching out to her and then finally there was no more pain.

Poppy was numb. She couldn't believe he had gone and that once again life would never be the same. She kissed him gently on the forehead. 'Goodnight my love. Until we meet again,' Poppy whispered, weeping into his chest.

Poppy took a deep breath and went back through to the living room to tell the children but there was no need for words. They all knew and wept openly.

The young family were devastated to lose their father, the man they loved and respected most. He had always been there for them, guiding and nurturing.

Poppy was heartbroken. She told the children that their father would always be watching over them from heaven and the angels would be looking after him. She knew, deep in her heart, that the universe had a higher calling for him and that one day they would all be together again.

Over the next several days Poppy and the family made the funeral arrangements. Stuart Austin Bruce died as he had lived - with modesty, dignity and grace. His funeral's tone was low key, as he wanted it, with just close family and friends and no media allowed.

Karina kept the promise she made when she was younger and arranged for another star to be named, this time in their father's name, although she hadn't expected to have done it so soon. She was devastated. It was placed next to Amanda's, Gregory's and baby Gregory's so they could look up to the night skies and feel he was with them. Poppy smiled, through her tears, thanked her and told her three children he would always be with them in their hearts wherever they were.

The *New York Times* and other prominent papers ran the story of the passing of the quietly charismatic publisher who had done so many good things with his life.

The family somehow managed to get through the funeral and the sad and lonely days and weeks wore on.

When she was alone, Poppy missed her wonderful loving husband and was deeply grief-stricken but it wasn't the same gut-wrenching sudden shock it had been when Gregory had died. This time she felt she could handle it better, after all she was older, wiser and more prepared for it. They had a good life together and had had time to say goodbye. She had the support of the children and tried to put on a brave face for them, but she missed her Stuart terribly.

Poppy wrote to Gregory's elderly parents and told them of her sad news.

Nancy wept into Jim's arms. 'That poor girl, I can't believe this has happened to her again and Stuart was such a nice man,' she said, remembering the one time she had briefly met him many years ago.

'I know,' Jim said, holding his cherished, frail wife. It brought back painful memories of their own loss, not that it had ever really gone away, they had just somehow learned to live with it.

'I'll ring her,' Nancy said, blowing her nose, 'and try and offer words of comfort.'

Jim nodded in agreement. 'Tell her I'm thinking of her too.'

'I will dear,' Nancy said, getting up to make the difficult phone call.

Poppy was pleased to hear from her and couldn't help but cry into the phone as Nancy offered words of comfort.

Poppy knew the firsts of everything were the worst, including birthdays and anniversaries, but especially Christmas. She remembered every joyful Christmas with Stuart watching their children grow and enjoying this special time of year. And now she couldn't bear to spend the holidays in New York so decided to go back to Costa Rica for a few days and not be involved in the festivities, despite her children asking her to join them.

Over the next few years, Poppy slowed down a lot and felt it was more a time of quiet reflection. She spent time with her children and friends but her thoughts frequently returned to Stuart. She was grateful they had found each other and thankful for the time they had shared, and that he had lived to see their children grow up into fine young adults. However, she was distressed that he wouldn't be able to walk his girls down the aisle or see his grandchildren.

Poppy spoke to Sam now and again on the phone. He would console her and offer words of encouragement but she couldn't face the idea of seeing her closest friend. Her heart was continually heavy and sad. She felt like a ship adrift without an anchor.

Chapter 24
Penthorpe Hill!

One Saturday afternoon when Karina was visiting her mother she broached the subject of visiting England. 'I've wanted to go for ages Mom, even if it's just for a week! Rob can't get time off work at the moment so what do you think to coming with me?' Of course, it was an excuse but Karina thought a trip back to England would help cheer her mother up.

Poppy thought about it. 'Well, if you're sure, I would love to do that but I don't want Rob to think I'm monopolising his girlfriend!'

'He wouldn't think that and, as I say, he's so busy at work he wouldn't be able to get time off.'

'So whereabouts in England do you want to go to?' Poppy asked.

'Well, as we only have a week I thought maybe London and the Cotswolds. I did wonder if you would also like to go back to Penthorpe Hill?'

Poppy raised her eyebrows, thinking about the old place where her gran had spent her early childhood and remembering when she took her there when Poppy was in her teens. 'I would love to go back there but as I've visited England quite a few times I think it should be where you want to go!' Poppy replied graciously.

'Actually I would like to go there too! After all, I've seen the photos and heard the stories. I think it would be a nice thing to do, especially as I never got to meet my great-gran. It would almost be like tracing my family history! If we go next month the weather should still be mild and warm. What do you think?'

'I think it's a great idea and I would love to do it. It would give us chance to have some quality mother/daughter time together. Thank you sweetheart,' Poppy said as she hugged her.

Poppy was touched that her daughter wanted to spend vacation time with her.

Both Poppy and Karina spent the following weeks excitedly planning the trip and Poppy e-mailed friends and distant family back in the UK to tell them of their forthcoming trip and hoping they might all have time to get together.

Their day of departure finally arrived. Rob dropped them off at JFK airport and Karina kissed him goodbye. They both declared how much they would miss each other. Poppy really liked Rob and was pleased to see love blossoming between them.

After Rob left, Poppy and Karina got their boarding passes and bags checked before going into the airport lounge for a cup of coffee and discussing once more what they would like to do during their week together.

They were on a direct flight to Heathrow and both slept pretty much most of the way on the long journey to England.

When they arrived in London they checked into their hotel and were looking forward to visiting the sites of the exhilarating city.

Poppy showed Karina the places her and Stuart had visited and Karina took delight in following her father's footsteps. Poppy thought how Karina and her father were so much alike. Karina still missed him terribly and had only just got used to him not popping in at the publishing house to see how she was doing.

Poppy and Karina spent many hours during the next few days visiting the tourist attractions and reminiscing.

On the third day Poppy hired a car and drove them to Penthorpe Hill where Gran Jasmine had spent her early childhood. The quaint little village looked the same as she remembered when she had visited it with her gran so many years ago. The thatched roofs were neatly trimmed and the gardens had colourful late summer blooms, although the pub was now closed and she didn't know whether that was just for a short time or was permanent.

They turned the corner and walked up to the huge iron gates with the now tattered sign telling people to keep out.

Contribution

Poppy started to push the gate open.

'Mom are you sure we should be doing this?' Karina asked in an anxious tone.

Poppy smiled. 'That's what I more or less said to gran when she brought me here. I must have been about thirteen or fourteen then. And it was fine so I'm sure it will be now!'

They walked down the road past the cricket ground and to the right was an overgrown field where houses had once stood.

The enormous historic building, that was once a school, was empty and dilapidated. They made their way up the hill to the big house where Gran Jasmine had lived when she was a little girl. It now looked derelict, desolate and eerie. Poppy showed Karina around the outside of the house. The gardens were now overgrown.

Poppy then took her daughter across the road and through the battered old door to where the greenhouses were but which were now locked up. It all looked so much more rundown, bleak and neglected than she remembered.

However, the pond still looked the same dark green as the last time she had visited. There was no-one around and it didn't look like anyone had been there in a long time. Clearly all the people her gran had known had passed on. The place now felt broken-down, sad and gloomy.

They then went back to the house and Poppy stood staring at it.

'Are you okay Mom?' Karina was starting to wonder whether or not they should have come here after all.

'I'm fine thanks sweetheart. I was just remembering when I was last here and how much nicer it all looked then. That was the last time gran saw it.'

'You still miss her don't you?'

'Yes, sometimes it feels like it was just yesterday we were together and other times it feels like eons ago. But she's always in my heart – just as your dad is!'

Karina nodded, understanding.

Poppy continued, 'I was also thinking how much the place meant to her. But strangely it doesn't conjure up any feelings for me. I guess that's because I never lived here and had no attachment to it!'

Karina nodded again. 'I guess a place like this has different meanings for people at different times!'

Poppy nodded in agreement. 'I think so.' Poppy sighed, looking at the austere building. 'Come on, it's time we were getting back to the hotel.' Poppy took one last look, thinking she would never return.

At the hotel Poppy told Karina that she wanted to go to her room and rest for a while.

'Are you okay Mom?'

'I'm fine thanks sweetie. I'm just tired, that's all. What will you do?'

Contribution

'I think I'll go to my room and check on e-mails from work. I'll also Skype Rob and tell him what we've been doing.'

'That would be nice dear. Send my love too,' Poppy smiled at her lovely daughter.

Poppy took off her shoes and lay on top of the bed. Her thoughts were filled with Penthorpe Hill, Gran Jasmine and all the people in her life, especially those she had lost. She felt sad as she let her thoughts drift off to another time.

Poppy wasn't sure whether she was sleeping and dreaming but things seemed to make sense in that funny way they do in dreams. She was surprised when in a half-meditative state Poppy saw herself as she was in a different lifetime.

Her dark hair was thicker and longer and her eyes were larger and darker. She was shorter in stature with a fuller figure but nonetheless Poppy was sure it was her. She could feel her heart beat and the emotions she was feeling that day and a sense of contentment washing over her.

Poppy stood next to a dry stone wall by the ocean in a place she thought was Spain. A warm ocean breeze blew strands of her long dark hair and she smiled at someone approaching her.

The male figure came into view. The handsome and rugged-looking man sauntered towards her. His hair wasn't blond any more but more a sandy colour. She watched it softly blow in the warm wind. His eyes were an intense blue and she felt with every ounce of her being that it was Sam. He wasn't quite as tall as Sam was now but he looked as lean as he always did. He looked like a pirate, swaggering towards her. She knew his name wasn't Sam but couldn't remember what it was. He smiled and briefly kissed her full on the lips, asking if she was ready to set sail for England?

The scene then changed to a place which Poppy knew was Cornwall in England from the time she had visited with Gran Jasmine.

Poppy and the familiar looking man were in a huge dark cavern near the shore that had been turned into a makeshift drinking hostelry. There were crates of smuggled alcohol piled high and lots of laughter and merriment. People sat on the cold rocks in the cave, swilling rum from the glass bottles. Sam's best friend Henry was serving behind an improvised bar made from pieces of driftwood and empty crates.

Poppy could see herself leaning against the damp dark wall of the cave, dimly lit by candles. She was wearing a dress with a black and white full skirt and patterns of red and orange running through. The white laced bodice was provocatively open. Sam leaned towards her and was kissing her fully and passionately on the mouth.

The lookout suddenly shouted, 'Quick douse the candles. Soldiers are on their way!'

Everyone hurriedly snuffed out the candles and scattered when they heard the uniformed men shouting

Contribution

in the distance. Dogs were barking and gunshots rang out in the air.

'Come on, let's head through the tunnel,' Sam urgently whispered, taking Poppy's hand and leading the way. In the darkness Poppy put a hand over her mouth and stifled a scream as she felt rats running over her feet in her thinly strapped sandals.

Sam lit a small lantern that helped guide their way. 'Are you okay?' he whispered.

She couldn't answer but just looked at him with wild, scared eyes.

'We're nearly there!' he encouraged. They could hear waves crashing down. Then daylight suddenly appeared and they ran out onto the soft beach. There was a thick rope anchored into the sands tethering the ship he had sailed in on from Spain. They waded through the water and heard loud voices getting closer.

'Quick, pull yourself along the rope,' he told her, lifting her up to hold onto it. He also jumped up to the heavy twine next to her and they put one arm in front of the other and pulled themselves along.

They nearly got to the ship when simultaneously they felt bullets searing painfully through their backs. Shocked, they looked at each other.

'I love you!' she managed to say, realising life was rapidly slipping away.

'I love you too! It's not the end!' he mouthed to her as they plunged into the sea.

Looking into each other's eyes and deep into the other's soul they swiftly slipped down into the cold waters. They were engulfed in a bright light as water submerged them and they quickly lost consciousness.

The armed men pulled the lifeless bodies out of the water and dragged them onto the beach.

With a jolt Poppy sat up trembling, looking around the hotel bedroom. Her heart was pounding fast. It felt so real that she was pretty sure it hadn't been a dream but a memory from a past life. She remembered Gran Jasmine telling her about reincarnation and referring to her favourite book on the subject. Poppy racked her brains trying to recall the name of it and visualised it on the bookcase at their home in Costa Rica. Finally the name came to mind, *Same Soul, Many Bodies* by Dr Brian Weiss. She wished she had read it and made a note to buy it tomorrow.

Poppy lay on the bed for quite some time before Karina knocked on the door to check on her mother. The sudden noise startled her and interrupted her unsettling memories.

'Yes!' Poppy shouted in a disconcerted voice.

'Mom it's me!'

'Come in,' Poppy beckoned her daughter.

Karina noticed her mother's pale face and dishevelled hair. 'Sorry Mom, did I wake you?'

Poppy smiled. 'No, I've just been lying here with my thoughts,' she said, deciding not to tell Karina about her vision. She was still trying to formulate the information in her own mind.

'Are you okay?' Karina was concerned at the sight of her mother's unusual dishevelled state, and thought a change of scene would do her good.

'I'm fine thanks dear.'

'Good, well how about us finding somewhere to have a traditional English tea?

'That sounds lovely,' Poppy said, getting off the bed and combing her hair.

The next morning, before setting off to visit the Cotswolds, Poppy told Karina that she would like to buy a book for the remainder of the trip. She didn't find the one she intended to buy but instead found *Karma and Reincarnation – Unlocking Your 800 Lives to Enlightenment* by Barbara Y. Martin and Dimitri Moraitis.

Every moment Poppy got she would read it and was amazed at how much sense it made and how the truth of it resonated within her soul. She was now absolutely sure that her time as a pirate's woman was a memory of a past life. However, she still didn't say anything to Karina.

Poppy and Karina enjoyed their last few days together exploring the English countryside and taking in all the culture, especially visiting Stratford-upon-Avon and watching *A Midsummer Night's Dream* at the Royal Shakespeare Theatre.

But Poppy's thoughts always returned to the vision and she found herself replaying it in her mind over and over like a scene from a movie with Sam's final words, 'It's not the end,' still echoing in her head.

All too soon mother and daughter were on the plane heading home.

On the flight back home to New York Poppy began thinking about her earlier life, Sam and her gran. She now had a yearning to go back to Costa Rica and spend some time in her old family home. Poppy asked Karina what she thought of the idea of her going back.

'I think it's a good idea, Mom. You love being there and it always seems to do you good!'

Chapter 25
Karma!

Poppy took comfort in returning to her family home in Costa Rica overlooking the ocean, although she missed seeing Karina, Joshua and Sonia so often.

She reconnected with friends and quickly returned to her daily schedule of walking along the beach and meditating at her favourite rock.

Poppy was glad Sam was away in Australia for a few months. This gave her time to try and make sense of everything in her current life, ponder on her memories of a past life and what she wanted to do with her future, without any influence from him.

The charities were so well established they almost ran themselves and she was pleased that Joshua now headed the finance department of the Trust. She had a permanent full-time staff dedicated to her world vision but promised she would make occasional appearances back in New York to connect with her organisations and see her family.

Karina was doing well with Stuart's publishing company and was very much in love with Rob. Poppy hoped they would get married and she would one day have grandchildren. Joshua had a string of girlfriends and Poppy couldn't see him settling down for a long time. Sonia was so totally dedicated to the medical profession working out in the field that at the moment she didn't have time for any serious relationships. But more than anything Poppy was grateful that her children were happy and doing well in their chosen careers.

All in all, Poppy's life settled into a comfortable and relaxed routine but she was starting to feel restless. She knew she needed to do something. 'But what?' she pondered to herself while she sat on her bedroom balcony with the familiar view of the ocean, sipping an ice-cold glass of lemonade.

She no longer felt she had the energy or enthusiasm to start new projects or charities the way she had after Gregory died. Besides, she felt she had done everything she wanted to do in that direction.

Poppy contemplated the family home here in Costa Rica. It held so many memories for her. She knew she wanted to keep it for her children and future grandchildren for their family vacations. But it was starting to look shabby. It hadn't had any real work done on it in years – they had all been so busy coming and going.

Excitement started to stir within Poppy, thinking about remodelling her home and bringing it up to date with new cabinets, drapes, furniture and a fresh coat of paint. She had never really refurbished a whole house on her own before and she was starting to look forward to tackling this latest project.

Contribution

Over the next few weeks Poppy scanned through home decorating magazines, collected swatches of material and paint chips. Colour schemes for each room were starting to form in her mind. She received quotes and booked in contractors and very soon work started on the family vacation home.

Poppy enjoyed supervising the work and watching the transformation occur.

Weeks later Poppy stood back and admired the makeover. It looked fresh, inviting and modern. It had everything to make the perfect family vacation.

Sam returned from Australia where he had helped direct and produce a film on the world's greatest surfers. He was always trying something new but never drifted too far from surfing and anything creative.

He was enjoying being back in Costa Rica and spending quality time with his now grown-up children and doing some much needed "soul surfing". He still loved surfing and was very fit and probably now more graceful and less aggressive in his style than in his younger years. He didn't think he could ever stop surfing such was his love of the sport and the feeling of oneness with the universe.

Sam and Poppy would occasionally meet up for coffee at one of their favourite beach hang-outs but Poppy felt apprehensive about spending too much with

Sam after Stuart's last words and the vision that had so unsettled her.

Now that the alterations at the family home were finished, Poppy volunteered her time teaching young people to speak English and also educating them on environmental issues. When she wasn't doing this, Poppy spent her free time visiting places in Costa Rica she hadn't been to since her youth. She loved seeing the spectacular volcanoes, wandering along the beaches and exploring the jungle.

Sam unexpectedly visited one late Sunday afternoon and she took pleasure in showing him around her newly refurbished home.

'Wow, it looks gorgeous,' Sam enthused. 'What a difference! I never really thought it needed any work but now seeing the new fresh colours it feels so light and airy!'

'Thank you!' Poppy smiled, pleased with his compliments. She had been unsure but had put so much of herself into it that she was glad of his approval.

It always amazed Poppy how quickly time flew by and once again another year had swiftly passed. She shyly asked Sam if he would like to share a joint birthday party with her as his birthday was only two weeks later. He thought that was an excellent idea.

Contribution

A lot of their childhood friends had moved away, but those who were left, including neighbours and their children, were invited to her home. She also invited her children over from the States.

Poppy used the same caterers she had used for her wedding to Gregory all those years ago but now it was their children who owned the business.

The party was in full swing with good food and lots of lively chatter. Everyone had a wonderful time catching up with each other's lives. There was music, laughter and much reminiscing as they sat on the candle-lit deck overlooking the ocean on the star-filled night.

The party eventually came to a close and friends said their farewells. It was just the grown-up children and Sam left. Everyone stayed up late talking and then said goodnight and went to their rooms. Sam was happy to sleep on the hammock on the lower deck after saying goodnight to everyone.

The next day her family tearfully said goodbye before catching a flight to return to their busy careers. They missed their mother and worried about her but she assured them she was fine.

Poppy was immensely proud of all her children and felt they had been her greatest accomplishment. As always, Poppy found it hard saying goodbye to her family but she knew they had to get back to their lives and make their mark in the world.

Karina still enjoyed editing and being in charge of her father's publishing house. She and Rob were now engaged and everyone was looking forward to their wedding in the summer. Her life was idyllic.

Joshua had been promoted to CEO and was doing a fine job of heading the family's Charitable Trust which had now merged with their other charities, including the ones that Stuart had created, and now they were all under one roof. Altogether they now employed over five-hundred staff worldwide. Joshua had recently met a wonderful girl and Poppy was hopeful that this would be the special lady in his life.

Sonia was still happily married to her profession and had inherited her grandparents' love of the medical profession and helping people. Like her grandfather, Toby, she had specialised in emergency medicine. She had now joined an international organisation that sent doctors to natural disasters and was kept busy throughout the world, being one of the first on the scene. She thrived on the adventure and adrenalin rush as well as the challenges of working in the field with little equipment. Poppy couldn't see Sonia getting married and settling down for a long time, if ever.

After everyone left, Poppy and Sam found themselves alone in the house. They walked back into the kitchen, and Poppy sighed, 'Ah, peace and quiet!'

'I know what you mean,' Sam agreed in his amiable way. 'It's great to see everyone but then nice to get back to normal again!'

Poppy smiled, nodded and started stacking the dishes.

Contribution

'Here, let me help you,' he offered helpfully.

'Thanks,' she smiled and they continued in their comfortable, easygoing manner that comes with being lifelong friends.

When they had finished clearing away, Poppy turned around and Sam was standing at the kitchen cabinets opposite, staring at her. 'Thank you for a lovely time,' he said.

'You're welcome!' She smiled, feeling there was something more he wanted to say.

'Wait! With all the excitement, I forgot to give you your birthday gift!'

Sam quickly ran over to his day pack and returned with a small, neatly wrapped package.

Poppy smiled, unwrapping the gift. It nearly took her breath away when she saw the intricately carved and polished white marble angel.

'Wow, it's beautiful, Sam. Thank you!'

'You're welcome. I felt I had to do it after having a dream about your gran telling me the angels would always be watching over us!'

Surprised, Poppy looked up at Sam. With tears in her eyes she embraced him tightly, feeling full of love. She stepped back and he looked longingly at her.

'Gosh Poppy you take me back. You look just like you did when you were sixteen!' She hadn't had time to tie her hair up and, unusually for her these days, she had left it loose. The sun was shining down on her and she noticed Sam looking at her with a look of love in his clear blue eyes.

'Hah if only! Oh my goodness... that's nearly forty years ago! Now I've wrinkles and grey hair that I have to dye, to say the least!'

'I don't see that - all I see is the radiance of your inner beauty!' he said softly.

'Sam?' she barely whispered. He had never spoken like that to her before. Poppy blushed, suddenly feeling flustered.

'I still see you as I did back then.' He paused, not sure whether to go on but on the other hand they had missed so many chances. 'Do you remember that day when we were down by the river and we stood naked in front of each other?'

She felt her stomach turn and her heart beat uncontrollably fast. She berated herself for feeling like that at her age. 'How could I not?'

'I thought then you were the most beautiful girl in the world and I truly loved you with all my heart.'

'And then straight afterwards you broke mine!' she quickly shot back, without judgement or condemnation.

He looked down briefly. Even after all these years, he still hated how he had hurt her back then.

Poppy continued, 'For a long time I hadn't understood how you could do that to me or why you did it!'

'But you knew we had to go our separate ways so that we could do the things in life that we wanted to!' Sam tried to reason.

'I do now but at the time I didn't see why we couldn't have done them together! It took me a long time to realise that you were probably right, which was just before I met Gregory!'

He nodded. 'Do you still think of him?'

'Oh yes, every day and Stuart too. I was very lucky to have loved and been loved by two very special men in my life. It's strange, they were so different but both marriages worked really well in different ways.'

Sam nodded again. They stood looking at each other, remembering, and bringing their past thoughts to the present.

'But I guess we all have the capacity to love totally and completely more than just one person in our lives!' Poppy added, after some thought.

'You're absolutely right,' Sam agreed and then he finally took the step they had both longed for all those years ago when they were sixteen. He tenderly put his hand behind the back of her neck, letting her long hair fall over his hands and igniting the deep desire between them that had been buried for so long. His lips gently found hers, first kissing her tentatively and then passionately. They embraced each other and, pulling back, Poppy looked at him steadily. They looked deep into each other's eyes. Then she took his hand and slowly led him to her bedroom.

They didn't say a word. They didn't have to. Their connection was a deep lifelong and unwavering love for each other.

Sam continued to kiss her lips, her face and her shoulders. Their clothes softly fell to the floor. Once again they stood gazing at each other and it was like the years had rolled away and they were sixteen again but this time he didn't run. He simply smiled and said, 'Poppy, my love...'

She smiled in return, letting him pick up her lithe body and lay her on the large bed. The sun shone through the large patio window highlighting their naked bodies while they gently explored and caressed each other until they were finally making love. All the years of hurt and desire melted away as they became one with each other and the universe.

Later lying in each other's arms, the late morning sun continued to shine through Poppy's bedroom window.

'Are you okay?' Sam asked.

'Oh yes,' she said, smiling and looking up at him. 'I feel like all the years have suddenly disappeared and I'm totally relaxed with nothing to prove any more.'

'I know what you mean. I feel the same,' he smiled, holding her.

They lay together for a long time and then drifted off to sleep with the warm tropical breeze blowing through the open patio doors caressing their bare bodies.

Contribution

After their relaxing siesta they made a late afternoon lunch and ate at the small round table on her bedroom balcony.

'Poppy, you know I think you are the most amazing woman I have ever met! All the things you did in your life for other people were just phenomenal. You made a great contribution to the world!'

'Thank you, but you know I couldn't have done it without all my friends and family and, of course, you. You were always pushing me!'

'Well, I had to keep you busy and remaining focussed but you could have done it without me - I just reminded you of the tools in the toolbox!'

'But the remarkable thing was that everything just fell into place. It was like Gregory or the universe was helping me make everything happen!'

'That's because you were always doing things for the highest good!'

She added in agreement, 'Yes and I feel truly blessed.'

He smiled wryly. 'So do you have anything else in the pipeline?'

She smiled. 'You really never stop pushing do you?'

He smiled back. 'No. I used to do it to keep you going but now I know you always have something in mind! So what is it this time?'

'Well, Joshua is doing a great job with the charitable foundations and he'll continue to take care of them long after I'm gone. So I thought I might stay a little closer to home. There are plenty of things to keep me busy here. Also Karina wants me to write my biography, so she can publish it. I'm thinking that maybe now's the time!'

'That's a wonderful idea. So what's your title going to be?'

'I think it will be *Poppy Anderson Taylor Bruce - One Step at a Time*!'

'Mmmm, not sure about that, it's rather a long title, although it's very you! What do you think to calling it *Contribution*? After all, you have spent most of your life contributing to the needs of others!'

'That's not a bad idea. I'll give it some thought! So what about you?' Poppy asked, for once turning the tables. 'Did you do everything you wanted to?'

'Yes, I think I did! Well, all except for one thing!'

'Oh and what was that?' She couldn't really think what it could be. He'd done everything possible from travelling the world, raising a family, having lots of exciting adventures, climbing many mountains and having his artwork and furniture sold all over the world.

'Getting married!'

She raised an eyebrow. 'But I thought you never wanted to!'

'I don't know. The timing was never right and although I loved Maria, marriage just didn't feel right at the time. And, to be honest, it was you I was always in love with. It's just that we always had so much to do in life and we were always out of sync with each other. I was about to tell you how much I loved you and what a mistake I'd made when you rang me and told me you'd met Gregory and were in love with the most wonderful man in the world! You were so happy I didn't want to do anything to spoil it.' Sam paused, remembering. 'Even after Gregory died, the timing wasn't right and then, of course, you met Stuart. Sometimes though, I do think that if I'd married you in the first place then you wouldn't have had the agony of losing two husbands. And honestly there were times I wasn't sure you were ever going to recover from the loss of Gregory.'

She was shocked, and tears stung her eyes. She had never thought of it that way. 'Sam, please don't feel guilty about what I went through after they died. They both gave me so much joy when they were alive. Besides, I don't regret a single thing and if I had my time all over again I would do exactly the same. I feel blessed to have been loved by two very special men. If I hadn't have been loved by them I wouldn't be the person I am today! And if it meant it was just for a short time then so be it! People die! We can't escape it… but it is a reminder that we should always make the most of every day!'

Sam absorbed everything she was saying.

Poppy paused, thinking. 'You know, I've met so many people who have survived natural disasters, personal tragedies and terrible human suffering but you know what?'

Sam shook his head.

'I learned that the human spirit is far stronger than we ever believe possible. I've seen people overcome such terrible situations. I once read that we are never given anything that we can't ultimately cope with. I think that's true!'

Sam nodded. 'I agree,' Sam responded, thinking about so many people he had met on his travels. 'But going back to you, I wanted to tell you that I'm so proud you lived and loved well and did it all with a sense of passion and spirit! You gave the greatest gift of all - your love - your love for your friends, family, mankind and our wonderful planet. You really cared and touched others. They felt the resonance of truth within you and as a result they trusted you. You truly made a difference in the world! And after Gregory died you showed such courage!'

'Thank you. I guess it was all about growing and being the best I could possibly be – even when times were really bad! I also found out that it doesn't matter whether you give of yourself, your time or your money but whenever you give with an open heart it helps you heal and your generosity makes you feel better!'

Sam smiled, before she continued, 'So maybe it was for selfish reasons!'

'Well, whatever the reason, it worked - for all concerned!' He thought about it some more before continuing, 'Your gran used to say: love, create, experience and develop an attitude of gratitude for everything that comes your way, even challenging situations, because it's all for our growth and learning!' Sam said, fondly remembering one of the old lady's favourite sayings when they were growing up. Jasmine had as much an influence on him too, he recalled.

'That's right and I was lucky too! I had the gifts that gran had given me. Then meeting Gregory and having the most exciting time. It's strange, I still remember him as he was - a vibrant, creative twenty-six-year-old. I can't imagine him growing older. However, trying to keep his memory alive helped me make a difference! Then I met Stuart. We shared a very deep special love and had three wonderful children together. I didn't think I could have been so fortunate as to have had two incredible loves in my life. But I did!'

Sam agreed. 'Yes, there are different kinds of love and they fill a different need in our lives at the appropriate time,' he said, thinking back to Maria.

She smiled, grateful he understood.

They once again fell into a comfortable silence and then she decided to broach the subject she had wanted to since her time in England with Karina. She had still not told anyone about her vision of a past life.

Poppy cautiously went on to describe her visit to Penthorpe Hill and the vision she had at the hotel afterwards of being a pirate's woman in Cornwall. She still felt absolutely sure it was Sam who had been there.

He smiled and nodded in acknowledgement, as though it was the most natural thing in the world.

'You remember it too?' she asked in a shocked voice. That thought had never occurred to her.

'Well not actually that incident. But I knew we'd been together somehow, somewhere in a past life. Why do you think we always had such a strong connection?' Sam said knowingly, 'Karma!' He smiled, delightedly. 'We keep coming back into each other's lives in various forms and relationships until we learn the lessons we're supposed to!' Sam paused. 'But that was back then and another story… I want us to continue with this stage of our lives, to continue to learn the lessons we need to and to finish where we left off!'

She smiled. It now all made sense to her.

He thought about things for a few more moments. 'Poppy I want to ask you something.'

She looked up at him.

'Have you ever thought about marrying a pirate?' He grinned, with a sparkle in his eyes, not sure whether she would marry a third time.

She looked at him, again shocked.

'A pirate?'

'Well, not literally a pirate this time!'

'You mean marry you?'

He nodded, 'If you'll have me!'

'Well, I've heard of some crazy proposals but that beats the lot!'

He smiled. 'I think it's about time... don't you?'

'But you know my husbands have a habit of dying on me?' she said, stalling for time.

'I'll take my chances!'

They viewed each other steadily with a feeling of completeness and a look of total love. They had finally come full circle.

'So is that a yes then?'

'Yes, of course, it's a yes!'

He looked to the ocean, raising his hands, shouting, 'fantastic!' Sam turned and swept her up in his arms, kissing her all over her face.

She smiled back at him, as they embraced and kissed passionately.

The past rolled into the present and they looked forward to the remainder of their life journeys together... no matter what the future may hold.

The End

Bibliography

As A Man Thinketh by James Allen (ISBN 978-149046-651-4) is 'suggestive rather than explanatory, its object being to stimulate men and women to the discovery and perception of the truth that "They themselves are makers of themselves" by virtue of the thoughts which they choose and encourage...'

The Road Less Travelled by Dr. M. Scott Peck (ISBN 978-184604-107-5) is 'the classic work on relationships, spiritual growth and life's meaning. Drawing heavily on his professional experience, Dr M. Scott, a psychiatrist, suggests ways in which facing our difficulties – and suffering through the changes – can enable us to reach a higher level of self-understanding. He discusses the nature of loving relationships; how to recognize true compatibility; how to distinguish dependency from love; how to become one's own person and how to be a more sensitive parent.'

Do Dead People Watch You Shower? And Other Questions You've Been All But Dying To Ask A Medium by Concetta Bertoldi (ISBN 978-006135-122-8) 'Concetta Bertoldi has been communicating with the "Other Side" since childhood. In *Do Dead People Watch You Shower?*, the first ever book of its kind, she exposes the naked truth about the fate and happiness of our late loved ones with no-holds-barred honesty and delightfully wry humor, answering questions that range from the practical to the outrageous.'

Proof of Heaven by Dr Eben Alexander (ISBN 978-145169-519-9)

A SCIENTIST'S CASE FOR THE AFTERLIFE

'Thousands of people have had near-death experiences, but scientists have argued that they are impossible. Dr. Eben Alexander was one of those scientists. A highly trained neurosurgeon, Alexander knew that NDEs feel real, but are simply fantasies produced by brains under extreme stress.

Then, Dr. Alexander's own brain was attacked by a rare illness. The part of the brain that controls thought and emotion — and in essence makes us human — shut down completely. For seven days he lay in a coma. Then, as his doctors considered stopping treatment, Alexander's eyes popped open. He had come back.

'Alexander's recovery is a medical miracle. But the real miracle of his story lies elsewhere. While his body lay in coma, Alexander journeyed beyond this world and encountered an angelic being who guided him into the deepest realms of super-physical existence. There he met, and spoke with, the Divine source of the universe itself.

'Alexander's story is not a fantasy. Before he underwent his journey, he could not reconcile his knowledge of neuroscience with any belief in heaven, God, or the soul. Today Alexander is a doctor who believes that true health can be achieved only when we realize that God and the soul are real and that death is not the end of personal existence but only a transition.

'This story would be remarkable no matter who it happened to. That it happened to Dr. Alexander makes it revolutionary. No scientist or person of faith will be able to ignore it. Reading it will change your life.'

Dr Alexander also includes in his book the poem *When Tomorrow Starts Without Me* by David M. Romano 1993

www.eternea.org is a valuable resource co-founded by Dr Eben Alexander and John R. Audette which offers help on furthering spiritual awakening and offering helpful thoughts on dealing with the death of a loved one.

Same Soul, Many Bodies by Dr Brian L. Weiss (ISBN 978-074326-434-1)

'How often have you wished you could peer into the future? In *Same Soul, Many Bodies,* Brian L. Weiss, M.D., shows us how. Through envisioning our lives to come, we can influence their outcome and use this process to bring more joy and healing to our present lives. Dr. Weiss pioneered regression therapy -- guiding people through their past lives. Here, he goes beyond that to demonstrate the therapeutic benefits of progression therapy - guiding people through the future in a scientific, responsible, healing way.

'Through dozens of case histories detailing both past-life and future-life experiences, Dr. Weiss shows how the choices that we make now will determine our future quality of life. From Samantha, who overcame academic failure once she learned of her future as a great physician, to Evelyn, whose fears and prejudices ended after she envisioned prior and forthcoming lives as a hate victim, Dr. Weiss gives concrete examples of lives transformed by regression and progression therapy.

'A groundbreaking work, *Same Soul, Many Bodies* is sure to deeply affect peoples' lives as they strive toward their future.'

Karma and Reincarnation – Unlocking Your 800 Lives to Enlightenment by Barbara Y. Martin and Dimitri Moraitis (ISBN 978-158542-816-8) is a 'practical hand guide to the ins and outs of the karmic cycle, and a field guide to the spiritual planes and description of precisely how reincarnation works.'